ONLY A PAWN

Marie W. Watts

**LAS TORTUGAS
PRESS**

Cover and interior design by Studio 94 - Lindsey Fojtik
ISBN   978-0-578-65540-6

To all who are victims of discrimination

PREFACE

Didn't read the first novel in the *Warriors for Equal Rights trilogy*? If you want to read it now, go to mariewatts.com to get your copy of *The Cause Lives*. If not, or if you need a refresher about the characters, here's a brief summary:

EQUAL EMPLOYMENT OPPORTUNITY COMMISSION (EEOC)
The EEOC is a federal agency dedicated to protecting employees from discrimination based on race, color, religion, sex (including pregnancy, gender identity, and sexual orientation), national origin, age (forty or older), disability, or genetic information. The agency also protects individuals who face retaliation because they've complained about discrimination. The ability to find "cause" (i.e., prove discrimination) is the gold standard for investigators. The characters in *The Cause Lives* work as investigators in a makeshift office in Austin, Texas, established to enhance President Obama's legacy as a civil rights champion.

ALICE ANTOINETTE ARDEN – A white enforcement supervisor conned into leading the Austin, Texas, office. Suffering from severe stress and a disability that leaves her unable to walk, she drinks Singapore slings to ease her angst and prays she can last until retirement. She suspects her boss, EEOC Chair Ami Saitou, does not want the office to succeed and has been denying adequate funding to sabotage their success

ESPIE GOMEZ – A millennial, Hispanic investigator who is an eighth-generation Texan and does not speak Spanish. Her secret passion is reading romance novels.

QUIANA JONES – An African American clerk who suffers from sociophobia. She works behind a Chinese screen and attends office meetings via webcam.

JJ JORDON – An African American investigator who joins the staff after having been incarcerated for twenty years on charges of sexual assault. Chair Saitou foists JJ on the office as part of her plan to show the commission supports reentry of prisoners into society.

JORGE MACIAS – A Hispanic investigator and family man who has an aversion to homosexuals.

INMAN PARKER – An African American attorney who joined the office to discover what was missing in his life, leaving his wife and family behind. To complicate matters, he learns of a daughter he never knew about in the process. To irritate Alice, Inman calls her "A Plus" because of her initials.

GAYE ROHATQI – A millennial, Asian investigator who struggles as she is torn between doing what her parents want (marry a nice Indian man) and what she desires.

DEXTER – Alice's miniature bulldog who acts as an emotional support animal for Quiana.

But it ain't him to blame
He's only a pawn in their game

-Bob Dylan

Chapter One

"Just get rid of it." Hank shoved an envelope at Espy. "Now."

"But you—"

"Just do what I say." Hank stood and threw a hundred-dollar bill at the check. "Call me when it's gone."

Espy choked back tears, staring at him as he threaded his way through the crowded dining room. *That bastard.* All his big talk about the sanctity of life. What a bunch of crap. Touching her stomach lightly, she felt a wave of relief that it was still trim.

Once positive Hank had exited the parking lot, she retreated to her car and drove aimlessly. Her cell rang.

"Espy, where are you?" Quiana asked. "Alice was expecting you fifteen minutes ago."

"Oh, I forgot. Just tell her I'm not feeling well. I'll probably be in tomorrow."

"Are you OK? You haven't looked well all week."

"I'm fine. Just caught a bug, I think." Espy didn't want to tell Quiana anything. While the clerk was a great person, this coworker seemed to get into everybody's business, and that was the last thing Espy needed now.

Turning into her apartment complex, Espy parked under a tree and cracked the window slightly. The summer was already brutal.

Once inside, she peeled off her clothes and donned an oversized T-shirt. Grabbing her iPad, she slumped onto the couch and began to surf, typing in "Hank Robbins." At the Texas House of Representatives website, his picture came to life on the screen, those blue eyes giving him a rather mischievous look. Another image showed the lawmaker and his family, indicating he had been happily married to his wife, Marisa, for ten years. Punching another button brought her to his latest pro-life diatribe. The hypocrite!

But what was she going to do with only six weeks to decide? Although she was no longer a practicing Catholic, the idea of an abortion unsettled her. Reluctantly, she googled Planned Parenthood. Hank and his self-righteous band of male chauvinists hadn't been able to close it—yet.

Skimming the abortion procedures, Espy paled. A sonogram was mandatory. Then they'd shove a speculum up her vagina for an exam. Even worse was the next day's protocol: enduring the indignity of the doctor describing the image and explaining the size of the embryo or fetus and the presence of organs and limbs.

Angrily, Espy threw her tablet on the couch. She had only herself to blame. After she'd tried to break it off, Hank had pursued her unmercifully. She'd always known that dating him would be playing with fire.

Moving from El Paso to work at the Austin EEOC office meant leaving a long-time boyfriend and a host of close acquaintances behind. Her boyfriend, she didn't miss so much; what Espy missed were her friends. It was harder to develop confidantes in Austin than she'd imagined. Her coworkers were great, but meeting them outside of office hours didn't appeal to her. After all, they had their own lives. Then she'd met Hank during one of her lunches at the state capitol's cafeteria, and he filled the void.

Espy turned off her device and cried herself to sleep, but troubling dreams disrupted her fitful slumber. Finally, she arose, fixed a cup of decaf tea, and curled on the couch. Her mother had dominated her nightmare; bits and pieces of Mom's criticisms of cousins and neighbors who'd had children out of wedlock had flashed through.

While sipping tea, Espy recalled her mother's reiterations regarding her high hopes that Espy would "marry up," better than she had. If Espy kept the child, what would her mother's reaction be? Espy shuddered.

If she kept the baby and stayed in Austin with no family support, could she manage her job and single motherhood? The thought of moving back to El Paso and facing her friends and family terrified her.

Chapter Two

Alice glanced at her ringing phone and grimaced. Jack Caulfield, Janine Lipscomb's attorney. Alice so dreaded the conversation that she had put it off. Telling Caulfield that she was closing the Bighorn Outfitters investigation was admitting defeat. Alice was confident that Lipscomb's snake of a boss, Davis Cummings, had forced Janine to simulate oral sex with a stuffed lion in the store's big game exhibit.

The only evidence Alice had to prove Cummings had given false witness was telephone records. They indicated he had initiated telephone calls while attempting to hire Lipscomb. The jackass had claimed that Lipscomb had called him and pursued the job. But there was no other corroboration to move the case one way or the other, and her boss, Saitou, had made it perfectly clear the "he said she said" testimony was insufficient to make a "cause" finding. *I bet the woman is scared to find discrimination because of the snake's grandfather, Republican donor and billionaire Jack Stewart IV. She'd rather us fail than draw any attention to her and the commission.* Defying orders, Alice had held the case open, hoping for a miracle.

"Hello, Mr. Caulfield. I've been meaning to give you a call."

"Ms. Arden, I have some news for you. I just got a call from Janine. She said that she got a call from Ellie, one of the employees at the Bighorn store in Houston. Ellie and Janine were close. Ellie told Janine that she called the LA store to see if they had a particular boot in stock.

"Ellie and the employee helping her, Cedric, got to gossiping about the company. Cedric told her that, when he started with Bighorn, a woman named Karen Sims was the manager. He'd heard rumors she was dating Cummings. I'll e-mail you Cedric's contact information. You really need to speak to him."

"Thanks for the information. I'll see what I can do," Alice said. The news thrilled her. This might be the opportunity she was looking for.

Alice was in the process of sending the information to Espy for a follow-up when her cell rang. It was Jane Wilson, the chair's secretary. Reluctantly, Alice answered.

"Good news, Alice. The chair is sending you a new investigator."

"You know, Jane, I really don't think we need any more staff. We're doing fine here. Besides, I have nowhere for a new investigator to sit." This couldn't be good. The last new employee had turned out to be an ex-con. Although JJ was working out OK, Alice was skeptical about taking on someone new.

"Nonsense. We have just the person you need. Her—uh, his name is Royce. Royce Atkins."

"Another ex-con?"

"No. Actually, he's an investigator in the San Francisco office."

"So, why isn't he staying in San Francisco?"

"Really, Alice, you should be glad you're getting some help. The chair noticed your inventory is aging and really thinks you could benefit from having a seasoned investigator."

"So, what's wrong with Royce?"

"Nothing. Nothing at all."

"So, are you paying his moving expenses?"

"Alice, you are so funny. Royce has family in Texas and just wants to move closer to home, that's all."

"Do I have any choice in the matter?"

"Well, actually, no. He'll report to work Monday."

As soon as Alice hung up the phone, she sent an IM to Quiana, asking her to check out Royce Atkins.

Quiana responded quickly:

> This is interesting. San Francisco says they have no Royce Atkins, only a Royce Ann Atkins. She does good work, apparently.

4

Alice typed back:
> That's strange, I could have sworn Jane said a Royce Atkins was transferring and kept referring to "him." I guess we'll find out soon enough.

Alice leaned back and stared out the window. The office was in a slightly seedy part of town, nestled between a rundown home and a weedy, fenced-off vacant lot. Traffic was minimal; the clientele who patronized the nearby dives were undoubtedly still sleeping off last night's binges.

Glancing at her watch, Alice noted that her favorite dive, Rebels, wouldn't be open for another hour. Just as well. She'd promised herself she wouldn't touch the booze anymore, but staying sober was harder than she'd imagined. The stress had been building lately, and without a luscious Singapore sling, she was having a difficult time keeping her nervousness under control.

Hearing a ding, Alice checked her e-mail. The contact information in the Bighorn case.

Good. Alice started to assign the work to Espy, but she had second thoughts. The woman had seemed a little frazzled for the past couple of weeks. *And she didn't call in this morning to say she wanted to take off. I need to speak with her; her work is slipping,* Alice thought. Instead, she asked Gaye to come to her office via IM.

When Gaye arrived, Alice asked, "Have you spoken to Espy lately? Is something wrong?"

"Not that I know of," Gaye said. "Quiana said she called in sick; hopefully it's just a bug."

"OK, well…some good news." Alice proceeded to explain the new lead on Bighorn. "I want you to take over the case. I'm not sure JJ is ready for this type of interview. I want you to get this done as quickly as possible."

"Sure, no problem," Gaye said.

"Let me know what he says. Saitou has been calling, asking when we are closing the case."

***

Gaye settled at her desk. She hadn't wanted to admit it to Alice, but she, too, was concerned about Espy. Lately, her coworker had been distracted, detached. It wasn't at all like her. Gaye dialed Cedric.

"Hello, my name is Gaye Rohatqi. I'm an investigator at the EEOC. I understand you might have some information regarding a former manager at Bighorn."

"Who gave you my name?" Cedric said.

"You talked to an employee at the Houston location, Ellie. She gave me your name and number."

"Damn. I don't want any trouble…I can't talk now. I get off at three. Call me after that, on my cell. 213-555-1243." He hung up.

He sure seemed scared, Gaye thought. Maybe there is something to this case.

Gaye tried to turn her attention to work, but she couldn't focus. Tommy, the love of her life, had finally convinced her to introduce him to her parents. They were leaving for Dallas right after work, and Gaye sensed disaster. When she'd told her parents they were coming, her mother had launched into an inquisition, firing questions as rapidly as Gaye could answer. Her mother had become silent, distant, when Gaye admitted that Tommy was Caucasian. Then she'd asked if the two of them were serious. When Gaye said they were, her mother said, "We'll see." She hadn't mentioned they were living together; her mother would have had a fit. Knowing that Gaye had accepted Tommy's marriage proposal would most likely have given her mother a heart attack.

Gaye glanced at Espy's empty desk. Something was going on, but Gaye didn't know what. Espy was an intensely private person and didn't share much of what she did after hours, even though Gaye felt they were good friends. When she'd told Espy that Tommy had proposed, pain had appeared to emanate from behind Espy's forced smile.

At the appointed time, Gaye placed the call to Cedric. "Thanks for speaking with me. Tell me what you know about the manager. I believe her name was Karen Sims."

"All I know it is that there was a rumor she and Cummings were dating. He came to the store quite often. They would be behind closed doors when I would leave for the evening. Then one day she was gone. Richard Cantu was hired shortly after that."

"How long ago did this happen?"

"I'd say about two years ago."

"So, what were the rumors about why Karen left?"

"No one really knows what happened. Must have been a big falling-out. They were joined at the hip."

Do you know how to contact Karen?"

"All I have is her cell phone number. I don't even know if it's still good. I'll text it to you."

"Thanks, Cedric. You're a big help."

Looking at the text, Gaye took a deep breath and made another call. "Hello."

"I'd like to speak with Karen Sims," Gaye said.

"This is she."

"Ms. Sims, my name is Gaye Rohatqi. I'm an investigator with the Equal Employment Opportunity Commission. I would like to ask you a few questions about Bighorn Outfitters. Would this be a good time?"

"How did you get my name?"

"Someone at the company gave me the information."

"Do I have to talk to you? I'm not sure who you are."

"If it would make you feel better, you can call the 1-800 number and verify I work there."

"I really don't want to get involved."

"I do understand. But this is rather important, so please don't forget we can subpoena you if necessary." Gaye crossed her fingers. She knew getting money to do out-of-state depositions would cost a fortune and the idea would be quickly nixed. "I know that you used to work at the Bighorn Outfitter store in Los Angeles, and Davis Cummings was your boss. I have a complaint that has been filed by another female manager who alleges that Mr. Cummings sexually harassed her. I need to ask you some questions about your relationship with Mr. Cummings and the reasons you left Bighorn."

"I'm not going to talk to you without an attorney present."

"I understand. That is your right. Can we schedule a time to talk next week? That should give you plenty of time to obtain legal counsel."

"This makes me so angry. I don't want to have anything more to do with that man."

"I understand, but the other woman is very upset. This has been a difficult ordeal for her. I'm sure your testimony will clear up some questions for us."

"I'll think about it."

"Thank you. I'll follow up next week." Gaye hung up the phone. Her hands were shaking.

Ms. Sims knows something. Alice will be so happy. Perhaps we can salvage this case.

Chapter Three

Espy rolled over and eyed the clock, amazed that she'd been able to sleep so late. So far, she'd been blessed with no morning sickness. A glance at her cell phone revealed that Hank had called at least three times, leaving messages. *Guess he wants to know if I got that abortion, the bastard.*

As Espy rose, she spotted her autographed copy of a romance novel by Caridad Piñeiro. The cover revealed a man and woman sitting on the lakeshore, holding hands. *That's what got me in trouble. Looking for Mr. Right. Thinking that I could live happily ever after. Listening to the line of crap Hank fed me. He was going to leave his wife. He really loved me.* Espy grabbed the book and threw it against the wall.

She dressed, made a grocery list, and headed to Target. As she pushed her cart toward the grocery section, her eyes wandered. A mother with a baby snugly attached to a car seat nestled in the basket passed by. The baby let out a cry, and the mother cooed. Espy had always wanted to be a mother; that wasn't in question. Finding the right partner was the problem.

Maybe there's no one out there for me. What if it's just the baby and me? Perhaps it would be better that way.

She thought about her coworker, Jorge. As mad as he made her sometimes, she envied him with his wife and four children. He had everything Espy ever wanted.

Impulsively Espy wandered through the infant section. Car seats, strollers, blankets, crib pads. And the items weren't just pink and blue anymore. A jumble of colors jumped out at her.

It was all so overwhelming. Who would keep the baby while she worked? She'd find the best care possible, even if she had to get a cheaper apartment.

Diapers? Espy studied the myriad of disposables available. Didn't people use cloth ones anymore? They seemed so much more environmentally friendly. Everything looked so daunting. Going through this by herself would be hard. Was she up to the challenge? If she kept the baby, she'd be forever linked to Hank, and the baby would never have the father he or she rightfully deserved.

Reluctantly, Espy returned to her original chore of grocery shopping. She decided to download some books on parenting this afternoon. Maybe that would help her decide once and for all.

***

Gaye stretched as she wrested herself out of a fitful slumber. Night terrors of her mother and Tommy had left her exhausted. Scrambling up, she dressed rapidly, intent on beating Tommy downstairs and heading off any trouble.

Gaye's mom, Nila, had expected them to sleep in separate bedrooms, and Gaye wasn't about to insist otherwise. The evening had been awkward. Her father, Sanjit, had asked Tommy pointed questions about his education, career, and family pedigree. Dad had held his cards close to the vest; Gaye couldn't tell what he was thinking. Her mom, on the other hand…

Entering the kitchen, Gaye was relieved to be the first one present. She started the coffee and then perused the cabinets and fridge for breakfast food. Tommy ambled behind her and eased his arms around her waist, kissing her on the neck.

"Don't," Gaye said, twisting away.

"What's wrong?" Tommy asked.

"It's just that…"

"That your parents wouldn't like it if we were married. We've been through this a hundred times before. I thought you didn't want to live your life based on what your parents want? You're not going to break our engagement, are you?"

"No, but I have to find the right time to tell them."

Tommy sighed. "It shouldn't be this complicated."

"What do you want for breakfast?" Gaye was anxious to change the subject.

"I have no idea. Is there some kind of Indian breakfast your parents eat?"

Gaye laughed. "No, they're completely Americanized. My mom doesn't like to cook anymore since us kids are all grown up. There's a choice of cereals, toast, and even some eggs."

"Oh, in that case, why don't I fix breakfast for everyone?"

"You don't have to do that."

"I insist."

"Well, OK." Gaye was worried that her mother would be upset. Not that she should be—it was just that her mother's body language told Gaye that Mom detested Tommy, and Tommy was in Mom's territory.

Tommy began bustling around the kitchen, gathering ingredients for a veggie omelet. Gaye helped him select spices that her parents would like. After pouring them each a cup of coffee, she sat at the bar to watch. *I do love him.* He was smart, funny, and extremely caring. And that red hair! He tried hard to learn her culture, too; most men wouldn't do that.

Just as Tommy was whipping the eggs, Nila walked in. "What's going on?"

"Good morning, Ms. Rohatqi. I thought I'd fix breakfast for everyone. I'll fix your omelet to order. Just let me know what you'd like in it."

"Out of my kitchen. Now! How rude of you to assume you could—"

"Mom, he was just trying to be helpful," Gaye said. "He didn't mean anything by it."

"If he wants to be helpful, he'll leave. He's unsuitable for you. You deserve better."

Gaye stared at her mother in horror.

"I understand, Ms. Rohatqi. We'll leave if that's what you want," Tommy said. Looking at Gaye, he said, "Are you coming with me or staying?"

At that moment, Gaye realized that failing to take a stand would condemn her to living her mother's life forever. That's not what she wanted. "Go pack your bag. I'll join you in a few minutes. I want to have a word with my mother first," Gaye said.

Tommy nodded and soundlessly left the room.

"Good riddance. He's not right for you. You can do better," Nila said. "I've got a line on a nice Indian man who just finished medical school. I understand he's handsome and comes from a good family."

Gaye glared at Nila. "How could you? How rude. You and Dad came to this country. If you wanted me to marry an Indian, you should have stayed in India. This whole thing makes me sad." Gaye headed out of the kitchen.

"Don't leave when I'm speaking to you. Come back," said Nila. Gaye ignored her and kept on walking.

Later, when Gaye and Tommy had finished packing, Gaye led the way down the stairs, and they slipped out of the house undetected. When they had left the neighborhood, Gaye burst into tears.

"I'm sorry," Tommy said. "I tried as hard as I could to be pleasant. I don't know what else I could have done. Forgive me. You warned me, but I wouldn't listen."

"It's not your fault," Gaye said. "You didn't do anything wrong. It's just going to take me some time to process all this."

"I'm not giving up. They've just got to come around. Besides, I plan to spend the rest of my life with you." Tommy reached over and put his hand on Gaye's, giving it a firm squeeze. "You're not thinking about postponing the wedding, are you? We're still on for September, aren't we?"

Gaye stared out the window, trying to determine her plan of action. She didn't want to choose sides, but there was no other recourse. "We are. I just want to see if I can smooth things over with my parents."

***

Quiana looked at herself in the mirror, satisfied that the blue in her shirt complimented her dark complexion. Would she ever be comfortable allowing others to see what she saw? Despite all the years of counseling, Quiana still couldn't handle knowing that someone else was looking at her.

Her coworker, JJ, was the only one who really understood. They'd watched a movie at his apartment several weeks ago. Just friends. Still, she had not let him glance at her face, choosing instead to hide behind a floppy hat.

Despite Quiana's excuse to JJ about not dating anyone at work, she could see herself dating him. But as long as she was unable to come out from behind the Oriental screen and the headpiece, dreaming of a relationship was useless. Maybe one day…

Grabbing her armor and pulling the brim low to hide her face, Quiana joined her sister, Chivann, in the car.

"You're sure about this?" Chivann said.

"I'm sure. JJ needs to practice driving before he takes his driver's license test," Quiana said.

"He's got a crush on you. You know that, don't you?"

"No, I don't."

"Well, he does, and I don't like it. The last thing you need to be doing is getting yourself mixed up with an ex-con."

"He's totally rehabilitated. Look, he's been at the office for nearly six months. He's polite, punctual, and he's learning the job. Everyone deserves second chances. Besides, with my sociophobia, there's no way I can get 'mixed up' with him."

"Quiana, I know you can lick it. Look how far you've come. I wish you'd go back to therapy. Maybe you can make some more progress. It's been a while since you've been."

"Just drive. I told JJ we'd pick him up in twenty minutes."

Quiana sat silently as they rolled through the Austin traffic. Was Chivann right? Would more therapy help? She doubted it.

Chivann eased the car to the curve and rolled down the window. "Hi, JJ. How long has it been since you've driven?"

"Hi, Chivann. Hi, Quiana. Thanks so much for helping me practice. Uh, let's see, it's been about twenty-one years."

"OK," Chivann said. "I think we better start out at a parking lot, somewhere where there's no traffic."

"It's like riding a bike," JJ said. It won't take me long to get up to speed."

After fifteen minutes on the parking lot, Chivann let JJ take the auto out on the streets. When she was satisfied that JJ was ready for his driving test, he asked if he could take them to lunch, and Quiana readily agreed.

Soon they were digging into a soul food meal of fried chicken and catfish.

"This is good," Quiana said. "Thanks so much. I didn't know this place was here."

"My neighbor told me about it, but I hadn't tried it yet because it isn't easy to get to on the bus," JJ said.

"So," Chivann said, "Are you going to buy a car?"

"Uh, I don't know."

"So why are you getting a license? If you don't get a car, it's not worth the trouble."

"Alice got mugged a while back and tore up her bad leg. She's on a scooter, but she can't drive to onsite investigations. Me being able to drive would really help her out," JJ said.

"Are you scared about the buying process?" Quiana asked.

"Yeah, I guess, a little. It sounds complicated…but I can do it," JJ said.

"I'll ask my brother to help you. You just look around and find a car that you like and think you can afford, and he'll help you through the negotiations."

"Thanks, I'd like that." JJ leaned over his plate and glanced up quickly. Terrified, Quiana lowered her face and situated the brim further down on her brow.

Chapter Four

Alice glanced warily at Inman, who was hovering over her desk. Her interview with Karen Sims for the Bighorn Outfitters case was in twenty minutes. She'd decided to do it herself because the stakes were so high.

"Let's go over the questions for Bighorn," Inman said. "Even if he did not sexually harass the witness, maybe something he did with her as a partner was similar to what he did to Lipscomb."

"I don't need any help from you. I know my job," Alice said. *And I don't trust you, either,* she thought. *I just know you're in cahoots with Saitou.*

"OK, don't get so defensive. I'm just trying to help," Inman said. Alice glared at him until he left.

She reviewed the Bighorn case once more and glanced over the list of questions. Inman had been right about how the questioning should go, of course. Still, Alice didn't want to give the attorney the satisfaction of hearing her agree.

Karen had finally acquiesced to speak with Alice after realizing Alice reiterated Gaye's threat to subpoena her. Thank goodness the bluff had worked, because the chances of getting any money for the process were slim to none. While preferring to meet Karen in person and watch her body language, Alice had been forced to settle for a video interview. The Denver office couldn't be trusted with such a critical mission,

Karen answered promptly. After explaining the process, Alice began. "First, let me ask you if you know Janine Lipscomb."

"No, I don't."

"Have you ever talked to her?"

"No. I told you I don't know her."

"Sorry. I just wanted to be real clear on that point. So, tell me, how did you get the job managing the LA store?"

"I had been the assistant manager in New York. Rocky thought I was doing a great job and recommended to Davis that I be moved to the new store."

"Rocky? Is he the New York store manager?"

"Yeah, Rocky Hart."

"So, how was your working relationship with Mr. Cummings?"

"Fine. We got along well, and he was pleased with my work."

"Did he ever make any unwelcome sexual advances or use any sexually oriented language around you?"

"No."

Alice became alarmed. The witness was not being terribly helpful, nor was she saying what Alice had expected her to say. Spasms rippled through her leg, and, gripping it, she willed herself to be still. She remembered the rumors that Karen and Davis were dating. "So, did you and Davis ever go out together after working hours?"

A long silence ensued. "Yes."

"Tell me about the first time you went out after work."

"We went to eat at a Japanese restaurant in Hollywood. The food was terrific."

"Do you remember the name of the restaurant?"

"Why does that matter? I think the name is Yamashiro. It's been there a long time."

"So, did you and Davis begin dating?" Another extended pause. "Yes, we did."

"Was this consensual?"

Karen sighed. "Yes, I was in love with the man. I knew he was married, but I thought he was going to leave his wife. He was always complaining about her. He said she didn't understand him."

"So, what happened to make you leave Bighorn?"

"Davis's wife apparently found about us and flew into a rage. Then, out of the clear blue, Davis's grandfather, Mr. Stewart, called me. He told me that if I would sign a release and never see Davis again, he would buy me a house. Free and clear." Karen stopped and cleared her throat. "I tried to call Davis, but he wouldn't answer the phone. I spoke to Rocky, but he said he didn't want to get involved. He told me that if it were him, he'd take the house and forget about Davis. I finally took his advice. I was afraid if I didn't, Stewart and his crew would make my life miserable. I decided to move back to Denver—that's where I'm originally from."

"I hate to be nosy, but how much was the house?"

"I was so mad, I wanted to make them pay, big time, but I can't say. That was part of the agreement; I can't talk about it."

Stewart wanted the woman out of their hair badly, Alice thought. "So, I'm just curious. You said that Davis didn't feel like his wife understood him. What was this all about?"

"Uh, well…you see, Davis was into the sadism thing. Not physical. He liked to humiliate women. His wife is a lawyer. She wasn't about to do stuff that would humiliate her. He'd tell me sex with her was boring. I didn't care. It was just a game for me, and it made him happy."

"So, what scenario did he like best?"

"That's hard to say. He liked just about anything that was a put-down."

Alice waited patiently.

Then, Karen spoke up. "For instance, he'd have me beg his forgiveness for screwing up a sale. He wanted me groveling on the floor. While I was groveling, he would masturbate."

Bingo! Alice tamped down her elation. "What did he have you wearing?"

"This is really embarrassing. Do we have to go into this?"

"Ms. Sims, I believe something similar happened to the other lady, but it was not consensual."

"Oh, I see…He liked to see me in my panties and high heels."

"Ms. Sims, you've been extremely helpful. I'm going to get a statement written up for you and get it out for your signature. Be sure you make a copy for yourself before you send it back."

Alice was positively ecstatic! What Lipscomb said had happened must be true! Cummings liked to humiliate his sex partners. And the panties and heels! How could Lipscomb make up something like that without knowing Sims? And the restaurant…it was his modus operandi.

She'd need to get Quiana researching it in the morning as well as pulling the records for the house in Denver. They'd need to be really sure Sims was telling the truth and not just trying to get back at Cummings for dumping her.

Chapter Five

Someone rapped at the office door promptly at eight o'clock in the morning. Jorge, who was pouring himself coffee, opened it. He stared at the coughing man who was waiting in the putrid entrance.

"Come in. It smells outside," Jorge said. "Uh, people who are bar hopping use the entryway for a bathroom." Jorge would have to remind Alice to get the entrance power-washed again. With the grueling heat, the smell was worse than ever.

"Hi, I'm Royce Atkins, the new investigator." Royce stuck his hand out to Jorge, who immediately sensed something out of place. Royce appeared to be a little over five feet tall, and his hands—they didn't seem to fit his body. Jorge shook the outstretched hand with the slender, dainty fingers. And the shape of his face…odd.

"Hi, I'm Jorge Macias. Put your things on the conference table. I'll tell Alice you're here." Jorge ducked into Alice's office and then hurried to tell the others the new investigator had arrived. After getting Royce a cup of coffee, Jorge settled at the far end of the conference table, where he could observe the most recent arrival.

While everyone was settling at the table, Royce stood up. He said, "I want to introduce myself. I'm Royce Atkins. I've been with the EEOC for eight years. I asked to transfer out of San Francisco because of all the discrimination I faced there. I'm trans and proud of it. Until three months ago, I was Royce Ann. I've been undergoing hormone treatments in preparation for gender reassignment surgery and was ready to make the transition to male in the workplace.

"I thought people who fought against discrimination wouldn't discriminate against me. I guessed wrong. I got some nasty notes left on my desk—unsigned, of course. Some people avoided me. A couple of them even continued to refer to me as "she" and "Royce Ann." Royce glared around the room. "If anyone does that to me here, I'm filing another EEO complaint."

Jorge, frozen, dropped his eyes to the table. How disgusting. No wonder his hands—its hands—were weird. Jorge began to rub the hand he had used to greet Royce on his pants.

Furtively he glanced at the group, praying for a time to excuse himself and wash up. The bathroom! Thank God it was a single stall with a lock on the door. Finally, Jorge focused on Alice, who had introduced everyone in the group and begun speaking.

"Royce, you're welcome here. I'd ask that you give us a chance. Uh, why don't you team up with Gaye and let her show you the ropes and tell you about her cases? I'll have you working with her, and you will eventually take her place when she goes back to school. After you learn what's going on, please drop by my office so we can chat."

Gaye broke the uneasy silence. "Royce, glad to have you. I've got some interesting cases. I share an office with Espy, so I'll bring some of the best ones out to the conference table. That way we won't disturb her."

The group began to dissipate. Jorge hurried to sanitize his hands.

***

Alice maneuvered her scooter back into her office and cursed. So, Royce Ann was now Royce. How convenient for the chair to use Alice's group as a dumping ground for employees who didn't fit in elsewhere. *That shrew…and I bet they did pay his moving expenses.*

Inman rushed into Alice's office and slammed the door. "What the hell! Why did you ever agree to take this he/she whatever it is? JJ was bad enough, but now we have to put up with some transgender with a chip on his shoulder? Give me a break. I don't believe anyone should alter the body God gave them."

"Shush!" Alice said. "He might hear you. Do you want an EEO

complaint? Remember what happened with Quiana when you harassed her and told her that her sociophobia wasn't real? The woman didn't file against you, but Royce will at the drop of a hat. We're going to have to be real careful."

"Humph. That woman shouldn't be hiding behind the screen. I still think that's a bunch of hooey."

"Why don't you call your boss and see if you can get rid of Royce? He certainly wouldn't get rid of JJ."

Inman glared at Alice and stomped out of the office.

***

"This case is interesting," Gaye said, opening the file and perusing it. "It's the Rojas Tortilla Factory in Houston. They got a new Hispanic manager. According to the Charging Party (CP), he's been cutting hours from African American employees and giving them to Hispanic employees. I just got the payroll records and need to analyze them. Perhaps you'd like to do that?"

"That Hispanic guy, Jorge, he didn't seem too friendly to me. Doesn't he like me?" Royce asked.

"How can you say that? You just got here."

"I get these vibes when homophobes are around. I bet he's one of them…OK, I'll be glad to do the analysis for you."

The pair reviewed a few more cases.

"That's all of the decent ones. What if we work the tortilla factory together and split the rest? Will that work for you?" Gaye said.

"Sure," Royce said. He stood. "I'll go speak with Alice if we're through."

"Good idea. You'll like her. She's one of the best supervisors I've ever had."

"We'll see," Royce said.

Gaye watched as Royce headed to Alice's office. *He's so touchy. With that kind of attitude, he's going to make some enemies.*

***

Alice looked up when she heard a knock. "Come sit down," Alice said, motioning to the chair in front of her desk. "We're glad to have you. Can always use another hand. Unfortunately, it's going to be somewhat crowded until Gaye leaves. She's getting married, you know, and decided to take a leave of absence to finish her degree. We'll miss her." Royce said nothing, so Alice continued. "San Francisco said you were a good investigator."

"Really? That's surprising. They sure didn't treat me like that."

"Royce, I get that you've had a difficult time. However, this isn't San Francisco. Why don't you give everyone a chance? I think you'll find they're great to work with."

"What if they're not? I don't think Jorge likes me."

"What makes you think that?"

"The vibes he put out. I know those kinds of people."

Alice trembled. An unsettling feeling like the one that had plagued her when Jorge had worked on the male-on-male harassment case reappeared. She'd had to assign him to the case because Espy didn't speak Spanish. That move had forced her to send two investigators out of town when only one investigator had been authorized. Alice hadn't trusted that Jorge would put his heart and soul into "the cause." Hopefully, the man wouldn't do anything to set Royce off.

"Please, Royce. At least give everyone a chance."

"The people in my support group told me it would be like this."

"Please don't just jump to conclusions. Let people get some time to know you. Have you found a place to live?"

"Not yet."

"Why don't you take the rest of the day off? No need to use leave. It's always easier to concentrate on work when you have a permanent place to live. Hotels are so uncomfortable."

"Thanks. I appreciate it. See you tomorrow." Royce exited the office.

Alice waited until Royce was gone and then summoned the investigators to the conference table. She already knew what Inman thought.

"I want to make myself perfectly clear," Alice said. "Royce is to be treated with dignity and respect, just like all the other employees."

"He's really defensive," Gaye said. "He thinks Jorge doesn't like him."

"He doesn't," Espy said. "Jorge's got this thing about the LGBTQ community. He can't stand them."

Jorge scowled at Espy. "What I think is none of your business. But, since you've made it your business, I'll tell you how I feel." Jorge looked Espy in the eye and said, "Do you believe in God?"

"What does that have to do with anything?"

"Just listen. Jorge withdrew a piece of paper from his pocket and began to read:

> · "Thou shalt not lie with mankind as with womankind: it *is* abomination. Leviticus 18:22.
> · If a man also lie with mankind as he lieth with a woman, both of them have committed an abomination: they shall surely be put to death; their blood *shall be* upon them. Leviticus 20:13.
> · A woman shall not wear a man's garment, nor shall a man put on a woman's cloak, for whoever does these things is an abomination to the Lord your God. Deuteronomy 22:5.
> · Therefore God gave them up in the lusts of their hearts to impurity, to the dishonoring of their bodies among themselves, because they exchanged the truth about God for a lie and worshiped and served the creature rather than the Creator, who is blessed forever! Amen. For this reason, God gave them up to dishonorable passions. For their women exchanged natural relations for those that are contrary to nature; and the men likewise gave up natural relations with women and were consumed with passion for one another, men committing shameless acts with men and receiving in themselves the due penalty for their error. And since they did not see fit to acknowledge God, God gave them up to a debased mind—"

"Stop!" Quiana said. The electronic camera roamed the table.

"That's Romans 1:24, verses 24 through 32," Jorge said.

"Yes, but what about the golden rule: 'Do unto others as you would have them do unto you'?" Quiana asked.

"What about it? The Bible clearly condemns homosexuality and all that other stuff," Jorge said.

"Oh my God, you are a bigot," Espy said.

"Am not. Take that back. That's the word of God. It has nothing to do with discrimination. It has to do with my right to religious freedom," Jorge said.

"You should be ashamed of—" Espy started.

"Quiet! All of you!" Alice said. She looked around the room at each of them. Jorge looked down at his lap, and Espy shifted in her chair. Gaye wore a pained look. JJ's eyes were as wide as saucers.

"Jorge, what you believe is your business. I can't tell you how to think. But as long as you work in this office, I expect you to treat Royce with dignity and respect. That means speaking civilly to him and not avoiding or ignoring him. When you go home you can say or do anything you want. But not here. Got it?"

Jorge nodded.

"We're here to fight discrimination against everybody—including against members of the LGBTQ community. It's the law. If any of you can't handle that, you need to transfer out ASAP. We've got a mess on our hands as it is with the Bighorn case, and we don't have any more 'cause' cases on the horizon…Now, everyone get back to work. If you don't find some more 'cause' soon, we'll all be heading home."

The group sat quietly. "Get going," Alice said.

Alice rolled into her office and lifted Dexter onto her lap. "Dex, I'm so screwed. That Royce is so touchy, so defensive. I don't think Jorge can treat him like he wants to be treated."

Alice's hand began to shake as it ran down Dexter's sleek brown-and-white coat. Suddenly her heart began to pound violently, heavy bands tightening in her chest. Death seemed imminent. She set him down, grabbed her purse, and fled the office.

Alice rolled into Rebels and secured her preferred seat. Within minutes Jake had set her favorite concoction in front of her.

"Alice, long time no see." When there was no response, he said, "You look frazzled. Bad day?"

"You won't believe it. Another new employee. Remember when I went through that?" Alice pressed her hands against her thighs to get them under control.

"Yeah, but it turned out OK, didn't it? Isn't the ex-con doing well?"

Alice sighed. "Yes, but the new guy. He's a transsexual who has just started presenting as a male. One of the other investigators is real religious and has taken offense. When I hear all that religious talk, my stomach turns. What hypocrites." A large gulp of her Singapore sling soothed her.

"Sounds like you have a bias against those who seriously practice their faith." Jake grinned.

"No, I…yeah, I guess I do. I'll have to work on it. Thanks, Jake. You know how to help me keep my head on straight." Alice could feel the alcohol surging through her, stilling her trembling hands.

"My pleasure." Jake left to tend to the couple who had just entered the bar.

Alice guiltily took another sip. She'd managed to stay off the sauce for several weeks, keeping the anxiety and stress under control, but this thing with Royce had pushed her button. *I know the stuff is bad for me…just this once.*

Alice ruminated about Bighorn while sipping the tasty drink. Since Saitou had ordered Bighorn closed, was pushing the case through without alerting her possible? Once the evidence was revealed, Saitou would be furious, but she wouldn't be able to shut it down without making Commissioner Feldstein angry. Thank goodness he was friends with the Charging Party's attorney and was pushing for the team to find merit in the allegations.

On top of that, if they didn't find some more discrimination quickly, Saitou could use the fact as an excuse to close the unit. That just couldn't happen.

Her thoughts turned to Art. He was much more fun to think about. Her attraction to this man with a kind face and salt-and-pepper hair had been instantaneous. Alice had long since abandoned the dream of finding a soul mate, but Art had her all atwitter. They'd gotten to know each other intimately as Alice had helped him out of a deep depression when he lost his job. Suspicious, her team had opened an age discrimination case against

Art's former employer and found he had indeed been let go because of his age. Nothing sexual yet, but Alice wasn't giving up on the idea. She looked forward to seeing him tonight at the dog park.

If Saitou closed the unit, would they send her back to New Orleans? If so, did Alice want to return? The San Antonio office was a possibility, but transferring as a supervisor was difficult. At this point, retirement was not affordable. One more year to go. Thank God. Sighing, she quickly finished the rest of her drink and waved for another.

Chapter Six

Statement in hand, Alice approached Inman, who, for some reason, appeared distracted. *He's been that way a lot these days. He hasn't called me A Plus in weeks.* "You think this is enough to find cause?" She tossed the Sims statement across the desk.

Inman perused it slowly. "Hmm. Very interesting. It is the same MO, humiliating his partner...Have you spoken to Saitou?"

"Yes. She felt it was clear and convincing evidence," Alice said. *Forgive me for lying.* Because Alice was convinced that Inman was in on the plot to get the office to fail, Alice believed the attorney wouldn't take any action without Saitou's blessing. But she knew her boss would object strenuously, even though they had convincing evidence.

"That surprises me. So, are you saying Saitou thinks we should find cause?"

"Absolutely. But, of course, you are the one who makes the ultimate decision."

"Well, OK...Maybe I need to speak with the general counsel. I—"

"No," Alice interrupted. "We're fine. I'm going to call Cummings and do the predetermination interview; I'll tell him what we've found."

"Let me know what happens. I assume this one will be on a fast track. I suspect Bighorn won't consider a settlement."

"You're probably right," Alice said. *And I won't be here to find out what happens because once Saitou figures out that I lied to you about her approving the case, I won't have a job.* But Alice had promised herself to do everything in her power to find justice for Janine and others like her. She was not going to back down now.

***

After Alice left the office, Inman checked the website helping link adopted children with their birth parents. He was obsessed with finding his daughter. What if Grace had told him about her at the time she was born? What would he have done? A young African American impregnating a white woman in the 1960s? He'd finally forgiven Grace for putting the baby up for adoption. It was the only rational choice.

Thank goodness he hadn't told his family about his offspring yet. Hope of locating his daughter was fading. Was this child even alive? Hiring a private detective was a possibility. But that was expensive, and there was no guarantee that she would even want to speak with him.

Why did he insist on looking up Grace, who was now a law professor at the University of Texas? Ever since, his obsession with the search had taken precedence. This Bighorn thing really needed his attention, but it didn't engage him. Maybe it was time to return to the Atlanta office. He did miss his wife.

***

JJ was taking a break outside when Royce appeared, cigarette in hand. JJ handed him a tin can for his butts, and Royce slid into the lawn chair next to JJ.

"So, JJ, how long have you been an investigator?"

"About six months. I really like the job."

"What did you do before you started to work here?"

"Uh, actually, I just got out of prison." JJ stared out over the weeds. He needed to clean up again. Quiana liked to keep the area neat, and staying on her good side was important.

"That really surprises me. You must have had some good recommendations."

"Quiana told me the chair wanted me hired as proof of the EEOC's

28

commitment to the prisoner reentry program."

"So, where were you?"

"Ramsey unit in Rosesharon for the last of my sentence. Why do you ask?"

"My cousin works there. Shawn Hicks. He's a lieutenant. Do you know him?"

JJ felt his stomach churn. The name brought back some bad memories. "Don't think so. So, did you find an apartment?"

"I did. I'm moving in at the end of the month."

Quiana opened the door, and Dexter tumbled out. "Keep an eye on him, JJ," Quiana said. She shut the door.

"What's with Quiana and that screen?" Royce asked.

"She has sociophobia."

"What's that?"

"A fear of being around people. She gets extremely nervous when other people look at her, so she stays behind the screen. You just put documents in the inbox for her. She also does e-mails and IMs. The camera on the table is hers. She can participate in the meetings without us looking at her."

"Wow, that's weird," Royce said.

"She's smart and funny. She helps us solve cases." JJ said. And you're weird, too, he thought. JJ stood. "Come on, Dex. We've got work to do." He looked at Royce. "I hear you're working the tortilla factory case with Gaye. Is it any good?"

"It's going to be fantastic. I just finished analyzing the payroll records. They got a new Hispanic manager who's been cutting the hours from African American employees and giving them to the Hispanic employees. He's actually been hiring Hispanic people, and the number of hours worked has expanded in the last three months. I've got to interview the managers."

"Great. We need some 'cause' cases," JJ said. He opened the door and followed Dexter inside.

***

Inman checked his watch and then entered the adoption registry website yet again. This time, there was a message. His heart skipped a beat. He'd dreamed of this day, but what would his wife say? Did he really want to go down that path? Turning back was possible, but…Inman breathlessly read the short e-mail:

> My name is Martha Scott. I was born in Illinois on the date and place you posted. I know that my birth mother was white, and my birth father must have been African American because of my skin color and features. Before we go any further, I want to see if would be willing to complete DNA testing.

Without hesitation, Inman replied, "Yes," and ordered the kit that Martha suggested. Barely able to contain his excitement, Inman snuck out of the office without bothering to tell Quiana. He drove straight for the University of Texas campus to search for Grace. Nearing the LBJ fountain, he slowed. Should he tell Grace now or wait until confirmation that Martha was their daughter? She'd indicated being uncertain about reuniting with the child who had been given up so long ago.

Martha would be in her forties now. *What does she look like? Would my daughter have the same traits or personality as I do?* Suddenly, meeting her seemed overwhelming. Inman wandered aimlessly, imagining that moment. What would he say to her? "Hi, I'm your father. Sorry I'm so late in meeting you. I never knew about you."

Inman returned to the office; he'd just sit tight until they got the results of the DNA test. No sense in upsetting everyone until he was sure Martha was his.

***

Alice turned over Karen Sims's address to Quiana to do some research about her house and the restaurant Cummings had taken Sims to on the first date.

Several minutes later, Alice had her answer. The restaurant was a favorite of movie stars, a very romantic place. The house Stewart bought to get Sims to go away was worth $1,250,000. Alice was shocked. *If I go after*

Cummings, how much money will Stewart throw at his defense? I'd better be really sure of myself, or it's going to blow up in my face.

Alice's leg stiffened, and her hands shook. She reached into her purse, withdrew the mini flask, and took a sip. Eying Dexter curled in his bed, she said "I have to do it, Dex. If I don't, it means they were right...Saitou, Inman... If I don't, I'm nothing but a fraud, living on past glory, all dried up." She raised the flask again, but it was empty. Looking at her watch and gathering her belongings, she turned her scooter toward the exit.

"Quiana," Alice called out in the direction of the elaborate Chinese screens. "I'm going to take a ride. I need to clear my head. Could you take Dex out before you leave?"

"Not a problem. Alice, Saitou's office called again to confirm that you had closed Bighorn Outfitters. What do you want me to tell them?"

Alice rolled out the door without answering, not able to get to Rebels fast enough. Claiming her favorite stool, she asked Jake for her usual.

Jake looked at his watch. "You're really early. What gives?"

"Same old, same old," Alice said.

Downing the Singapore sling in record time, Alice motioned to Jake to whip up another tasty potion.

"Things not going well?" Jake said as he placed the glass on a dry napkin. Alice greedily took a long swig.

"You might say that."

"Want to talk about it?"

"Not now. Got to do some thinking on my own."

Alice stared at the TV. The images doubled and weaved out of focus. Finally, her agitation began to ebb. With shaky hands, she took another long draw, like a thirsty cowboy coming upon a full canteen.

Suddenly, loneliness enveloped her. Asking for help was out of the question. This was her decision. Doing the right thing was paramount. Failure meant not being able to live with herself. Memories of almost being raped at work when a teen confronted her. *If someone had been there for me then...*

A new bartender brought Alice out of her trance. "Where's Jake?" she asked.

"Oh, he has a test tomorrow and asked if I could cover for him.

"Want another?"

"Yes, please."

"What is it?"

"Singapore sling."

"A what?"

"A Singapore sling." Alice began to recite the recipe by rote: "One ounce of Bombay Sapphire gin, half ounce of cherry brandy, three ounces of pineapple juice, a quarter ounce of Benedictine, quarter ounce of Cointreau, and a half ounce of grenadine. You need to shake that well with ice and strain it into a tall glass of crushed ice. Fill the rest with club soda, and add two cherries."

Alice finished the last of her potion and started to slide off the stool, but she stopped, her head swimming. She hesitated, then tried to stand again...useless. Fear soared through her that, while attempting to make it to her scooter, a fall would further damage her leg. She fumbled in her purse, clutching her phone. The possibility of calling Quiana or one of the other staff emerged, but truth be told, it would be an embarrassment for them to see her like this. With no one left to help her out of the jam, she dialed Art.

Art wrestled the scooter into his trunk as Alice sat in the passenger seat, focusing on the AC vent to prevent the car from spinning. When Art eased into the front seat, Alice said, "We have to get Dex. How long has he been at the office?"

"No, we don't. I stopped by the office, and Quiana said she would take him home. I'm taking you to a rehab hospital." Art did not look at Alice.

"No, I can handle this myself, I just..."

"If you don't go, I'm done with you. I've been watching you tank for months. I thought you were getting better, so I didn't say anything. Alice, you're my best friend. I'm not going to put up with it anymore."

Alice closed her eyes; seeing a duplicate of Art's head was making her ill. Art was right. *I'm in a hell of a mess. It's all my fault...I know better. Thought I could handle it...keep it under control.*

If only Jake had been there, he would have stopped her. *I can't miss work...the crew can't pull it off without me...Saitou will find a reason to get rid of me. I'll really be a failure then. But I'll lose Art...Time's running out for me...I feel like it my last chance to have a human relationship. I love Dex, but...*

"Ok, I'll go. But I'm not staying long." Alice closed her eyes, passing into oblivion.

Inman glared at the group around the table. Eying the videocam, he said, "Quiana, how long is Alice going to be gone?"

"I don't know. Uh, maybe a week."

"So, who is going to do the PDI on the Bighorn Outfitters case?"

No one moved. They all averted their eyes, eager to avoid getting saddled with the predetermination interview. "Jorge, you're the senior investigator. I guess you need to do it," Inman said.

"I don't know anything about the case. I haven't worked on it at all."

"Inman, didn't you help draft the interview questions for the other woman? You should do it. You know the most about it," Espy said.

Inman was about to tell Espy that wasn't his job. Then he remembered how she'd shamed him into continuing the Hyperion male-on-male sex harassment investigation by telling him he was no Dr. Martin Luther King. "I guess I'll have to do it."

"Jorge, why don't you tell us about your new case?" Inman said.

"Sure. It's at a bank in College Station, Consolidated State Bank. Charging Party's a teller and said he was fired for making too many mistakes. He said his boss is a woman, and he's the only male teller. CP said some of the other tellers make more mistakes than he made and are still working there."

"How far away is College Station?" Inman asked. He looked expectantly at the digital camera perched on the conference table.

"About one hundred miles—an hour and forty-five minutes without traffic," Quiana said.

"Do you think you can tie this up in a day, Jorge?" Inman asked.

"Shouldn't be a problem if I take another investigator. I'll get CP's statement over the phone, and then he can just sign. I can do his rebuttal at the same time. I don't think the other witnesses will take too long with two of us interviewing."

"OK, onsite it is," Inman said. "Royce, why don't you go with Jorge?" Inman looked from Jorge to Royce. Neither seemed enthused.

"I'll drive," Jorge said.

"JJ," Inman said, turning to him. "What are you working on?"

"I don't have any cases of my own. I've mostly been helping the other investigators."

"Quiana," Inman asked, "have we gotten any new cases?"

"Actually, one just arrived—Logistic Construction. It's in San Antonio. The Charging Party, African American, said there was graffiti inside the porta can saying 'niggers stink.' The company painted over it, but it reappeared several days later. That happened a couple of times. Basically, his supervisor said there was nothing further he could do because he didn't know who was behind it. He just told CP to ignore it."

"Wow!" JJ said. "Sounds like a good one."

"I agree," Inman said. "JJ, would you like to take the assignment?"

"Oh, I'd love to have the case," JJ said.

"Put that on a fast track, and see if we can get it turned around quickly. The company can do a better job than that," Inman said.

After they had finished discussing the other cases, Inman dismissed the group and returned to his office. His irritation about the Bighorn PDI welled, but getting out of it would be tricky. One possibility was to wait for Alice's return, but since he was going to have to litigate it, he might as well get his feet wet. Nothing else pressing was on his desk.

***

JJ retrieved the Logistic case from Quiana and began to read. Then, he called the CP, Thaddeus Johnson. After the call ended, JJ made a few notes regarding the conversation and promptly freaked. This was the first case where he was entirely on his own.

Going over his notes, he calmed and began to develop his investigative plan. Thad said that they were at an office building construction site with approximately eight other subcontractors. The porta cans belonged to the prime contractor and were used by everyone on the building site. There were around six units. Thad's favorite one was second from the left. That's where he'd found the graffiti. After it was whitewashed, he used another stall, but several days later, the same message appeared.

Apparently, there were other African Americans on the site, but Thad didn't know whether they had complained or not. He was the only one on this particular Logistic crew, which was tasked with cabling the building for electronic devices.

JJ scratched his head. Thad had told him that no one had made any slurs or derogatory comments to his face. However, finding the graffiti had left Thad nervous, always looking over his shoulder.

He'd reinterview Thad, of course, and obtain his written statement as well as that of the supervisor. Interviewing others to verify that the graffiti continuously reappeared would be important. His plan complete, he turned it in to Jorge for approval.

Chapter Eight

Jorge stopped his car in front of the office and motioned for Royce to get in, Alice's warning ringing loudly in his ears. Being civil to Royce was going to take flat-out concentration. He was going to discuss the issue with his preacher next Sunday after church; he definitely needed guidance.

Once they were on the highway, Royce asked, "What about JJ? I understand he's an ex-con. Were you surprised he got hired?"

"It was the chair's decision, not Alice's. He's OK, though. He hasn't caused any trouble."

"Well, my cousin is a lieutenant at JJ's prison. I'll have to ask him if he knows JJ."

"You might want to read over the case before we get there. I've got a list inside the case of the witnesses for you to interview and some questions to ask."

To Jorge's relief, Royce stopped chatting and began reading. If they continued their discourse, Jorge feared he might accidentally say something that offended Royce, and Jorge didn't want to deal with Alice's wrath.

***

Jorge and Royce entered the bank and headed to a counter at the center of the lobby. The interior featured walnut-stained walls with contrasting gray-flecked white marble floors and counters. Jorge glanced around, noting three women tellers at the stations against the back wall. He turned his attention to the young receptionist.

"I'm here to see Gwen Roberts. My name is Jorge Macias, and this is Royce, uh, Royce Atkins." Royce gave the woman a small hand wave and a big smile.

"She's expecting you. Have a seat, and I'll let her know you're here."

The two sat as the woman made a phone call. "She'll be with you in just a minute."

Jorge said, "I'll take care of—"

Gunfire echoed through the cavernous lobby, and the security guard dropped to the floor in a heap. Royce dove to the ground while Jorge froze, staring into the wild eyes of a tall, beefy white man waving a .45-caliber pistol, a sweat-stained cowboy hat perched on his head.

"Move your asses. Get off the floor, girly boy. You and Pancho go stand over by those tellers. Empty those damn pockets, and put everything on the counter." He threw a large canvas bag at the nearest teller. "Honey, you better fill that to the brim, or I'll put a round between those bright blue eyes of yours."

Jorge tensed. Anger seethed through him. He hated bigots. Pancho. *Pancho!*

Royce rose and raised his hands. "Easy. We'll do just what you say." He stepped backward slowly. Jorge followed his lead. Two of the tellers were sobbing.

"Quit that sniveling, or I'll shoot your asses. Hurry, move it."

Jorge dumped the contents of his pockets; Royce followed suit. The sound of approaching sirens brought a flicker of hope.

"Goddammit. Who did that?" The gunman waved his weapon at his victims. Jorge grimaced. The bandit looked at the countertop and saw two badges.

"You fuckers the law?" He jabbed at Royce.

"Easy. No, we're fed—"

"Feds. Shit." The robber glanced over his shoulder. The wails became more intense, and red light began to bounce off the lobby walls. Again, he menaced with his revolver. "Y'all get to the back. No funny stuff. He grabbed the bag the teller had filled and herded the group to the rear of the building.

When he reached an office, he barged in. "Sit against the wall. *Now!* Keep your hands in the air where I can see them." The gunman glared at the elderly African American woman seated at the desk. "Heifer, anyone else but you back here?"

"No, sir, no one else is here. Everyone else took a early lunch," the woman said.

"Better not be lying to me, or I'll blow that 'fro 'do right off your head."

"Hey," Royce said, "I'm Royce what's your name?"

"None of your business." The man glared menacingly at his captives. One of the women stifled a cry.

"Shut up! Every single one of you!"

"Just trying to be friendly," Royce said.

"Don't need no friends. I'm just fine, fairy."

"Why don't you relax? Have a seat. Looks like we're going to be here a long time," Royce said.

"Why are you being nice? You got something up your sleeve?"

"No. Just want you to know I'm not going do anything to cause trouble for you. I'll do anything you say. My partner feels the same, don't you?" Royce looked at Jorge. Jorge swallowed. He wished Royce would have just kept his mouth shut.

"Yes, yes, I'm going to do everything you say. You can count on that," Jorge said. Suddenly the sirens died, and the room became eerily quiet.

The gunman eyed the women suspiciously. Any of you got guns on you? Hey, you feds, stand up. Jorge started to stand, but the robber pointed his weapon at him. "Not you, just him." He motioned at Royce.

Royce struggled to rise, hands in the air.

"Turn around and step backward, over here. Keep coming." The gunman waved his gun erratically, then, when Royce got close, shoved it in the small of his back. "One false move, and I'll blow your spinal cord in two." The bandit quickly frisked Royce, including a check of his ankles.

"I don't have a shiv if that's what you're looking for."

"Shut up, girly boy. You sit down. Pancho, I'm going to check you. Stand up."

The criminal followed a similar procedure with Jorge. When he was satisfied, he told the men they could put their hands down.

"Now, we're going to have some fun. You at the end. You stand up. Pancho's going to search you. Now Pancho, I want you to rub your hand up and down her body real slow-like. She might have some knife hidden in her titties or snatch." The gunman laughed loudly.

When Jorge hesitated, the gunman jabbed the pistol in his ribs. Jorge immediately did as he was told.

"OK. They seem to be clean enough. Y'all can put your hands down. I want everyone to take their shoes off and slide them over."

"Boy, Tom, you're thorough," Royce said.

"I'm not Tom, I'm Pete. Don't call me Tom again.

"Sorry, Pete. I won't, I promise." Royce took off his shoes and glided them across the tile floor.

The telephone in the office rang. "You, cotton top, answer the phone."

"Hello...My name is Gwendolyn Roberts. I'm the vice president.... Yes, there are seven of us in the office with Pete."

"Shut your mouth, you whore."

"Mr. Pete, would you like to speak with Nathan?"

"Give me the fuckin' phone. Go sit down. No funny business." He waved the firearm over the crowd.

"Nathan, this is what I want. I want a car and $500,000 in small bills." You need to have that here in two hours, tops. And I want a hamburger all the way, fries, and a large Coke. If I don't get everything I asked for, I'll start shooting the hostages. You got it?" Pete slammed down the phone.

Jorge's stomach roiled. And he was stuck here with this Royce person, someone he couldn't stand. Why had he agreed to bring him? Would they be able to get out alive? His wife would be worried when he didn't make it home on time—she always was.

"Hey, you, Pancho," Pete yelled and kicked Jorge's feet. "Get up. You and the fruit come with me. Any of you pussies move, I'll shoot these two fuckers. Cotton top, give me your keys."

Pete shoved them down the hall to the utility closet and unlocked the door. After canvasing the tight space, he shoved Royce and Jorge to the back and, swinging a broom handle, knocked out the light. "Have a nice life." Pete slammed the door, locking it.

Jorge sunk to the floor, brushing off the shards of glass that coated him. He could barely make out Royce with the feeble light emanating under the door. Royce tried the handle.

"We're stuck," Royce said.

"Really? I'd never have guessed."

"What's your beef with me, Macias? You've not said two words since we left this morning."

"Nothing."

"Well, I don't buy any of it. You're just like all those other bigots out there. You're all for stomping out discrimination when it's against Hispanics, but you're just fine when people like me are attacked."

"That's your opinion."

"Yeah, well, it's true. I can feel it. I've gotten bad vibes from you ever since I started working in Austin."

"Just drop it, OK? We need to be more worried about what that wacko out there is going to do."

"You're right...I got to go to the bathroom." Royce banged on the door until Pete showed up.

"Quit your bellyaching. I gotta have quiet so I can think."

"I have to go to the john."

"Too bad, so sad." Pete laughed. "You'll figure something out."

Jorge listened as Pete's footsteps faded down the hall. It was bad enough that he was stuck with a queer, but now they had to pee in the same room.

"Look," Royce said. "I saw a pail with a mop in it when we came in." He felt around until he located it. "I'll just take a leak in here."

"Gross." Jorge groaned.

"Got any better ideas?" Royce asked. "You can't see me anyway. Your turn will come when you need to relieve yourself."

"Just do it." Jorge put his fingers to his ears until he was sure Royce was finished.

Chapter Nine

Frustrated, Inman came out of his office to get a breath of fresh air. He'd just been on the phone with the asshole from Bighorn. The man proclaimed his innocence and said he was being framed. The bitch only wanted money, according to Cummings. The bully warned Inman that they would fight him tooth and nail. *I can't believe he called the CP a bitch! Let me just guess what he thinks about women.* Approaching the Oriental screen, he heard Quiana speaking to someone.

"What? Say that again?" Quiana asked. Inman listened as Quiana's nails clicked across the keyboard. "Holy crap…Thanks for letting me know." Then she called out, "Everyone to the conference room. Shit's hit the fan!"

"What's all this about?" Inman said.

When everyone had gathered, Quiana said, "The College Station cops called the Houston office because they found two EEOC badges at the scene of a bank robbery. They belong to Royce and Jorge. They may have been taken hostage. Has anyone heard from them lately?"

"No," Espy said. She began to text Jorge. Shortly, a text came back, and she read it out loud to the group. "Pancho ain't here. You squeal to the pigs and he's dead." She put down the phone. "They got him," Espy said. "And probably Royce, too."

"Oh, shit," Inman said. "And Alice isn't here. "What are we going to do?"

"It's what *you* are going to do," Quiana said. "You're in charge, remember?"

"Are you going to go to the bank?" Gaye asked.

"Well, that's the problem," Inman said. "The chair doesn't exactly want other people to know our office is here."

"I don't understand," JJ said.

"Here's the deal. This is a secret project. No one's supposed to know about it," Inman said.

"Why?" asked Espy. "I don't get it. We were asked to come here and work, so why all the secrecy?"

"If we succeed, they can tell everybody how good we are. But if we fail…" Inman said.

"I thought we had succeeded," JJ said.

Inman said, "All I know is that's what the chair said, she didn't want anyone to know about it. So, if I go to College Station…"

"I don't get it," Espy said. "Why does this have to be secret now?"

"I don't know, but someone needs to call Jorge's wife before the poor woman hears it on the news," said Gaye.

Does Royce have any family we should call?" Inman asked.

"No one I would want to call," JJ said.

"JJ, shame on you," Gaye said.

"Sorry, I don't like working with fags," JJ said.

"He is not gay he is transgender," Gaye said.

"Whatever," JJ said.

Quiana's phone rang. A look at the caller ID prompted her to answer. "I'm sorry, ma'am. Ms. Arden is not here…She's sick. But Mr. Parker is here. Would you like to speak with him? …Yes, ma'am. Give me just a minute, Chair Saitou, and I'll transfer the call to his office," Quiana said.

Inman sped to his desk, slamming the door. He listened to the chair yell and scream, unable to get in a word edgewise.

Minutes later, Inman exited his office and sank into a conference room seat. "We are in deep doo-doo. The media have been calling the chair, asking for a statement. She's livid."

"It's not our fault the bank got robbed when they were doing the onsite," Espy said.

"Yeah, but according to Saitou, it's our fault we did an onsite in the first place," Inman said. "The chair's been trying to reach Alice for over an hour, and she's furious that Alice is not here."

"Damn," Quiana said.

"Where is Alice, anyway?" Inman said. "We really need to get her in the loop on this."

"Well, she's really sick, but I'll see what I can do get hold of her," Quiana said.

"This has been a swell day," Inman said. "I finally did the predetermination interview on the Bighorn case. The guy was a piece of work. He accused us of railroading him with testimony from a liar—said we had no real proof. He threatened to sue us for defamation of character. I'm glad the chair made the decision to 'cause' the case and not me…OK, back to work…No one is to answer any questions from the media; you need to refer them all to headquarters."

***

Quiana's fingers rapidly clicked out a text to Art.

Quiana: Dragon lady looking for Alice. Big problem at office. Need to contact her STAT.

Art: No can do. She is really sick.

Quiana: She'll be sicker if dragon finds out she's not here. Jorge and Royce are being held hostage.

Art: OMG. Will call you. Go somewhere rest of office will not hear.

Quiana reached for her droopy hat and situated it low over her brow. Calling to Dexter, she crept out the back and settled in a lawn chair. The heat was already debilitating, and it wasn't even noon yet. Dejectedly Dexter sniffed a few of his favorite marking spots, but he soon slouched back and laid at Quiana's feet. The dog appeared grateful when his good friend leaned over and rubbed him under his chin.

"I know you miss her. I do, too," she said.

She punched talk on the first ring. "This is serious," Quiana said. "Apparently we are supposed to be a secret office, and nobody is to know we are here."

"Why?" Art asked.

"Haven't a clue. But the media is swarming, and Alice needs to know there is trouble. The chair has been trying to contact her."

Silence hung on the line.

Art sighed. "I told Alice I wouldn't say anything. You've got to promise not to tell any of the others…Alice is in rehab. I don't want to tell her what's going on. She'll get stressed. That's what started her drinking in the first place."

"I knew something was wrong. She just hadn't been herself lately."

"What are we going to do?"

"Why don't I tell the chair that Alice is having surgery? We'll say it's a minor procedure and she didn't want to bother the chair about it. I can probably buy her about twenty-four hours."

"OK. Keep me posted. And promise you won't tell."

Quiana thought about her own demons and how Alice had worked with her. "I won't."

***

Alice glanced at her watch while closing her journal. The evening group therapy session had been intense but satisfying. Sure, she missed her slings, but truthfully, she was feeling better. Stepping back from the precipice made her realize the extent of the damage that had been done to her body. Before bed, the idea hit her to wheel out to the patio and envision a plan to stay sober.

Nearing the nurse's station, she overheard a conversation among several of the counselors. One of their former patients was holding hostages at the Consolidated State Bank in College Station. Alice perked up. Was that the bank where they were doing an investigation? Snippets of the discussion drifted toward her. Hostages? Federal employees?

Alice froze. She punched hard on the scooter's accelerator and zoomed over to barge in on the exchange.

"Hostages? Who's been taken hostage?" Alice asked.

"Apparently, five bank employees and two federal employees. It's sad. We thought we had him out of the woods. I guess he just couldn't handle it when he got on the outside," a counselor said.

"Do you know who the federal employees are?" Alice asked.

"Why does it matter?" the counselor asked.

"They're with the EEOC," another said.

"Shit!" Alice screamed out. They stared at her. "They're my employees. They work for me. I've got to get out of here."

"Calm down," Beatrice, her group therapist, said. "They're being taken care of. You're getting too worked up. You're too vulnerable now to leave."

"I don't care. I'm out of here." Alice wheeled her scooter away and sped to her room, Beatrice jogging behind her.

"You can't do this. You—"

Alice screeched to a halt, the counselor slamming into the back of the scooter. "Yes, I can. I came in here voluntarily, and I'm going to leave voluntarily. End of story."

Alice grabbed a plastic bag and stuffed her belongings in it. All the while, Beatrice sat on Alice's bed, nursing a stubbed toe. Alice ignored the sound advice Beatrice was providing.

"Beatrice, I know you're right. Look, it's just that these people work for me, and I'm responsible for them. They were on a trip on behalf of the US government, and it's gone horribly wrong." Alice watched as the woman's shoulders sagged. "I promise I'll check myself back in just as soon as the crisis is over. You have my word on it."

"I do hope you come back. Much more of your past behavior, and you'll develop cirrhosis like your mother."

Alice nodded and avoided Beatrice's gaze.

Well, at least let me call someone for you," Beatrice said.

"Please call me a cab. And if you want me to sign some papers, you better have them ready ASAP."

Chapter Ten

Royce watched the light under the door grow dim as Pete paced by. The gangster had been plodding the hallway for what seemed an eternity. A glance at his watch showed it was close to eleven. Shifting, Royce tried to get comfortable, but his head hurt, and he was craving a cigarette. At least they had been able to dampen the pungent odor of their comingled piss by diluting it with cleaning chemicals.

"Guess Pete didn't get the money and car," Royce said.

Jorge moved but didn't respond.

Royce exhaled heavily. The tension of the whole situation was exhausting, and the fact that Jorge had remained silent for most of the ordeal was gnawing at him. All Royce wanted was to be understood. What if this was his last day on earth?

"When I was a kid," Royce said, "I didn't like to play with dolls or play school, for that matter. I just didn't feel I fit in. My girlfriends would talk about how they felt all the time. It made me uncomfortable. I felt more comfortable hanging with the guys, talking about things. The older I got, the more uncomfortable I became."

"I don't want to hear this," Jorge said.

"Well, you're going to, unless you want to knock on the door and have Pete save you." When Jorge didn't reply, Royce continued. "When I went through puberty, my world got turned upside down. I wasn't welcome to hang out with the guys anymore, and I was increasingly relegated to the sidelines.

"The boys wouldn't listen to what I had to say; they just didn't accept me. I felt like a loner. I started to dress like a boy, and my parents became angry. They shamed me. By the time I got to high school, I was suicidal.

"I know you don't get any of this, not being comfortable in your own skin. It's horrible...I finally got to the point where I was willing to risk everything to feel whole, to..."

"What did your parents say?" Jorge asked.

"My mother told me I was an abomination and she didn't ever want to see or hear from me again. I haven't heard from them since. That was fifteen years ago."

Silence enveloped the room. Royce listened to the steady click of Pete's boots slowly plodding the hall, resisting the urge to stand up and scream at the absurdity of it all.

"It's the bathroom thing that freaks lots of people out," Jorge said. "We shouldn't be going to the same bathroom."

"Yeah, that's what they say. But you couldn't see me peeing in the pail, so what big deal did it make? I couldn't see you either. It's the same way in a bathroom—there are doors. Nobody sees you doing your thing. We're not a bunch of loony rapists—no more than the rest of the population. I'm a human, just like you. I just want to live in peace. Just thought you should know."

Jorge shifted. "We may as well try to get some sleep. No telling what will happen tomorrow."

***

However, Jorge couldn't sleep. He attempted to plump the paper towel rolls under his head and ignore his hunger and thirst. Although he was aching with fatigue, his mind wouldn't let go of what Royce had said.

He'd sounded so sincere talking about how he felt so disjointed and out of place in his body that he'd risk anything to feel whole and right. Jorge couldn't fathom those feelings. He'd always assumed that people like Royce just woke up one day and decided they wanted to change their sex for the hell of it.

Jorge's mind wandered to his family. What would happen if he couldn't get out of this mess? Why hadn't he told his wife he loved her before leaving the house?

***

Alice waited impatiently for the cab to arrive. Calling Art had occurred to her, but it didn't feel right. He'd try to talk her into staying, and she just wasn't going to do it.

As soon as her ride appeared, she began barking orders. "You'll have to load the scooter into the back. I need you to get me to the Consolidated State Bank in College Station yesterday.

"Ma'am? You know how much that will cost?" the cabbie asked.

"I don't care. You take a credit card, don't you?"

"Yes, but—"

"You going to drive me or not? I'll give you a generous tip for your trouble."

"Will I have to wait for you?"

"No, you'll be free to go."

"At your service." The cab roared into the darkness.

***

Alice peered out the window at the blinking red and blue lights bouncing off the nearby buildings, giving the area a surreal look. It was nearly one in the morning, and she was exhausted.

"You sure you want to get out here?" The cabbie asked.

"Yes. Pull over there. That looks like the command post," Alice said.

The cabbie complied, and Alice soon found herself rolling full steam toward a knot of officers. The media were gathered a short distance away.

A patrol officer blocked her progress. "Sorry, ma'am, you can't enter. Authorized personnel only."

Alice dug in her purse and flashed her EEOC credentials. "My employees are the ones who are being held hostage. I came as quickly as I could."

The officer viewed her credentials and then got on the radio. "You can go on in. Chief Carson is the Incident Commander. He'll speak with you."

***

Pete jerked open the door, and a bright light hit Royce, who winced and covered his eyes. "God, it stinks in here," Pete chuckled. "You two been having a pissing contest?" He laughed and, waving his gun, pointed at Jorge. "Pancho, I got a job for you. The cops put some eats in the lobby; I need you to go get 'em. Any funny business, and I'll blow you away."

"Hey, fairy boy," Pete jerked his weapon toward Royce. "You wait in the room with the women. You keep those heifers quiet and inside. If they so much as put their little toes out the door…"

A rage so profound welled within Royce that he shook. If Pete hadn't been pointing that pistol at him, Royce would have charged the bastard.

Pete stepped back into the hall as Royce and Jorge stumbled out of the closet. At least Royce had felt safe there. The last time he had been this frightened was when a group of toughs followed him and his friends after an evening at a gay bar.

Pete gestured Royce into the office with the women and then proceeded to walk away with Jorge. The ladies appeared worn and tired.

"What's it been like?" Royce asked Gwen.

"He's real jumpy. Been on the phone with the hostage negotiator, but that pacing is driving me up the wall. I'm afraid he's going to snap. The lack of sleep is making him punchy. Things aren't going his way. The food is the first concession he's gotten out of them," Gwen said.

Royce looked around the stale, squalid office. Candy wrappers littered the floor. The contents of the top of the desk had been swept to the ground. He could hear Pete yelling directions at Jorge.

Grabbing a nearby stapler, Royce motioned to Gwen and whispered, "When Pete steps in the door, I'm going to hit him in the head as hard as I can. Try to go for his gun if he drops it. It's our only chance."

Gwen nodded.

"All right, Pancho, bring that box down the hall nice and slow. Put it down, and take out all the food. Want to be sure they didn't put any weapons or listening devices in there."

Royce flattened himself against the wall, hoping that Pete didn't realize where he was. Gwen was quietly giving instructions to the women. One of them had a phone-charging cord hidden in her fist.

"OK, Pancho, looks clean. Load it back up. Hurry. Damn, I'm hungry. You go first, you greasy Mexican." Pete laughed as he shoved Jorge through the door.

As Pete crossed the threshold after him, Royce sprang into action. *Thwack!* The stapler slammed into Pete's head, throwing him off balance. The pistol fired as Pete and Royce went sailing onto the floor.

***

"Oh my God. Gunfire." Alice watched in horror as the swat team leader yelled, "Go, go, go," and the heavily armed police vanished into the building. Tense moments ensued. Radios crackled. A call went out that the scene was secure but paramedics were needed.

Alice's heart sank. Jorge…Royce…Who was hurt? Was someone killed? By now, the media was swarming, reporters jostling for position. At long last, a stretcher appeared. Alice craned to see who was being brought out. Jorge. Shaking uncontrollably, she automatically reached for her flask, but it wasn't there. Setting her scooter at full speed allowed her to barge past a cop who was yelling at her to stop. She rode along beside the stretcher, peppering the paramedics with questions.

"It's OK," Jorge said. "She's my boss. Call my wife." He closed his eyes, grimacing in pain.

"What's his status? How badly is he hurt?" Alice asked.

"Ma'am, I really can't tell you anything," the paramedic said. We're taking him to St. Joseph's hospital. They'll do everything they can."

Alice stopped rolling and watched as Jorge was whisked inside the ambulance. Looking up, she realized the TV cameras were trained on her. Reporters were shouting, trying to get information. Additionally, a frustrated policeman admonished her for breaking through the line and ordered her back. Alice did as she was told.

Quickly she dialed Quiana. "Listen, I can't talk. Jorge's been hurt…."

No, I don't know about Royce. Have Inman call Jorge's wife and arrange for her to get to College Station. Make her some hotel reservations.... No, are you kidding? I'm not charging it to the government. I'll pay for it myself. I feel responsible. If only I'd...Yes. I guess you need to call Art. I'll be here. I have nowhere else to go. Thanks."

Alice hung up the phone and slumped. She was already in so much trouble with the chair. *How am I going to get out of this one?*

Anxious minutes passed; it seemed like an eternity. Finally, the swat members begin to escort the hostages from the bank. At least they appeared uninjured. Then Alice spied Royce moving under his own power. Her relief turned to alarm when she realized the extent of the cuts and bruises on his face. But this time Alice remained in her designated area.

When the cops were finished speaking with Royce, Alice managed to get his attention by waving. He limped painfully toward her but stopped as soon as he realized the media were about to storm him. A police officer then escorted him through the lines to Jorge's car. Royce struggled in.

Alice fought her way through the crowd, laying on her horn. The throng parted like molasses, but she finally wrestled her way to the automobile. Royce unlocked the door, and Alice hobbled in, batting away the microphones.

"Are you OK?"

"I am. But how is Jorge?"

"I don't know. He was conscious, and he recognized me. He's probably at the hospital now. What happened?"

"I decided I would jump Pete. That's the robber. He had Jorge walking in front of him with a box of food. I jumped out and hit Pete with the stapler and knocked Pete over. The gun went off. It hit Jorge. Next thing you know, the ladies had jumped all over Pete, tying his hands with anything they could find and sitting on him until the cops made it in."

"It's not your fault. You never know what will happen in a situation like that. He could have shot all of you."

Royce leaned his head back and closed his eyes. Finally, he said, "The cops are giving me some time to rest and clean up. Then I have to go to the station and tell them what happened."

Alice fished her telephone out of her purse and perused the hotels in the area. "Are you up to driving? There's a decent hotel about three miles from here. I'll book us some rooms."

Royce nodded and started the engine. Alice then rolled down the window and motioned to one of the policemen, asking that he load her scooter in the trunk.

Chapter Eleven

Once they had checked in, Alice pulled back the covers and lay down. Exhausted, she drifted off into a troubled sleep. Jorge…dead…memorial service…children crying…wife angry, cursing at Alice. Mercifully her phone rang, short-circuiting the disquieting dream.

"Inman, slow down, where are you?…OK, good. Royce has to go over to the police department so they can interview him later this morning. I'm hoping you can go with him…Good. I can't think. I'll text you the hotel address in a minute. I'll call and book two rooms…Yes, I'm paying for Jorge's wife. But you'll have to pay for your own. Alice held the phone from her ear…Well, you can try. I'm not even going to bother. They've been such pricks about our expenses…See you soon." Alice pushed the end button. "Bastard." She dropped her phone on the bed and put her head on the pillow, lost in thought.

***

Royce stood in the shower, letting the warm water wash away Pete's blood. But he couldn't rinse off the guilt he felt about Jorge. He'd let his hatred of Pete consume him; the man calling him a fag and fairy had sent Royce's rage spiraling to the boiling point. By the time Pete walked in the door, his fury was blinding, adrenaline surging. Despite his fatigue, Royce had swung wildly, clocking Pete in the forehead and opening a large gash. The force of the swing sent Royce crashing into Pete, who reflexively hit the trigger as they crashed to the ground.

I should have thought about that. I was so mad, I didn't think. Will the others believe I did this on purpose because Jorge's been such a shit to me? Royce climbed out of the shower, dried, and crawled into bed, naked. He couldn't stand to put back on his clothes, which were dirty and reeked of sweat.

His phone pinged with a text from Quiana asking about him. She'd seen the news. After some back and forth, Quiana said someone would bring him clothes and toiletries. Relieved, he closed his eyes and tried to sleep but kept reliving the moment the gun fired and Jorge screamed. The more he tried to block it out, the more persistent it became.

***

Quiana summoned the others to the conference table. The electronic eye roamed from one face to another.

"What's the problem? Has Jorge taken a turn for the worse?" Espy asked.

"No, no. Inman said his surgery was successful, and he's resting. But we're in a fine mess. What is Alice's saying? 'Up shit creek without a paddle'?" Quiana asked.

"Just tell us," JJ said. "Nothing can be as bad as Jorge getting shot."

"Well, this comes in a close second. Apparently, the chair saw Alice on TV. You know, all the news stations, even the Today Show, covered the story. She's furious. We were to keep a low profile, and I told her Alice was in the hospital having a procedure. She's been calling Alice nonstop, but Alice won't answer."

"Oh, we are in deep shit," Espy said.

"Where was Alice, anyway?" JJ asked.

"I really can't say," Quiana said. "So, what are we going to do? Any suggestions?"

"I guess we get ready to have a new boss," JJ said. "I don't see how this can have a happy ending."

"And I really like Alice," Espy said. "She's been the best supervisor I've ever had."

"Yeah, she really knows her stuff," JJ said.

"I can't believe you all are giving up so easily," Quiana said. "I plan to fight as hard as I can for Alice."

"We all plan to," Gaye said, "but there's nothing we can do now but wait."

Quiana said, "By the way, Royce needs a change of clothes and some toiletries. He has nothing to wear. Can someone take the stuff to him?"

"I'll run out and get a few things for him," Gaye said. "JJ, could you drive them over?"

"If I have to," JJ said.

"You have to," Quiana said. "Besides, it'll give you a chance to put that new car of yours through its paces.

***

As Inman headed to deposit his luggage at the hotel, his cell phone rang. Glancing at a number he didn't recognize with a Washington, DC, area code, he felt obligated to answer.

"Inman?"

"Yes."

"This is Ami Saitou. I've just landed in Houston. I'll be in College Station shortly. Please give me an update on what is going on. For some reason, I have not been able to reach Alice."

"You haven't? That's strange. I just spoke to her a while ago," Inman said.

"Humph. Well?"

"Jorge Macias is in the hospital. His wife came down this morning, and we've been to see him. He's in stable condition. Royce Atkins is OK."

"Which hospital?"

"Uh, St. Joseph's."

"I'll drive straight there and will meet with you when I arrive. The commission will be paying Mrs. Macias's expenses. I don't think we've ever had this occur in the history of the agency."

"What about mine?"

"We'll discuss that later. Sorry, I have to go. I'll see you shortly."

The phone went dead. "Witch," Inman said. Then he quickly dialed

Alice, who answered immediately.

"You told her what?" Alice asked.

"That I had spoken with you earlier. The chair said she'd been trying to reach you all morning."

"That was stupid. I didn't want her to know where I was."

"She already knew where you were. She saw you on TV."

"Oh, crap."

"Yeah, and the hag is headed to the hospital."

"OK, thanks for letting me know. Just take care of Jorge."

***

Gripped with panic, Alice turned off her phone. Her hands began to shake as relentless waves of anxiety crushed her chest. She wanted a sling. Pacing the floor to relieve the stress would help, but her feeble legs wouldn't let her. No, now was not the time for a drink. What would Art think? How was she going to explain why her employees were caught up in this mess? *Why didn't I answer the phone? If only Art were here. But I have to face this alone.*

Alice flipped on the TV and aimlessly watched the soaps. Their problems seemed tame compared to hers. Then the TV broke to special coverage. Alice sat up, horrified. Saitou was in town at the hospital!

Chair Saitou. Just seeing her scared the ever-living daylights out of Alice. Those slanty, piercing eyes. The prim, trim figure dressed immaculately in a powder blue business suit. The snake!

Alice listened as Saitou praised her investigators for disabling the robber and saving the day. As Saitou peered into the camera, Alice felt as if the dragon lady would jump out of the TV and grab her by the throat. Flipping off the box, she sunk deeper into the bed and tossed the covers over her head. *I'm dead meat. I'll never work in the government again. I'm a failure, just like Inman said.*

***

Inman sat uncomfortably in the only vacant straight-backed chair in the hospital waiting room. What a depressing place. Fluorescent lights accented the expressions of those worried about loved ones; the mood was subdued. At least Jorge was stable. His mind drifted to the impending results of the DNA test. If Martha were indeed his daughter, he'd eventually be forced to tell his wife…

"Inman?" The chair said.

"Yes, ma'am." Startled, Inman looked up and into the face of an ashen, angry woman. "I need a word with you." Saitou raced down the hall with Inman in hot pursuit. They entered a vacant room the chair had used earlier when speaking with the press.

Saitou slammed down her purse and jerked out her cell phone. Hitting speed dial, she pushed the speaker button. Inman's boss, General Counsel Weber, answered.

"Tell Inman what just happened," Saitou said.

"I got a call from the attorney from Bighorn Outfitters," Weber said. "I didn't realize you had found cause on that case. Why didn't you tell me? I was blindsided."

"Uh, sorry. I should have. I apologize," Inman said.

"I didn't know, either," Saitou said. Inman became frightened as the woman stared at him.

"But Alice said—"

"Alice said what?" Saitou said.

"That you knew. That she told you and you said OK."

"I did not," Saitou said.

"Damn," Inman said.

"We've now got a PR problem," Weber said. "Bighorn's attorney figured out from the TV coverage that Alice is based in Austin and that there's no official office in Austin. He's claiming that we're out to get Stewart on a witch hunt by going after his grandson. I hope you've got some strong evidence."

"I do, too," Inman said under his breath.

"You mean you haven't been over this with a fine-tooth comb?" Saitou was shrieking by now. "You'd better find Alice, and find her quick. I'll be at the Hilton doing damage control. I expect the two of you ASAP. Get that case down here immediately." Saitou grabbed her phone, ended the call, and stormed out of the room.

Inman slumped in his chair. How stupid he'd been. The obsession with his search for Martha had distracted him. He'd allowed Alice to talk him out of discussing the case with the general counsel. *Why in the world did I trust her?* Now shit was hitting the fan. *I might have been able to prevent it if only I'd...* Sighing, he called Quiana.

"I need you to get the Bighorn case down here immediately," he said.

"JJ just left town to bring Royce some clothes. I can try to see how far he's gotten and have him come back and get it."

"We don't have time. You need to have it couriered."

"Well, I'll have to get permission for that expense," Quiana said.

"Hang the expense. The chair wants the case, STAT."

"OK. I'll take care of it. Have you talked to Alice? She won't answer her phone."

"Goddammit! The chair wants to see Alice ASAP. What's gotten into her lately?" By this time Inman was pacing the floor, visions of a disgraceful end to his career rearing their ugly heads.

"I'll get her to answer. I'll get the case to you. You're in the same hotel?"

"Yeah, I'll go by and see if I can get her to talk to me. You just get the case here."

"Not a problem." Quiana hung up, but she hadn't a clue about what to do. She called Espy, who had left early.

"The only person who can get to her is Art," Espy said. "You could ask him to go down and to take the case with him."

"Yeah, but he's not an employee. Wouldn't we get in trouble turning over the case to him to transport?"

"True, but if you send it courier, you're doing the same thing."

"Except the courier is bonded and insured."

"Well, then use a courier."

"I don't even know what it's going to cost. I don't think the chair will be—"

Espy interrupted. "Just do what you think you need to do. I've got to go. I have something important to take care of." The phone went dead.

Stunned, Quiana took a deep breath. Espy had never been that abrupt with her before. *The whole office is going to hell.* She softly called to Dexter, who obediently trotted over. Gently lifting him and stroking his sleek fur gave her a chance to take deep breaths and steady herself. *I know what I have to do.*

***

Alice heard a knock, but she ignored it until Art called to her tenderly. Struggling, she limped to the door and unlocked it. Without acknowledging him, she wobbled back to the bed and climbed in, turning her head to avoid him.

He sat on the edge of the bed. "Alice, talk to me…please." When she did not respond, Art continued. "The chair is demanding that you and Inman present yourselves at her hotel suite immediately. I brought you some clean clothes along with the case." When Alice didn't move, he continued, "I believe in you and your investigations. I know if the case didn't have merit, you wouldn't have pursued it. You've got to stand up for the Charging Party like you stood up for me."

Alice finally looked at Art. "It's not that simple. I haven't followed orders. Whether I'm right or not, I'm going to get fired for insubordination."

"So, you're just going to take the Charging Party down with you? Is that it? What if there are other victims? What if that jerk goes after other women? How would you feel then?"

Alice sighed. "You're right as usual." She fumbled to a sitting position. "Let me get changed, and I'll be down in about fifteen minutes."

Alice lay in bed, feeling the bands of dread caress her. Did the heroes of the Alamo feel the same way as they faced death? *I'll have to make friends with the pain,* she thought, finally pulling herself out of bed and toward the suitcase Art had brought her. *It will be my red badge of courage.*

Dressed, she looked at herself in the mirror. Haggard, old. Maybe losing this job was for the best. *I can't keep this pace up much longer.* Climbing on her scooter, she wound her way to the hotel lobby.

Inman and Art looked up as Alice wheeled close to them.

"Here's the game plan," Inman said. "I've made a brief outline of the merits of the case. We're going to present it to Saitou in a positive light. I think we can get Commissioner Feldstein to support us on this. Regardless of where our office is, the case is still discrimination, and it still has merit."

"How are we going to handle the fact that I didn't tell her?" Alice asked.

"Oh, let's just say we had a bit of a miscommunication. You let me do the talking and keep your mouth shut, OK? She's furious with you."

Alice nodded. Silently they headed to the Hilton.

Chapter Twelve

Espy maneuvered in front of Planned Parenthood and shut the engine, her hands shaking. A female protester at the front door held a sign saying, "Babies are Murdered Here." Espy quaked. The thought of telling the woman it was Hank's baby and asking her to adopt it crossed her mind.

Impulsively, she dialed Hank. "Did you take care of it?"

"I'm sitting in the car in front of Planned Parenthood. There's a woman outside with a sign…I just can't—"

"Goddammit! You're running out of time. Just ignore her."

"Maybe if you came with me. If you—"

"Are you out of your mind? Going there would be political suicide."

"So, what are you going to do if I don't get the abortion?"

"Deny everything. Say you were stalking me. You're not going to ruin my life."

"But you can ruin mine?"

"It's your fault you got pregnant."

"I'm not the one who said he couldn't feel anything with a rubber on and refused to use it."

"I thought you were on the pill."

"I thought you were going to leave your wife and marry me."

With that, Espy pushed the end talk button and threw her phone onto the passenger seat. Sobbing, she hauled out of the parking lot, ignoring the ceaseless ringing from her cell.

***

Quiana read Art's text message with relief. At least he had arrived safely with the case files, and Alice was on her way to see Saitou. A stillness hung in the office. She and Dexter were the only ones there, as the others were out.

"Come on, Dex. Let's sit outside awhile. I'm so nervous I can't focus on work."

Settled in the lawn chair, Quiana watched Dexter make his rounds at the fence perimeter. *This building isn't so bad,* she thought. *If we'd been in a real office, we would have had to take Dexter out on a leash.* Unfortunately, JJ and the ugly things he had said about Royce continued to grate on her. She and JJ would need to discuss the matter sooner than later.

The door opened, and Gaye came down the steps, taking a seat next to Quiana. "Any news?"

"She and Inman are speaking with Saitou. It's been a while, and I haven't heard anything. It must be bad."

"Don't give up hope just yet." Gaye stared off into the distance.

"You don't look so good. This getting to you?"

"Yeah, and my parents. My mother was so ugly to Tommy that we walked out of the house."

"Oh, no. So, what are you going to do?"

"Tommy wants to elope, but I don't know…"

JJ came out, sat on the steps, and called to Dexter. The dog rushed over and nuzzled his hand.

"You get Royce's clothes delivered?" Quiana asked.

"I did. Then I went to see Jorge."

"How is he?" Gaye asked.

"Holding his own. His wife was there, so I didn't stay long."

"JJ, why did you call Royce a 'fag'?" Quiana asked.

"I don't like him."

"What, because he's transgender? He has rights, too. You better get used to it," Quiana said. "I am really disappointed in you." There, she'd said it. If they were ever going to have a relationship, JJ would have to get over his hang-ups.

"That's some of it. But I don't like him. I don't like the way he talks about how we're discriminating against him before anyone's even had a chance to do anything."

"We've been discussing in grad school how some people get fearful and paranoid while others always look on the bright side of things," Gaye said. "It's called the Pygmalion effect. You get what you expect. If you expect everyone to hate you, that's what you get."

JJ rose. "I need to get some work done. I was supposed to have a modified investigative plan written up for Jorge today." Without another word, he disappeared into the office.

Gaye stood as well. "I need to get ready for my onsite tomorrow. Royce and I were scheduled to visit the tortilla factory tomorrow, but I guess I'm going by myself."

"Let me know how it goes," Quiana said.

Quiana called Dexter, picked him up, and caressed his coat. "Dex, what in the world is going on with JJ? I've never heard him talk like this. Something else must be bothering him." Glancing at her watch, she said, "I hope your momma isn't in too much trouble. I don't want you to move."

***

Despite the repeated deep breaths, Alice's hands continued to tremble. Tucking them under her thighs didn't bring relief, either. Saitou had kept them cooling their heels in the lobby for forty-five minutes while she'd read the case. Alice wished she'd spent more time crafting the document.

Saitou rang Inman's phone and told them to come to her room. Alice entered and spied an alcove sporting a king-sized bed. Saitou was sitting at the desk with the case, a pile of scribbled notes littering the surface.

When Inman was seated, Saitou looked at Alice and said, "Where have you been? I've been trying to reach you."

"I've been sick."

"I had Jane check. She didn't see that you had signed out for sick leave. You should have asked me in advance for the leave for a planned surgery. That's policy."

"Sorry. You're right. I should have. I'll fill out the form first thing tomorrow." Alice could feel the anxiety coursing through her body and banding around her chest, nearly knocking the breath out of her.

"This case is weak at best. You've put the agency in a precarious position. I talked with Commissioner Feldstein, and apparently his friend already told him all about what you've discovered, so I can't pull it back, thanks to you." She motioned to Inman to get the case. "Alice, why did you tell Inman that I had approved the case?"

This was it—the beginning of the end. Alice took a deep breath. "I—"

"My mistake," Inman said. "We have another case working that I think we're going to find 'cause' on, in a tortilla factory. Alice told me she was *going* to tell you about it, but I thought she said she *had* told you about it. Just got my cases mixed up."

Saitou glared at Alice. If at all possible, Alice would have fled the room.

"I see...I want you to keep the general counsel posted on all moves you make on this case. Copy him on everything. Don't file anything or send any letters until you've cleared it with him." Looking at Alice, she said, "If the agency goes down, it will be your fault." Saitou rose and opened the door. Also, you're off the Consolidated case. Send it to Houston. The duo beat a hasty retreat.

When they arrived in the lobby, Inman sunk into a chair next to Art.

"What happened?" Art asked.

"I'm not sure," Inman said. "Apparently there was enough evidence and enough pressure from one of the commissioners to keep Saitou from closing the case. Now comes the hard part. I've got lots of work to do."

"I'm exhausted," Alice said. "I can't face the drive right now. Can you just take me to the hotel?"

"Sure, if you want," Art said.

"I'm headed back to Austin," Inman said. "I'll hate this town for the rest of my life. I don't want to stay here any longer than I have to."

***

Art helped Alice into her room. "You want me to get you something to eat?"

"I would love it. What about you? Do you need to go back tonight?"

"If I go back, how will you get home?"

"I'm not sure. Royce is still here and has Jorge's car. Jorge's wife drove her own here. Perhaps Jorge will be dismissed soon. I can probably get a ride home with one of them."

"Are you always so stoic? So self-sufficient? Don't you want me to stay?"

"I do. I just don't want to impose on you. What about Simon?"

"I've already made arrangements with Quiana. She and her sister will pick him up. So, it's all settled. I will rustle up something fabulous to eat."

After Art left, Alice changed into her pajamas and lay on the bed, her mind racing. Checking in on the tortilla factory case was priority. Royce felt it was promising. *Let's hope to God it is.* With a little luck, updating Saitou about it to cover their tracks would be a breeze. Then, she sent a text to Royce telling him to get a good night's sleep and to charge his meals to the room. They would touch base tomorrow.

Restless, Alice shifted on her side. The cravings she'd held at bay for a sling intensified. A call to Jorge's wife served as a distraction from the urge. He was doing well. She wished Art would return soon.

Alice drifted into a heavy sleep and didn't awake until Art nudged her shoulder. "You're back?" She struggled up on one elbow.

"Yes. I stopped by a cafeteria and got us some healthy food." He opened a container, and the aroma reminded Alice that she hadn't eaten in nearly twenty-four hours. She was famished.

"I checked on the dogs. Quiana says they are doing fine. I told her I would pick them up tomorrow. Do you know what your plan is?"

"I talked to Jorge's wife. Somebody needs to drive Jorge's car back to Austin. She doesn't think he'll be able to drive when he is dismissed. If Royce is rested and the police are finished with their interviews, I'll tell him to take it home tomorrow."

After their meal, Art removed the empty food containers and sat on the bed next to Alice. "I've been so worried about you. You shouldn't have left rehab. With all this stress, it will be too easy for you to start up again."

"I didn't have any choice. I know you're right, but I can't go back, not right now, with all this shit hitting the fan. I think I can do it myself if you'll help me." Alice put her hand over Art's, idly rubbing her finger across the top of his hand.

He leaned over and leisurely kissed Alice on the lips. Not pulling back, she caressed his cheeks.

Art drew back and said, "I'll go and let you get some sleep; it's been a long day."

As he rose, Alice reached out and touched his arm. "Please stay. I don't want to be alone tonight." Art sunk back next to her.

Chapter Thirteen

"Good morning, Mr. Rojas. I'm Gaye Rohatqi. Nice to finally meet you." The two shook hands.

"I've never done this before, Ms. Ro, Roh…"

"Just call me Gaye."

"Thanks. You can call me Andy. What do you want to do first?"

"I'd love a tour of your facility."

"My pleasure." Andy gave Gaye a hard hat and warned her not to cross the yellow line painted along the concrete floor. As they began, he shared the story of the plant. "My father started the factory twenty-five years ago because he was dissatisfied with the tortillas around here. It has always been a small, family business until ten years ago. After his death, my brothers and I decided to modernize and grow the company."

As they walked, Gaye observed silver machines spitting out round blobs of dough on a conveyor belt. The mixture was flattened and sent through the oven. A quality control employee inspected the tortillas as they progressed down a cooling belt, removing those with holes or other blemishes.

To Gaye's amazement, the machine even bagged the tortillas. Workers then placed the bags in boxes. The mechanically sealed boxes skated off the conveyor belt and onto a palette. Gaye noted that the line employees were all Hispanic women. A man on a forklift retrieved the full palette.

Next, they entered the warehouse, which was swarming with activity. The beep of forklifts and the hum of truck motors on the loading docks surprised her with their intensity. Gaye made a mental note that only men worked in this area.

Once they had left the deafening warehouse, Gaye asked, "How many employees do you have?"

"We're up to fifty right now. Business is good, and we are hiring more."

"That's great. So, who does your hiring?"

"That would be Juan Flores. Would you like to speak to him now?"

"Yes, please. I need a room where we can have some privacy, and I can set up my computer."

"My brother is not here today. You can sit in his office." Andy escorted Gaye to the office, where she quickly settled in while Andy went to find Juan.

"Come in, Mr. Flores, and have a seat. My name is Gaye Rohatqi. You can call me Gaye. Here's my card. I have a few questions to ask, and I will record your answers on an affidavit. After I finish, you will have a chance to read over it and make any changes. Once you are satisfied, I'll have you sign it. Then I'll give you a copy for your records."

"Fine." Mr. Flores said.

"So, I understand you are the general manager. How long have you held that position?"

"About a year."

"What does your job entail?"

"I'm responsible for being sure that the machines are maintained, and that production is up to Mr. Rojas's standards. I am also responsible for oversight of the warehouse. I am totally responsible for making and delivering the product."

"So, tell me how the hiring process works."

"The girls at the reception desk take applications, and when I need employees, I look through them, see who appears qualified, and then set up interviews. The foreman for whichever department is hiring will interview them first. If they believe the applicant is a fit, they will tell me, and I will do a second interview. Then, if I like them, I will offer them a job."

"Do you advertise the positions?"

"No, we haven't had to. We get enough walk-in traffic to fill the positions. It keeps costs down."

"So, tell me how you decide who works and who gets overtime."

"It depends on which line will be running in a given week. Some weeks we don't run but two lines; other weeks, we have all five going. Anyone who is interested in overtime tells me. I try to keep it at a minimum, though. You know, it keeps costs down."

"So, according to your records, you have very few white or African American employees. Why do you think that is?"

"I don't think they want to work for Latinos. We call them, they interview, and then they turn down the jobs when we offer them."

"Do you have any women working in the warehouse?"

"No. You've got to be able to lift seventy-five pounds, and they can't do that, so we don't put them there."

Gaye completed the statement and printed it out. After skimming it, Mr. Flores signed without making any changes.

"Thanks, that's all I need for now," Gaye said.

"Let me know if I can do anything else for you." Mr. Flores left the office.

Gaye was puzzled. The neighborhood was reasonably integrated. Did the prospective employees really turn down the jobs? The African American who filed the complaint said that a number of African Americans left because they weren't getting many hours.

OK, I've got so many issues here I don't know where to start, she thought. The first is cutting the hours, and it appears that it actually happened. From the review Royce did, it seems the hours were not equitably distributed. Then there's the issue of why more African Americans and whites don't work here. *And it bothers me that men and women appear to be segregated into jobs.*

Gaye asked Andy if she could review the old applications along with an organization chart. Had any men had been hired into the tortilla packing line?

One of the secretaries brought in a large box that held several hundred applications. Gaye frowned. Briefly glancing through them revealed ample non-Hispanic names. Another trip was warranted.

After informing Andy of the need for a return visit, she ordered him not to destroy any of the applications. After giving Gaye an odd look, he complied with her request for another tour of the warehouse.

Gaye noticed that pallets were moved into delivery trucks with a forklift. How did Flores come up with the requirement of lifting seventy-five pounds? The single tortilla boxes didn't look that heavy.

Returning to her car, Gaye made some notes. She called Quiana and gave her an update on her findings.

"Have you heard from Alice?" Gaye asked.

"Yes, she and Art are on their way. Royce has to go to the police station one more time, and then he'll be back. Alice said she'll come into the office, but she's given Royce the rest of the day off."

"Have you heard from Espy?"

"No, I haven't. Something's really wrong. She didn't call in this morning."

"I think maybe I better check on her. Alice has too much going right now to worry about anything else. I'll be in later."

Gaye started to call Espy when she neared Austin but thought better of it. It would be too easy for her not to answer. A visit to her apartment was the only solution. Spying Espy's car, she sent her coworker a text message. *I'm not leaving until you let me in.* A few minutes later, the door opened.

Gaye stared at her coworker in horror. She was disheveled, and her eyes were red and listless. Gaye made her way into the gloomy apartment and looked around. Espy's sophisticated, gray-toned living area was in disarray. Clothes were strewn everywhere, and the modern, glass-topped coffee table sported what appeared to be weeks of glass rings peeking out from under takeout containers.

"Espy, what's the matter?"

Espy slumped onto the sofa, and Gaye sat next to her. "I'm pregnant."

Gaye stifled a cry of surprise. That was the last thing she'd expected. Gaye reached out and touched Espy. "Want to talk about it?"

Espy began to weep. Gaye went into the kitchen, fixed them both a cup of tea, and settled on the couch. "You'll feel better if you talk. You don't need to go through this by yourself. I'm here to listen."

Haltingly, Espy relayed the situation to Gaye.

The two sat in silence. Then Gaye said, "This has got to be your decision and no one else's—not your mother's, not Hank's. Whatever you decide to do, I will support you. Does anyone else know?"

"No, you're the only person I've told. Please don't tell anyone else."

"I won't. How long do you have to make a decision?"

"Four weeks."

Gaye rose and opened the curtains. Despite Espy's protests, she began to straighten the house. Espy laid in a fetal position on the couch as Gaye cleaned, changing the linen and throwing all the bad food in the trash. "I'm going to the store. While I'm gone, why don't you take a bath and get cleaned up? This is not the end of the world."

While she was in the car, Gaye called Quiana. "Espy's really sick. I'm going to the store for her. Just put her on sick leave. I'm not sure how long it's going to take for her to pull out of it."

"Sounds serious. What's wrong?"

"Don't know. She has an appointment with the doctor scheduled." Gaye felt guilty lying to Quiana, but she didn't have any choice. Gaye wondered what she would do if she were in Espy's situation. *I hope I never have to find out.*

Later, Gaye brought in a couple of bags of groceries and set about stowing them away. Espy had cleaned herself up, thank goodness. Encouraged, Gaye prepared breakfast for her distraught friend.

"One thing you might do," Gaye said, "is to make a list of the pros and cons of keeping the baby. That way, you could look at it more rationally." Gaye was relieved to see Espy eating the eggs and toast heaped on her plate.

"One con is that I will be forever linked to Hank. Do I go after him for child support and force him to be a part of the baby's life, or do I try to keep him out of the picture? I'd never really thought about how expensive children are. Is it fair to separate the child from her father? One day I'm sure she'll ask. What will I tell her?"

"My personal opinion is that he should be financially responsible. I don't think he should get off that easy."

"On the pro side, I've always wanted to be a mother. Seems like I've been thinking about it more and more lately." Espy sighed. Gaye gathered the dishes and put them in the dishwasher. When everything was clean, she sat at the table and took a sip of her tea.

"All I know is sitting here locked up in your apartment isn't going to help. You should at least come to work. You'll drive yourself crazy thinking about this twenty-four-seven. Sometimes when I have something that is bothering me, the answer comes when I quit thinking about it."

Espy nodded. "How did the meeting between Tommy and your parents go?"

"A complete disaster. My mom was so rude to Tommy that we left."

"Oh, sorry to hear that. So, what are you going to do?"

"We're getting married, anyway. I can't worry about what my parents think. I have to follow my heart."

Espy grinned. "Good for you. I'm sure your parents will come around. Mine did after my brother married a black girl. Took them several years, but eventually, they accepted her into the family."

"I sure hope so."

"Trust me. They will."

Chapter Fourteen

The drive home gave Royce time to think. While Alice had been decent enough, he still didn't trust her. Then, there had been the brief meeting with Saitou before leaving College Station. *She was just trying to make nice; she didn't seem to care about me one iota.* Finding a support group with people who understood his journey, who were trustworthy, was crucial.

Even though surgery was almost a year away, the thought made Royce anxious. Being a man felt right. And people who didn't know about his past took him more seriously as a man than anyone had as a female.

He was convinced the others in the office would blame him for Jorge's gunshot wounds even though it was an accident. No one ever believed him. He wondered how long Jorge would be out, praying there would be no long-term damage.

And what about that JJ? Royce didn't know what to think. According to his cousin, the man was dangerous. Should he tell Alice? What if something happened? The possibility of Alice retaliating against Royce for raising the alarm convinced him to keep quiet.

***

"Hi, Dex," Alice said. Her best friend perked at the sound of Alice's voice, jumping and barking. Simon, hearing the commotion, rushed to join the fray, howling with delight upon seeing Art.

"I'm going to take Simon home and head to the office. See you at the dog park tonight?"

"I'll be there."

"Don't be late."

Alice caught Art's pointed meaning—don't stop by Rebels before coming. After a brief hello to Quiana, Alice went to her office and closed the door. Picking up Dexter, she began to cuddle and baby him, stroking his head.

The ride home had been awkward. While the night before had been heavenly, Alice didn't know how to broach the issue of the future. They were no longer friends, but lovers. It had been so impulsive. Alice had been wishing something like this would happen. But now that it had, what did it mean? Would they revert to the way things were?

Alice perused her e-mails; there were several hundred. As she was working her way through them, a message appeared from Wilson. Anxious bands flicked across Alice's chest.

An audit! Saitou had ordered an inspection of the whole office. Timekeeping, everything. Alice lowered Dex to the ground and darted out the door.

"Quiana, you there?" Alice asked.

"Yes. What's up?"

"Saitou has ordered an audit."

Silence emanated from behind the Oriental screen. "We are so screwed. When they get to the travel and find that you sent three people and only had the money for two, we'll never hear the end of it."

Pain shot down Alice's leg; the bands engulfed her chest. She began to feel nauseated. Visions of a Singapore sling followed by relief battered her brain.

"I'll be back." Alice gunned her chair, scraping the doorframe on the way out of the building. The disgusting odor of the entryway heightened her nausea. *I've got to get that taken care of.* Throwing the acceleration switch into high gear, Alice flew toward Rebels, hitting every chink and crack on the sidewalk, careening crazily. She could hear footsteps behind her.

"Stop!" Quiana said, catching Alice and shoving her hand off the accelerator. "I'm not letting you go in there."

Horror crept over Alice. How did Quiana know? She tried to push

Quiana's hand away. "I made Art tell me about the drinking. I had to know so I could run cover for you."

Close to tears, Alice drooped in her chair. She looked up, but she could only see Quiana's hat. "You of all people should understand. I can't break this; it's got me just like the sociophobia has got you."

"I'll call Art."

"No, don't do that."

"What do you want, Alice?"

Alice burst into tears. Quiana turned and walked away.

What did she want? She wanted the stress to go away. She wanted to live happily ever after with Art. She wanted to find cause cases. She wanted… By going to Rebels, she risked losing Art. Of all the things she craved, it was Art.

Alice turned the scooter around and crept to back the office.

***

Gaye checked on the steaming broccoli and then opened the roasted chicken. Thankfully it was still warm. Quickly setting the table, she went into the spare bedroom where Tommy was studying. He looked up. "Dinner is ready."

"Good. I'm starved." He settled in and cut the chicken for both of them. "So, what are we going to do about your parents?"

"I don't know. I've been racking my brain."

"You're still willing to go through with the wedding without their blessing, aren't you?"

"I am. I do love you. I just wish it were different, that's all. I at least need to tell them we are getting married. Somehow I've got to get up the courage."

"But I'm guessing their blessing is what you really want, isn't it?"

"More than anything in the world."

"Before you talk to them, let's think about this some more. There must be something else we can do."

Gaye nodded. The whole thing saddened her no end. Living her life estranged from her parents was unthinkable, but living without Tommy was impossible. She chose Tommy.

***

Anxiously, Inman settled on the park bench just outside Townes Hall on the UT campus. Although the area was shaded, he was sweating profusely. Unfurling the morning's newspaper and perusing the headlines helped divert his mind from the impending meeting. The tactile act of reading soothed him, somehow.

And calming he needed. Bernie Sanders and Hillary Clinton were still battling it out even though Obama had endorsed his former Secretary of State. Clinton would be a shoo-in for president, Inman thought, once she eased past the upstart who was too liberal even for Inman.

Looking up, he rose as Grace approached.

"I'm glad you agreed to meet me," Inman said. He sat, and Grace joined him on the bench.

"You have news about our daughter," Grace said.

Inman nodded. "I've found her. Her name is Martha Scott. I've confirmed it with DNA. Do you want to see her picture? She looks like you."

"Not now." Grace lowered her head. The two sat soundlessly.

"I'm going to meet her this weekend. She lives in Chicago and is a nurse. She's married to a high school coach. They have two boys." When Grace did not reply, he continued. "She's not ready for me to meet her husband or children yet."

"Did you say anything about me?" Grace asked.

"No, I wanted to ask how you want to handle it."

"I think I want to meet her, but I'm scared. She must hate me. I don't think I could take that kind of rejection."

"I understand. I'll see if I can explain it to her. If she's not angry, do you want to meet her?"

"I think so. Just don't say anything about me until you find out how she feels."

"I understand."

The two sat quietly. Inman's thoughts drifted to that day that had changed his life so long ago. Finally, Grace rose.

"I need to get to class. Call me after you meet."

"I will." Inman watched as Grace entered the building. *Our lives will never be the same. I started this quest, and I will follow wherever it leads me.*

Chapter Fifteen

Inman boarded the plane and checked his e-mail one last time before turning off his phone. He had told his wife he would be at a conference all weekend and could not be reached. Important business. Maybe after he'd gotten to know Martha, and if she wanted a relationship with him, he would let Shirley in on the secret. At this point, however, Inman was worried. While he wanted to meet his daughter, misgivings abounded. What if she rejected him? After all, he had not known she existed until recently. Hopefully, she would not hold him responsible for being absent from her life.

He pitied Grace but understood her decision to put Martha up for adoption. It was the right decision to make in the 1960s. Things were different now; single women could keep biracial babies. Inman closed his eyes and played the meeting in his mind.

As Inman deplaned and strode into the terminal he eyed the crowd apprehensively. There she was! Smiling. Joy welled within him. This was going to be a good visit; he just knew it. He approached Martha and gave her a big hug. "I'm so glad I found you. I'm staying at the airport hotel. Let's go over there so we can talk. I want to hear all about you and your family. I want to tell you about my life."

A few minutes later, they were seated in the hotel restaurant. "I never thought this day would come," Inman said. "I can see some resemblance between you and my son. I'm still in a daze. This is all so unreal."

Martha took his hand and squeezed it. "Thank you for coming."

They spoke for hours about their families, Inman sipping iced tea while Martha drank water. Martha explained that she was raised in a decent, working-class family. Her father was employed in sanitation by the city of Chicago, and her mother cleaned houses. While her parents worked, her grandmother kept her. Because her father had lighter skin, she escaped the usual harassment and teasing. The family adopted one more child, a boy. She'd excelled in school and earned a scholarship to the University of Illinois in Chicago. She was the first one in her family to go to college.

Inman told Martha about his childhood in Tougaloo, where his father had been a professor and his mother a stay-at-home mom. He also talked about his children. "I can see a resemblance between you and my daughter, too."

"So, how did you find out about me?"

"On a whim, I looked up your birth mother and contacted her. We met during a civil rights march. I only saw her that once, and I never even knew she'd gotten pregnant. I met her recently and she told me about you. Do you want to meet her?"

"I don't know. All these years, I've harbored anger about being given up for adoption, feeling that I wasn't worthy enough."

"It was different then. Unwed mothers were pariahs, outcasts. And as a biracial baby, frankly, you would have suffered badly."

Martha sat silently, running her finger through the puddle of water that had collected next to her glass. "Tell me about her."

"She's a law professor at the University of Texas. She never married, never had children. She's still haunted about giving you up." Inman reached over and laid his hand over hers. Martha gently withdrew.

"So, what's next?" Martha asked.

"Do you want our relationship to go further? I do, but only if you are comfortable."

"I think I do, but I need some time to process everything."

"I'll be honest with you. I haven't told my wife and children yet. But I plan to soon."

After the goodbyes, Inman went to his room. His first instinct was to call Grace, but he hesitated because of the late hour. *I'll do it in person. What am I going to tell Shirley?* He'd have to tell his wife soon, but how he would do it was chafing at him. What would the kids think? No matter, he owed Martha that much. Failing to acknowledge his daughter to those closest to him would reinforce her belief that she wasn't good enough to be loved.

Inman emptied his pockets and took his cell phone off his waistband. Eying it, he realized he had failed to turn it back on after landing. When he did, the screen exploded with texts.

Goddamn it! His boss. Six texts. On a Saturday. Something was wrong. Inman swiftly scanned all the communications. Then he frantically booked a flight to Washington, DC, early the next morning.

***

Tommy adjusted his tie and wiped his hands on his pants; they were perspiring freely. Clearing his throat, he rang the doorbell. Mr. Rohatqi answered. Relived not to see Nila, Tommy said, "Mr. Rohatqi, thanks for seeing me."

"Come in, and please just call me Sanjit." Sanjit ushered Tommy into his office and motioned for him to take a seat in one of the chairs next to his desk. His future father-in-law sat in the other. "Now, what can I do for you?"

"Gaye has accepted my proposal of marriage. We plan to marry in September. I am asking for your blessing. It would mean a lot to Gaye…and me, too."

"I guess you know her mother is opposed to this union?"

"I do. But I'm hoping she will reconsider. I really love your daughter and was hoping to surprise her with a traditional Hindi wedding."

Sanjit stared at Tommy, unnerving him. "Did Gaye say she wanted a traditional wedding?"

"No, sir, it's my idea. I'd like to surprise her."

"And what do your parents think?"

"Actually, they really like Gaye, and they are happy for us. I'm hoping you and Nila will be happy for us, too."

"So, do you know what goes into a Hindu wedding?"

"I think so. I've been reading about it on the Internet. But I'm sure Nila will want a say in the preparations. Honestly, I want things to be right with you and Nila. Gaye does love both of you."

"I must say this is a surprise. I'll give you my answer within a week.

Give me your phone number." Tommy read it out to Sanjit, who entered it into his telephone. Then Sanjit rose and escorted Tommy out.

Back in the car, Tommy undid his tie and breathed a sigh of relief. He hadn't told Gaye what he was up to, just in case it backfired. Tommy had been so sure, but now…

The ride home gave Tommy time to consider their predicament. While they were tossing around a few ideas about the wedding, Tommy had pressed for Dallas, where Gaye's family and old friends were. However, she had balked, saying it would be awkward if her parents chose not to attend. Other family members would then be forced to choose sides, and that drama would be unbearable.

Now, Tommy agreed with her. He would suggest they elope. There was always Vegas, but Gaye wasn't a Vegas kind of girl. Maybe they ought to go to the justice of the peace and then take a quiet few days to themselves. His mother had offered to spring for a bed and breakfast in Fredericksburg as a wedding present.

Tommy glanced at his phone. Gaye. He started not to answer but changed his mind.

"I thought you'd be back hours ago. I was beginning to worry. Is everything OK?" Gaye asked.

"Sorry, the study marathon ran over, and I'm so worried about the test I decided to stay a little longer. I'm on a roll. I'll give you a call when I wrap it up." Tommy glanced at the mileage sign. It would take him another hour to get to the outskirts of Austin.

"I can't believe you really need to study anymore. Relaxing and getting away from it all would probably do you more good than rehashing what you already know."

"You may be right, but I really need to ace this. I promise I won't stay too much longer. Love you. The sooner I get back to work, the sooner I can come home."

"OK, but please don't stay too long."

Tommy hated lying to Gaye. Not such a good start in a relationship, but it was necessary.

***

Gaye punched the end button and settled on the couch. Tommy seemed so intent on having a wedding in Dallas, thinking her mother would change her mind. Gaye knew better. Tommy's mother wanted a big wedding but, without her family, a large affair just didn't feel right. There'd be a hole in her heart when she saw the empty space reserved for family. Gaye wiped her eyes, then returned to her textbook.

***

Inman arrived at Weber's office at one o'clock sharp. Jason, one of the other HQ attorneys, was sitting at the conference table. Weber glared at Inman and motioned for him to sit.

Clutching the table tightly, Weber said, "I can't believe you failed to tell me about this case before you issued a cause finding. Do you realize what a firestorm you unleashed?" Weber didn't give Inman time to answer. "Stewart has brought in the big guns. He hired Vincent, Vincent, and Vincent to defend his grandson. They're going full-court press. They're giving Fox News an exclusive interview tomorrow. I have no idea what they're going to say, but it won't be good."

Inman felt his stomach tighten. Three V was the nastiest law firm in the country, known for their underhanded smear campaigns in the press. The last two times the EEOC went up against them, the commission came out with a black eye. They were in deep trouble.

"What are you going to do about it?" Weber asked.

"The case has merit," Inman said. "We had a miscommunication in our office. I thought the chair was aware of it. We should be able to defend it. The CP is a strong witness." At least he hoped he could trust Alice on this. He hadn't spoken to her himself. *Damn! I should have paid more attention.*

"They really don't care whether there's merit. What line of attack do you think they may take?"

"My guess is that they will go after the fact that we have an office in Austin that no one knows about."

"Shit. That's what Saitou said. How did they find out?"

"Well, the robbery our investigators got caught up in blew our cover."

"We are screwed." Weber threw down his pen and jumped up, pacing. "We've got to come up with a story to explain everything."

"A secret unit?" Jason asked.

"Apparently the White House wanted to beef up Obama's legacy by having the EEOC find lots of discrimination. The office was formed to do just that." Inman said. "We've had some pretty good success so far." The glare from Weber was so intense that Inman felt like shriveling into a fetal position.

"Oh, great," Jason said. "I know Three V, and that's right up their alley. We need to go into full crisis management mode. We've got to do a better job than we did last time."

"I wish we could just close the damned case," Weber said. "But Commissioner Feldstein got an update on it from his buddy. He's already been politicking to handle the case here at headquarters."

Inman could feel the anger whaling within him. They were going to take the case away from him! The bastards. They wanted to close it? A case with merit? The spineless creeps. Just out to save their own skins. Rather than say something he regretted, he clenched his hands on the chair and peered at the documents in front of him.

"I'm going to alert Saitou to tell the employees in Austin to keep their mouths shut," Weber said. "Jason, you contact the PR staff and have them report within an hour. We need to strategize."

Chapter Sixteen

Alice stirred and glanced at the clock. Seven thirty. Art had already left. What a sweetheart, staying with her the whole weekend, keeping her away from the booze. Despite Alice's protests, he had cleared every drop of alcohol from her apartment. She'd left her computer and cell phone off for the weekend, for fear that any work-related matters would push her over the edge. Just one day at a time. *That's all I can focus on.*

Before heading to work, Alice turned on her cell phone, which ignited. There were at least ten calls from Saitou's personal cell and two this morning from Wilson. Noticing a phone message from Inman late last night, she listened, then paled, frozen. She and Art had talked about what might happen if she lost her job...

Alice flew into the office, dumping Dexter on the floor. "Everyone, emergency meeting. STAT." Not bothering to maneuver into her office, Alice drew up to the conference table and asked Royce to bring her some coffee. The staff, bewildered, settled around her.

"Inman is in Washington as we speak. It's the Bighorn case. Stewart, who owns Bighorn, has hired Vincent, Vincent, and Vincent to represent him."

"You mean, the ones who—"

Before Royce could finish, Alice interrupted him. "Yes, Three V. We are not to give out any information regarding the office. Do not talk to anyone about what you do. Not reporters, not curious outsiders. Three V probably has private detectives swarming the place as we speak. Also, we're having an audit. Quiana, do you have an update?"

"The auditor will be here soon. We're not to destroy anything—e-mails, travel vouchers, that kind of stuff."

Everyone was motionless. Alice herself felt as if she were moving in slow motion, a feeling she'd had just before the auto wreck that had ruined her leg. *I'm going down; I know it. And there's nothing I can do about it.*

"So, just what could Three V do to us?" Royce asked. "We haven't done anything wrong."

"We're a secret location," Espy said. "No one was supposed to know we were here. According to what Quiana heard on the grapevine, Stewart's son, the harasser in the Bighorn case, saw Alice on TV when you and Jorge were at the bank. He heard that you had come from Austin. They'll be all over that."

"What can we do?" JJ asked.

"Absolutely nothing except keep your mouth shut," Alice said. "Get back to work. I've got to call Saitou."

***

After Alice left, JJ said, "This audit, will it get Alice in trouble?" No one answered. Finally, Gaye nodded an affirmative.

"We'll just have to cook the books. I've seen it done all the time on TV," JJ said.

"You really want to lie during a federal investigation?" Espy asked. "I thought you'd had enough of jail."

"I have, but there must be something we can do. It's not fair. Those idiots in Washington wouldn't give us enough money to do our jobs, and now that we've made it work with what they gave us, they're coming after us. I guess we were just supposed not to do our jobs and keep good books."

They all stared at each other.

"I don't understand," said Royce.

"Alice sent three of us to Corpus Christi on a hot case when we only had the budget for two. She shorted me, Inman, and Jorge travel money. Also, Inman paid his own plane fare once for government business," Espy said.

"You were OK with that?" Royce asked.

"Yeah, I was. It was a horrible case; these men were being forced to perform oral sex on their boss. I'd have paid my own way to stop that abuse."

"Maybe we should all be on an onsite investigation when the auditor comes," JJ said. "That way, we don't have to say anything."

The roving eye of the webcam focused on JJ. "Forget it," Quiana said. "The auditor will be here for days. Even if you try to stall, she'll catch up with you."

JJ looked over at Royce, and he could swear that Royce was giving him a critical look. "What's your problem?" JJ said.

"Nothing. Are you blaming me for Jorge getting hurt? I bet you are. It wasn't my fault."

"Nobody's blaming you," Gaye said. "It was an accident."

Rising, JJ said, "Whatever. I'm going back to work."

JJ acted busy on the case, but, he couldn't concentrate. Ever since discovering that Royce was related to that prison lieutenant, JJ had been on edge. His mind drifted back. It was a hot, sweltering summer in the un-air-conditioned prison, and everyone was cranky. For some reason, Shawn had taken a disliking to JJ and was always on him, needling him. Issues erupted when Shawn thought he was walking too slow. The guard would insult JJ and make fun of him over his missing tooth. When JJ ignored him and tried not to react, Shawn changed tactics, targeting JJ for shakedowns several times a day, even though he never found anything.

One day after JJ had returned from an especially brutal work detail in hundred-degree heat, Shawn shoved JJ away from the water fountain. He heaved him against the wall to perform a pat search. JJ reached the breaking point when Shawn squeezed his genitals and commented that JJ had a small package. JJ decked Shawn, breaking his jaw.

Of course, the only witnesses were inmates who wouldn't testify against Shawn. JJ was then routinely bypassed by the parole office as he was deemed a dangerous risk to society. So far, he had the confidence of everyone in the office. But if they found out why he'd served his full sentence...

An instant message from Quiana appeared, asking him to meet her on the back porch. JJ found Quiana in the lawn chair, a bottle of water in her hand. "What's wrong with you? Talking about tampering with federal records? You really disappointed me."

JJ badly wanted to explain the situation to Quiana. Still, he didn't want to disappoint her any more than he had when he had gotten robbed while out on the town. "This whole situation with Alice has gotten me down, I guess. And Jorge. You just don't think about that kind of stuff happening to people like him."

"I get it. But that doesn't give you an excuse to behave like a fool."

"Sorry. Can I get you some lunch? I was going to pick up Subway, but I can get you anything you want."

"No, thanks." Quiana rose and disappeared into the office.

Stung, JJ fell into despair. If Quiana didn't support him anymore, he would be lost.

Chapter Seventeen

Espy struggled to concentrate on the latest piece of evidence. It didn't seem like this case was going anywhere.

"Espy, you want to go out for lunch?" Gaye asked.

Glancing at the computer screen, Espy realized it was almost one o'clock. "I'm fine, really. Thanks for asking, though."

"I shouldn't have asked you—I'm telling you we are going out to eat. You need a break."

Espy started to protest, then thought better of it. Her Herculean efforts to keep her mind off the impending decision had failed. Only by talking to Gaye the other day had she maintained some piece of her sanity.

Gaye drove them to a quiet, out-of-the-way coffee shop that served sandwiches. After ordering at the counter, they chose a table in the corner, away from prying ears.

"If you want to talk, I'm here to listen. I've been thinking about your dilemma, and honestly, I don't know what I would do," Gaye said.

Espy closed her eyes and took a breath. She wanted to pretend nothing had happened. "Thanks. I know you're a good listener. It's just...I don't want to think about it right now. What we need to talk about is what we can do about the office. Everything is a mess. Jorge will be back Monday, thank goodness. But JJ, I don't know what's gotten into him. I've been looking after him since Jorge's been gone, and he hasn't done any work. And Royce is still so defensive. Every time I try to talk to him, he bristles."

"He's a tough one, isn't he? I don't get it. He thinks you're out to get him if you say 'good morning' and out to get him if you don't. I am honestly scared to say anything to him anymore. Can you believe he thinks we blame him for what happened to Jorge? That we think Royce did it on purpose?"

"It's unreal. I talked to Jorge a couple of days ago. He didn't say anything like that to me."

"How is Jorge, by the way?"

"I'm not sure. He was so quiet. But I don't know how he's going to act around Royce."

"Well, we'd better stay on guard and be sure we run interference between the two of them." Gaye looked around and frowned. "See that woman over there?"

"The one with the green shirt and jeans?"

"Yeah. I think I saw her coming out of Rebels just as we were leaving the office."

"Think she's following us?"

"I don't know, but we'd better keep an eye out. I hear Three V is vicious."

Espy shivered. Three V nosing into everyone's life could be disastrous. Especially for her. The last thing she needed to see on the front page was her affair with Hank.

"Do you have any other good cases besides the tortilla factory right now?" Espy asked.

"No, I think I'll have that one finished up next week, but with Inman gone and Alice preoccupied, I don't know if it will get any attention."

"I just got an interesting one. The CP is an older African American woman who works in a warehouse ordering inventory. A twenty-something Hispanic coworker sings along to hip-hop lyrics, which include the "N" word, while wearing ear pods. She has complained to the white managers, but nothing has been done."

Gaye looked at the time on her phone. "We'd better get back. I've got a lot to work on, and I need to leave early for class.

***

Jorge gingerly fingered the bandage around his chest as he listened to the children argue over a board game. The torrid summer heat kept them from playing outside. With luck, his wife would take them to the swimming pool soon, giving him some quiet time. He'd be glad to get back to work. Although he loved his family dearly, hanging around the house with them was driving him batty.

The shooting had changed him somehow. He'd never realized just how fragile life was. One moment you could be healthy and energetic, and the next, you could be dead. His purpose in life hadn't been on his radar. Working until he could afford to retire had been his only goal. But, surely, there must be something else.

Reading the Bible hadn't helped him work out the Royce thing. He'd never really been around anyone from the LGBTQ community. In fact, he'd tried avoid those people, if at all possible. But that night in the closet, listening to Royce and his pain, something was different somehow. Jorge couldn't put his finger on it.

The church taught love and compassion and doing God's work. But it also said that Royce's lifestyle was a sin. How were you supposed to treat sinners? If you acted friendly to sinners, were you condoning their sin? Wasn't it your responsibility to proselytize and try to turn them away from wickedness? Should he try to do that with Royce rather than ignore him? He would talk to his preacher the first chance he got.

Chapter Eighteen

Gaye's cell phone rang on her way to class. Her father. He never called in the middle of the day, so she answered, concerned. He and her mother were on their way to Austin and would be at her apartment by eight. He gave no hint as to the reason for the visit.

Trepidation enveloped her. Her parents didn't know she and Tommy were living together, much less engaged. Class wasn't over until seven-thirty, and her love's belongings were strewn over the living room. Sending Tommy a quick text to hide his possessions seemed prudent, but then she thought better of it. She would have to inform her parents of their living arrangement sooner or later. But Gaye did let him know of the impending visit, leaving the decision to be present to him. Tommy's response that he would tidy up and go to the library to study relieved her.

When Gaye arrived at the apartment, her parents were waiting in their car. Her mother appeared to be in a foul mood. Cringing, Gaye realized it was going to be a grueling visit. Unlocking the door and ushering them in, she offered something to drink. To her surprise, both declined. Nila surveyed the room, noting Tommy's belongings.

"Your mother has something to say to you," Sanjit said.

Looking straight ahead and avoiding eye contact, Nila said, "I'm sorry for the things I said to Tommy. I only have your best interests at heart. I didn't mean to offend him."

"Your apology is accepted."

"Tommy came to visit with me last week," Sanjit said. Gaye gave him a puzzled look. "Weren't you aware of his visit?"

"No, he didn't say anything." Then Gaye remembered he had supposedly had an epic study session.

"He came to tell me that the two of you are getting married. He wanted our blessing." Gaye froze. She didn't know what to say.

"Is this true? Were you were going to get married without saying anything to us?"

"Dad, this has been so difficult for me. I wanted to tell you, but after what happened, I didn't know how. If I told you, I thought you'd find some way to stop me. Then, if I had a wedding and you and mom didn't come, it would break my heart. I thought that if we went somewhere and got married privately, you might warm up to the idea later."

"Do you love him?" Sanjit asked.

"I do. He's a kind, thoughtful man. He makes me happy. I've never met anyone like him."

"You have our blessing," Sanjit said. Then he looked at Nila.

"You have my blessing as well."

Gaye shot up and ran to her parents, hugging and thanking them profusely.

"So, I hear the big day is coming up soon," Sanjit said.

"Yes, I have lots of work to do, but first I have to finish my classes. I've been approved for leave without pay for the next school year, so I can finish my degree."

"Tommy asked that we have a traditional Hindi wedding," Sanjit said. "He did?"

Sanjit laughed. "He did, indeed. I've asked Nila to begin working on it, if that's OK with you."

Gaye looked at her mother. "I would like that very much." For the first time, her mother looked pleased in spite of herself. Gaye called Tommy and asked him to come to the apartment as soon as possible.

When he arrived, Sanjit stood up, put his palms together while bowing slightly, and said, "Namaste. Welcome to the family."

***

Alice and Art sat at the dog park, holding hands and watching Dexter and Simon cavort. Things had been moving so fast that Alice didn't know what to think. Had Art just stayed at her apartment to keep her from drinking, or did his presence mean more? Was this a fling or something serious? Alice wanted to broach the subject but was terrified of the answer. Art had gone back to his own apartment Monday night, but did that really mean anything?

"How did things go at the office today?" Art asked.

"Not too well. An auditor is coming to look over the books. I fudged some of the travel expenses. I'm sure I'll catch hell for that."

"What do you mean?"

"They wouldn't give us enough money for travel to send three people, so I sent three people on money for two. Inman even paid for a plane ticket out of his own pocket."

"And that's a problem?"

"In the government, it is. Each employee is entitled to be paid per diem and travel expenses. After the audit, the EEOC will most likely be required to reimburse the employees' money. I will be in big trouble as I authorized more than I was told I could."

"Oh."

"Yeah, and that's not the end of it. The chair is angry that I did not properly contact her regarding sick leave, not to mention the case I didn't close. Then the company hired Three V to defend them."

"That's that real nasty law firm, isn't it?"

"Yes. We think they have some people snooping around. Gaye saw a woman coming out of Rebels the other day and then saw the same women where she and Espy were having lunch. I'd like to see if they've been snooping around Rebels, but I don't dare go in."

"I can swing by one day this week and check it out. What's the bartender's name?"

"Jake. I'd appreciate it if you could do that."

"No problem." Art squeezed Alice's hand. "I need to get home; I've got an early morning meeting. You'll be OK tonight?"

"Sure, I'll go straight home. I should be fine."

"I wish you'd check back in and finish the rehab program."

"I just can't. There's too much going on. Besides, I'd have to ask Saitou for leave, and that would be a disaster."

Art leaned in and gave Alice a quick kiss. "I expect you to be here tomorrow right after work—no stopping at Rebels."

"I promise."

Alice watched as Art walked Simon to his car and left. She browsed her e-mail quickly. Thankfully, all was quiet. There was nothing to do about the audit, so there was no use worrying about it. *I'll just have to take whatever punishment Saitou has in store. I just hope it isn't my job.*

Chapter Nineteen

JJ rifled through the kitchen drawers, gathering silverware and napkins. Gaye had prepared a cinnamon coffee cake in honor of Jorge's return. Its aroma, as well as that of freshly brewed coffee, permeated the office. JJ wished Jorge would hurry; he was starving. As he returned to the conference table, the door opened. Jorge walked through with a wide grin on his face.

"I'm so glad you're back, man," JJ said.

Espy and Gaye appeared and gave Jorge hugs. Inman patted him on the back and stuck out his hand.

"I'm so glad you're OK," Inman said. "You really had us worried for a while."

The back door opened, and JJ looked up to see Royce entering the area hesitantly, focusing on Jorge. Suddenly the crowd grew silent. *Did Jorge really blame Royce?* JJ wondered. Glancing over to the Oriental screen, he hoped Quiana would say something to break the tension, but then he realized she couldn't see what was going on.

"I know what you think," Royce said. "You think I shot you on purpose."

JJ sensed a sharp edge to Royce's voice. He swiveled his head to glean Jorge's reaction.

Giving Royce a critical look, Jorge said, "Where'd you come up with that idea? I never said that."

"I know you thought that. I'm always to blame for everything."

"Everyone, sit down," Gaye said. "We thought we'd celebrate Jorge's homecoming. We've got coffee cake." Gaye motioned to the table and began to cut generous slices. The others busied preparing plates, and JJ put one into Quiana's inbox. Royce finally sat with a piece but remained soundless.

"Look," Jorge said. "If you hadn't jumped that piece of shit, he'd have probably shot us all. You did the best you could, and we're alive. So, let's just forget about it."

Relieved, JJ watched as Royce seemed to loosen up. They'd had enough drama in the office to last for a thousand years and didn't need anymore.

***

JJ looked up as Jorge handed him the investigative plan for Logistic Construction. He could see that Jorge had made a few changes.

"What do I do now?" JJ asked.

"What do you mean? You need to follow the investigative plan," Jorge said.

"It's just that I haven't done a case totally by myself before."

"I suggest you get on the phone to the company and find a few things out about the prime contractor who owns the porta cans. It could be that we need to file another charge against them."

"But the CP doesn't work for the prime contractor."

"It doesn't matter. The prime contractor, as well as Logistic, is responsible for assuring there's no hostile environment. The prime has more power over the other contractors to stop the graffiti. After all, they're the ones who set the porta cans out."

"That makes sense."

"Hey, I gotta run a quick errand. Should be back in about thirty minutes."

"OK. See you in a few."

JJ made a call to Logistic and spoke with Sarah Barnes, the HR manager, who was rather upset to find out about the graffiti. Apparently, the supervisor hadn't informed her of the problem. She pledged full cooperation. However, as the HR manager had pointed out, it was hard for

Logistic to deal with the situation because they didn't control all employees on site. Carmichael Incorporated, the prime contractor, had that power.

He found the company's number on the web but hesitated. Jorge had just returned and settled at his desk. JJ was uncomfortable sitting next to the man, afraid Jorge would eavesdrop and then criticize his handling of the call.

Scooting out of their office, JJ wandered to the backyard. It was hot, however, and the sweltering environment forced him back inside, where he slid into a conference room chair. He so wanted to ask Quiana what to do, but he felt ashamed. He shouldn't need to have his hand held.

What's wrong with me? JJ thought. The incident with Royce had left him with no confidence whatsoever. *I've got my dream job, and now I'm just giving up.* What had he told Quiana about stepping out? "Just do it." Shouldn't he take his own advice?

JJ went back into his office and made the phone call. After several transfers, he reached Jose Vega, the human resources manager at Carmichael.

"Mr. Vega, my name is Joseph Jordon, with the EEOC. I'm calling about a case that I'm working on with one of your contractors on the Stone Creek job site, Logistic Construction."

"What can I do for you?" Jose said.

"One of the Logistic employees filed a complaint because racist graffiti has been found in the porta cans at the job site. I understand that, as a prime contractor, you provide them."

"I'll have to check. No one has reported any racist graffiti to me. If that really happened, it's a big concern."

"Look," JJ said. "I was hoping that maybe we could get this taken care of without having to file a complaint against Carmichael."

"I'm all ears. What do you want me to do?"

JJ froze. He wasn't expecting this kind of cooperation. Taking deep breaths, he began to relax. "Let me give you the number of the Logistic HR manager who is handling the complaint on their end. Their supervisor acknowledged the graffiti and tried to cover it up several times, but it keeps coming back. After you confirm it's legit, perhaps the three of us can get together and work up an action plan to get this taken care of."

Jose exchanged information with JJ and agreed to get back with him by tomorrow afternoon. Relieved, JJ let out a sigh.

"You realize, don't you, that if you settle this case, we can't litigate it?" Jorge asked.

JJ slumped in his chair. "But we settled the case where the employee was using the word *niggardly*, and everyone thought that was good."

Jorge sighed. "They've put us in an awkward position, for sure. The right thing is to settle the case, but they are judging us based on how many lawsuits we file. The *niggardly* case wouldn't have made a good court case; it was different from this one."

"What should I do?" JJ cringed at the thought that he might be hurting the office by initiating a settlement. But it felt right; both companies were being so cooperative.

"You might want to discuss this with Alice," Jorge said as JJ's phone started ringing.

JJ answered to find Jose Vega of Carmichael on the other end.

"Mr. Jordon, I did speak with Sarah at Logistic, who has spoken with her supervisor. We have a plan to present to you. Carmichael will require all companies onsite to give a brief talk to employees about the graffiti and make it clear that it is to stop. We will remind employees that if they are caught, they can be subjected to discipline, up to and including discharge. Then we'll put a videocam outside the porta cans, so we will know who goes in and out each day. Every morning the Logistic supervisor will check to see if there is any graffiti. That will narrow down any suspects. We are hoping to take care of the problem this way without you having to file a charge against Carmichael, and you won't need to conduct an investigation. What do you think?"

"Let me discuss it with my supervisor first, and I'll get back to you." JJ hung up and went to Alice's office to explain the proposition.

Unfortunately," Alice said, "we're going to have to file a complaint against Carmichael. There's no way we can write a settlement agreement that includes them unless there's a charge on file."

"But I told them we wouldn't have to file a complaint against them."

"You'll just have to tell them otherwise. I do agree that settling the case is the right thing to do. When you write up the agreement, put some timelines in it. What if, for instance, we say they agree to order the other companies to do the training within fifteen days and to monitor the porta cans for ninety days. Oh, and they should put up a big sign saying the cans are being monitored, and anyone found posting graffiti will be subject to discipline, up to and including discharge. Think the CP would be willing to agree to such a settlement?"

"I can ask."

"Just remind him that this will stop the graffiti quicker than an investigation would. Also, if the graffiti returns at some point in time, he can file another charge."

"Will do."

Chapter Twenty

Royce had become increasingly uneasy about JJ. The expressions, the talk about doing something illegal. Staying silent any longer was impossible. He stuck his head in Alice's office. "Do you have a minute?"

"Sure, come in."

Royce shut the door and then sat down. "My cousin, Shawn Hicks, is a lieutenant at the prison where JJ was. He said JJ was bad news."

"Really? What did your cousin say about him?"

"He attacked my cousin one day for no reason. That's why he had to serve his full sentence."

Alice was stunned. This wasn't the JJ she knew. She hadn't seen that kind of temper. "That's surprising." Then Alice thought about JJ being assaulted and robbed and not remembering anything. Did JJ start that fight, too? "Thanks for letting me know."

"Personally, I'm afraid of him. He broke my cousin's jaw. I expect you to do something about this. We shouldn't have to work with these kinds of people."

"Royce, I will look into it. I assure you that I have not seen anything of this nature from JJ, and he's been here over six months. You have to remember that the EEOC supports prisoner reentry. These people need to work."

Royce stood. "OK, but if he so much as looks at me crossways…"

"Thanks, Royce. I promise I'll look into it."

After Royce left, Alice scooped Dexter in her arms. "Dex, this can't be true. What am I going to do? How in the world am I going to handle this?" Her hands trembled; that longing for her favorite concoction surged through her body.

Alice shot Quiana an IM.

> I need you to come into my office. This is important. I can't talk to you from behind the screen.

Shortly, Quiana appeared, hat low. "What on earth is so important? Is it the chair again?"

"No, something much worse. Royce just came in and said that he talked to his cousin, who was a guard at JJ's prison. Apparently, the cousin said JJ was violent and attacked him. Said he broke his jaw."

"I don't believe it one iota. I haven't seen him get angry or violent."

"So, what are we going to do?"

"I don't see how you can do anything. JJ hasn't done anything wrong."

"Problem is, Royce says he is scared of JJ, and that I need to do something. I told Royce I would look into it."

"I guess you could ask JJ about it."

"OK, thanks, Quiana. Just keep an eye on the two of them for me, OK?"

"Sure."

After Quiana's departure, Alice drooped, fighting the urge to hightail it to Rebels. But Art was taking her to dinner tonight, and she didn't want to chance drinking more than she should. Thank God it was Friday. She'd deal with the situation on Monday.

***

Alice sat close to Art as they watched the dogs romp around the park. They'd had a fabulous weekend, which had unfortunately come to an end. Still, she felt unsettled. What did he envision for their relationship? If it was only a fling to him, she would be devastated, unable to cope. *I can't ask. The answer might destroy me.*

"Oh, by the way, I did stop by and talk to Jake," Art said. "As you feared, someone has been nosing around the bar, asking questions about the office. A blond woman."

Alice slumped. "Espy and Gaye thought a woman was following them, and Espy believed she had seen the same woman coming out of Rebels."

"You still have your stun gun cane?"

"I do, but I don't have a reason to carry it anymore now that I'm on the scooter."

"Well, just keep an eye out."

"So, you all packed for your trip?"

"I am. I have to be at the airport at 6:30 a.m. Are you sure it will be OK for Simon to stay at the office with you while I'm gone?"

"It's no problem, really. Don't give it another thought."

They walked to the parking lot, where Art loaded all Simon's food, toys, and bedding as well as both dogs into Alice's disability van. He leaned over and gave her a kiss on the cheek. "See you Friday. Call me if anything comes up. I love you."

Alice watched as Art walked to his car. *Just how much does he love me?*

***

Espy lounged on the couch, reading the evidence she'd collected for the San Antonio hip-hop case. Unfortunately, her spotty attendance had put her behind. While she was aware that working off the clock was forbidden, she needed to take her mind off her own situation. Besides, guilt about her lack of attention to her work was nagging at her.

The CP was in her fifties and had worked at the warehouse for about ten years. About a year ago, the company had hired Rodrigo, a twenty-three-year-old Hispanic, in the warehouse. Rodrigo listened to music on his iPhone with ear pods during the workday. The problem was, Rodrigo listened to rap music and sang along with the lyrics. When he sang the "N" word in CP's presence, she became upset.

CP's boss was white, and when she complained to him, he brushed her aside. After all, she played religious music on her portable radio, and anyone passing her desk could hear it. CP had taken her complaint to human resources, but nothing was done.

Best Espy could tell, no one else had complained about Rodrigo's singing—or CP's music choice, for that matter. Espy had grown up on hip-hop, so she hadn't realized the extent some people could be upset by the "N" word.

She'd had a talk with Inman about the case. He'd explained that the word was linked to violence and brutality against African Americans, and older people, especially, were deeply offended by its use. He wholeheartedly supported finding "cause" on the case.

Alice will be relieved, Espy thought, because it had been a while since they had had a "cause" case.

Espy heard a ping and glanced at a new text message. Hank. She'd been ignoring him for days. This was the fourth text this hour. He was begging her to call him. Espy dialed his number.

"What do you want?"

"I know the scene around the Planned Parenthood office has you upset. Look, I think you should go to New York for the abortion. They don't ask questions there, and there's no waiting period…Espy, are you there? Did you hear me?"

"So, that's how desperate you are. Isn't your wife going to miss that money?"

"That's none of your business. But she'll never know. You just need to get it done and fast. I'll transfer the money for the trip to your account."

Espy punched the end button, knowing she needed to make a decision soon. Time was running out. Focusing on her work, she began to write her "cause" case.

***

Royce walked to the conference table where JJ was sitting and talking to Quiana.

"My cousin says you should know him," Royce said.

"Really?" JJ tried to ignore Royce.

"You broke his jaw. That's why you had to serve your full sentence."

JJ sat silently.

Quiana said, "Is that true, JJ?"

"But you don't understand…"

"What's to understand?" Quiana said. "You attacked a prison guard."

"Yeah, but he—he was always riding me; he pushed me over the edge," JJ said.

"See, I told you," Royce said. "JJ's a dangerous man. We all need to keep an eye on him. I can't believe he's allowed to work here." Royce went to the backyard.

When Quiana heard the door slam, she said, "JJ, I'm so disappointed. I've stood up for you against everyone around here. Then I find out you did something like this. And you've been acting like a fool lately, saying we should tamper with government records and being against Royce, who's done nothing to you. I guess you're just showing your true colors. I don't want to talk to you anymore. I'm going to listen to some music over my earbuds."

Tears rolled down JJ's cheeks. *I knew this was going to happen.* He wanted so badly to explain to Quiana precisely what had occurred, but he knew she'd never believe him. The prison officials certainly had not accepted his explanation. Why should she?

What hurt worst was the fact that Quiana didn't believe in him now. The more JJ thought about it, the angrier he became at Royce. If that queer hadn't shown up, everything would have been just fine. That *whatever-he-is* came in here, chip on his shoulder, threatening everyone. Royce expected to be respected and given a chance, but he wouldn't give anyone else the same courtesy.

Finally, JJ could stand it no longer. He stormed out the back door, nothing to lose.

"You think you're just hot shit," he yelled. "That you've had hard knocks in life and that everyone should bow and scrape to you. You don't know anything!"

Royce jumped up from the lawn chair, knocking it over and stepping back several paces. "You stay away from me, you maniac!"

JJ made fists and took several steps toward Royce. "I'm not a maniac. I bet you don't know what your cousin did to me, do you? You think he's so innocent. Well, he's not. He harasses all the prisoners. He even grabbed me by the balls and told me I had a small package. I'm surprised someone hasn't killed him by now. He deserves it."

"Leave me alone!"

"I haven't done anything to you, you asshole. Maybe if you weren't so wrapped up in being sure no one was stepping on your toes, you'd see how others are feeling and that you're not the only one with a hard life…I—"

"Hey, what's going on?" Jorge asked. He'd heard the ruckus from inside and felt the need to intervene.

"The guy's a lunatic. He was going to hit me. He's dangerous," Royce said.

"He's a liar. I wasn't going to hit him. He's just a scaredy-cat who talks big," JJ said.

"JJ, go take a walk. Come back in thirty minutes when you've cooled down," Jorge said. After JJ had gone, Jorge asked, "What happened?"

"I was just sitting here taking a smoke break, and JJ came out, menacing me and insulting me, saying I thought I was hot shit, that I didn't know anything. I thought he was going to deck me."

"I don't understand. That doesn't sound like JJ. Did something happen between you earlier?"

"He admitted to Quiana that he had attacked my cousin. I guess he wanted to take it out on me. I'm going to call the union. This is unreal."

"Attack your cousin? I don't understand."

"My cousin is a guard at the prison where JJ was. JJ went off on him and broke his jaw."

Jorge was shocked. He was glimpsing an unknown side of JJ. "Royce, why don't you take a break and cool off? Alice isn't here yet. Let's see what she has to say."

"OK, I'll wait, but I don't think she's going to do anything about it."

Jorge returned to his desk, on edge. Royce always thought everyone was out to get him. *Thinking I blamed him for the shooting? And now accusing JJ of threatening him? What's wrong with him?*

***

Alice settled at her desk and looked around. Putting her finger in the ivy, she realized it was dry. Hopefully that was the worst thing that would happen today; she couldn't take any more drama.

Alice heard a knock, and Jorge entered when she gave the go-ahead. "We've got an issue." Jorge took a seat.

Alice could fill her anxiety kick up a notch. "Now what?"

"It's JJ and Royce. They got into an argument this morning. Royce said JJ threatened him, which JJ denies. Royce said he's going to the union, but I talked him into waiting until he talked to you."

"Oh, my God." Alice's shoulders fell. That's the last thing she needed. "What happened?"

"I'm not really sure. Both were tight-lipped. Apparently, JJ confessed to Quiana that he had hit Royce's cousin, the prison guard, and that set JJ off. I really didn't get into it, and I figured you'd want to hear everything firsthand from all parties involved."

"Thanks. Are they in?"

"Yes."

"I'll take it from here."

Alice slumped in her chair. *I should have dealt with the situation Friday.* Now it was out of control. *How much more of this can I take?* She didn't understand what was going on with JJ; it wasn't like him at all. And Royce was so touchy that he was impossible to work with. Her fear was saying anything that might send him running to headquarters screaming discrimination.

Not knowing what to do, she decided to start with Quiana.

Alice stared at the hat drawn over Quiana's face, wishing to see her eyes, her expression. Anything to give Alice a clue as to what she was really thinking.

"So, what happened?"

Quiana sighed and then explained what occurred.

"So, what's your take? Do you think JJ is dangerous?"

"Alice, honestly, it doesn't make sense. JJ was so different until Royce showed up. Now, he's cranky and acts like he doesn't give a shit. I'm still having a hard time wrapping my head around the whole thing."

"What do you think I should do?"

"My heart wants to give JJ the benefit of the doubt, but my head says otherwise. And frankly, Royce is a pain in the ass. All his threats and his attitude have soured the office."

Alice couldn't agree more, but she didn't dare say that to Quiana. After Quiana left, Alice felt a strong urge to head to Rebels. Maybe Jake would have some sage advice and, of course, an elixir to calm her nerves. Then thoughts of Art intruded. Instead, she picked up the sleeping Dexter, rubbing his coat, willing her fearfulness to ebb.

Finally, she called in JJ. Maybe understanding where he was coming from could better help her handle the fiasco.

"JJ, we've got a lot to discuss. I'm not sure where to start…Why don't you tell me your side of the story about what happened between you and Royce's cousin."

"You wouldn't believe me even if I told you. No one ever believed me. Royce is going to have me fired even though I've paid my dues. That son of a bitch."

"What happens is not up to Royce. So, tell me what went on."

"Basically, Shawn, his cousin, was harassing me constantly. One day he did a pat search on me, grabbed my privates, and said I had a small package. The day was hot; I was tired. I lost it and took a swing at him."

"Did you report him to the authorities?"

"It didn't do any good. They believed him."

"For what it's worth, I believe you."

"Really?"

"Really. I haven't seen that kind of behavior out of you since you've been here—at least, not until Royce arrived. What's changed?"

"I don't know. When I learned who his cousin was, I just figured the whole thing would get out, and everyone would turn on me. Then, with the audit and everything, it just didn't seem worth it to keep trying."

"So, you're just going to give up, huh?"

JJ sat silently, and Alice watched a tear roll down his cheek.

"OK, tell me what you said to Royce when you were outside. He seemed really upset."

"I told him that he wasn't the only one with a hard life, and if he'd just quit focusing on himself, he'd find out others had it tough, too. I told him what Shawn had done to me."

"Did you raise your voice?"

"Uh, yeah. I was mad. He can be such an asshole."

"Did you get in his face?"

"No."

"So, if you were me, what would you do?"

JJ hung his head. "I don't know."

"I expect you to treat Royce civilly and respectfully. Also, I expect you to put your heart and soul into your work. Got it?"

"Yes, ma'am."

"OK, get back to work."

Suddenly sinister and foreboding thoughts enveloped Alice, causing her heart to beat rapidly and sending bands of anxiety rippling through her chest. She grabbed her purse, checking to assure herself that Quiana was not at her desk, and fled the office.

Pushing the throttle full tilt, she thought about Art. He would be so disappointed in her. Would a call to him help bring her down from the brink? *But it's my problem, not his.*

Jake approached as Alice settled on her favorite stool.

"Haven't seen you in a while," Jake said. "Has everything been going OK?"

"Well, it could be better."

"Your usual?"

"Uh, it's kind of early. Let me start out with iced tea."

"When Jake brought her drink back, Alice said, "I've got a real dilemma on my hands. I thought I could use some of your thoughts on the problem."

"Shoot."

"You remember the ex-con, right?" Jake nodded. "One of our new employees found out that he had to serve his full sentence because he attacked a prison guard. When I spoke to the employee about it, he said the guard goaded him until he just lost it. Personally, if the guard did do what the employee alleges, grabbing his genitals, I don't blame him for swinging."

"I can understand why he'd do that. So, what's the problem?"

"The new employee is demanding I do something about the ex-con. There really wasn't much I could do about it until the two employees got into an altercation today."

"Seems like you should punish the one who started the altercation."

"Problem is, the new employee needled the ex-con, and, frankly, the new employee is tough to deal with. Everyone in the office finds him obnoxious."

"Ouch! That's a tough one."

Alice finished off her tea. "I think I'm ready for your work of art."

"Coming right up."

When the drink arrived, Alice took a large gulp. *Nirvana!* Her agitation dropped a notch. She began to relax.

How in the world am I going to handle Royce? A written warning for JJ about his behavior toward Royce was probably in order. But, damn it! Royce was a whiney, self-centered employee who had everyone on edge. It wasn't healthy for team morale.

How was she going to handle him and keep Saitou off her back? Acting soon was a given. Royce was threatening to call the union again, and their meddling would complicate the situation.

Turning to the TV, Alice watched the news as she nursed her drink, taking in more information about Donald Trump's wide-ranging campaign rallies and his insulting remarks about people of color. *Disgusting.* She'd be glad when the election was over. Would Hillary allow Saitou to continue as chair? Surely not.

Alice heard a slurping sound and realized her nectar was no more. Greedily she thought about another one but thought better of it. After leaving Jake a generous tip, she returned to the office.

***

With Royce, Alice decided to take a different tactic. She asked him to meet her at a quaint little restaurant away from the office, where they could speak unobserved.

"Royce, lunch is on me. I know you have lots of concerns, and I want to hear them out and see if we can get things resolved."

"If we can't, I'm calling the union right after this meeting."

Now or never, Alice thought. "Royce, I'm meeting with you in good faith. I've tried to do everything in good faith, but you're always threatening something—calling the union, filing an EEO complaint. It makes me feel like you don't trust me to do the right thing."

"I don't. I've been screwed over so often it isn't even funny. People say things to your face and do other things behind your back. No one respects me. They treat me like shit."

"Do you respect other people?"

"Huh?"

"My personal belief is that you have to give respect to get respect. You expect me to treat you with dignity and respect, but you don't feel you have to treat me that way."

Royce stared at Alice, glaring. She could feel her heart began to thud. Rather than babbling on, she held back, hoping Royce would speak. When he didn't, she continued. "Look, let's start over. I am concerned about what happened, and I want to have a workplace where everyone is happy and productive. I'm here to try to figure out how we can make that happen. I just need you to work with me, put some faith in me.

"To be honest with you, your attitude has soured some people in the office. They've all had their crosses to bear, just like you. They want to accept you, but you're not making it easy. Can we start over?"

"JJ crossed the line. He needs to change his attitude and quick. I won't put up with his threats and bullying."

"Let's do this. You just worry about your own behavior. You can't change his. The only behavior you can change is your own. I promise I will take care of JJ. He won't behave that way again. Would you be willing to sit down with him and talk things out? I'll be the go-between."

"Let me think about it. I don't think I've done anything wrong, so I don't see why I need to sit down and talk."

"Fair enough. Royce, tell me about the journey that led you to change your sex."

As they ate, Royce poured out the painful story of his journey—the internal discomfort, self-loathing, suicide attempts, family rejection, and harassment.

Alice could tell that the wounds had not healed. To her, it seemed he really hadn't quite accepted what he had done, and he still felt guilty on a subconscious level. Maybe that was the reason for all the bluster—he had to ward off any negativity that reinforced his fear that he'd made the wrong decision.

"Royce, I admire your courage. It wasn't easy. From what I know, you did the right thing, being true to yourself. I'm not judging you, far from it. Just let me know if you are willing to sit down with JJ." Alice paid the bill and then rose.

"I will. And Alice, thanks for listening."

As they left, Alice noticed a car parked down the street with a blond woman in the driver's seat. She twitched, making a mental note of the woman's description.

***

Jorge observed that both Alice and Royce had returned to the office. They must have had a chat over lunch; Alice did that kind of stuff. He'd been pondering what went on between JJ and Royce and just couldn't make sense of it. It was so out of character for JJ to behave like that.

But why was Royce picking at JJ, bringing up what had happened in prison? *I guess I can see how he could be scared of him after hearing what his cousin said. If I'd heard that before I got to know JJ, I would have probably reacted the same way. And I remember how testy my brother would get when any of his past behavior came up.*

So, should he just stay out of it? *It's not my fight.* But Jorge liked working there and, if the issue didn't resolve itself, and if Royce kept up his lousy attitude, things were going to deteriorate quickly.

Then, there was the issue of Royce's sexuality that had been weighing heavily on Jorge's mind, so much so that he'd even discussed him with his preacher. According to the minister, transgender people reject themselves— their birth, their gender, everything God has beautifully made. Getting surgery to remove the organ God gave you is a form of self-mutilation and self-rejection.

The only way to salvation for Royce, the pastor indicated, was for Royce to accept himself the way God made him—as a woman—and to act like a woman. Somehow, Jorge couldn't see Royce doing this. It was as if Royce was driven to find peace within by making his physical self congruent with his internal self.

Then, there were left-handed people—about 10 to 12 percent of the population. Jorge had been surprised to learn that lefties had been discriminated against throughout history. And, in some countries, they were still facing harassment. God's error? Was Royce also God's error?

Jorge thought of his cousin, whose daughter was born with spina bifida. Did God make his daughter beautifully? Was his cousin's use of surgery to repair God's obvious error a sin? If not, why was it a sin for transgenders to do the same thing?

Hearing Royce's story and reading about others who'd had a sex change led Jorge to conclude that God made errors; you just couldn't see gender errors like you could see the spina bifida.

While the reverend did not come right out and say it, Jorge got the impression that he expected Jorge to engage Royce and lead him down the path of righteousness. Proselytizing was part of his religious beliefs, and Jorge knew it was expected of him.

The very thought of engaging Royce about the topic troubled Jorge. He understood what the minister had said, but still…trying to persuade Royce to follow God and not change his sex didn't feel right. Looking up, he saw Royce go outside for a smoke break and followed him.

Easing into the lawn chair, he said, "I hope things are going better today. I know what happened between you and JJ really upset you."

"Well, they're not."

"You know, how JJ acted really surprised me. I've never so much as seen him raise his voice since he's been here. It was really out of character for him."

"Not according to my cousin."

"You know, it's hard when you get out of prison. I watched my brother go through it. You've paid your time, and yet no one gives you a fresh start. People were always throwing it up in his face. I didn't even want to give my brother a chance. I didn't trust him; wouldn't let him get close to me. If it wasn't for my mother, I don't know what would have happened to him."

"That's how I feel. No one will let me have a fresh start. My past is always an issue."

"Then you two have something in common." Jorge didn't wait for a response. "I've got to get back to work."

***

Royce took the last drag of his cigarette and then ground it in the metal can. Loneliness engulfed him. He hadn't really made any friends since his arrival. The people in the office were nice enough, but his terror that they would wound him kept him on the offense. Admittedly, this tactic put emotional distance between him and the others. *Is that what I really want?*

Was Alice right? Should he try to start over? Whose responsibility was it to stick out the olive branch anyway? JJ surely owed him an apology. *Why shouldn't I be scared of him after what he did to Shawn?*

Royce checked his watch. Shawn wasn't on duty yet. He called. "Hey, Shawn, you know that guy JJ we were talking about?"

"Yeah, what about the douchebag?"

"He says you grabbed his privates during a pat down. Did you?"

"What of it? I was just having some fun with him. He was way out of line, swinging at me. Hell, he always walked around like a goody-two-shoes, but he's a rapist creep, the lowest of the low. He needed to be taken down a notch."

"That's all I needed to know." Royce punched the end button and drooped in his chair. *I can see why JJ hit him.* Shawn had always been a bully; Royce could remember Shawn teasing him and his sister until they cried. Maybe Alice and Jorge were right. *I need to give JJ the benefit of the doubt. But how?*

Chapter Twenty One

Gaye tried concentrating on the lecture, but her mind was elsewhere. With the wedding approaching, Nila had been pestering Gaye to take care of the marriage license sooner than later. Her mother was on the phone daily to the wedding consultant and was on top of every little detail. Her phone pinged, Nila asking if Gaye had gotten it yet.

Grimacing, Gaye made a quick search on her phone about marriage licenses in Travis County. The permit was eighty-one dollars. *No wonder people just live together,* Gaye thought. Then she noticed you could get a sixty-dollar reduction if you completed an approved premarital training course.

Intrigued, she did a little more digging about what went into the course. Knowing that her mother could make their lives miserable, she thought the eight-hour course seemed like a good idea. They could discuss it when she got home.

Gaye's thoughts drifted to Espy. What was her friend going to do? *I'm glad I don't have to make that choice.* The pressure Espy's religion put on her not to choose the abortion route must make the decision excruciating.

A mention of a test during the next class got Gaye's attention. She scolded herself for letting her mind drift. Between the wedding and everything that was going on at the office, her concentration had been minimal. At least, by moving ahead quickly with the permit, she could get her mom off her back. Hurriedly, she packed her belongings and made her way to the front of the building where Tommy was waiting.

"Mom again?" Tommy asked.

"Was I that obvious?" Gaye asked.

"Actually, yes. What now?"

"She's on me to get the marriage license taken care of early so there will be no slipups."

"That doesn't sound so bad. We had to do it anyway."

"I know. I just want to do it at my own pace, that's all."

As they headed to the car, Gaye explained the matrimonial class and how she thought they should take it.

"I can't ever imagine us not getting along, but you're right, it's probably a good idea. I'm game."

"Great! I'll get us enrolled. By the way, have you gotten the guest list from your mother yet? What about your friends? You haven't given me your list yet."

Tommy stopped as they approached the passenger door of the car. He put down his backpack and took Gaye into his arms. "Don't worry. It will all work out. The wedding will be fabulous."

She laid her head on his shoulder. "I know. I should just let my mother have the day she's been dreaming for. With everything going on at the office and school, I'm just stressed out."

They stood quietly. The heat from the pavement still oozed up despite the late hour. "Enough of the worry. Let's get something to eat. I'm starving," Tommy said.

***

Yesterday, Quiana had received a cryptic IM from Alice:

Ask JJ to tell you exactly what the prison guard did to him.

Quiana wanted to, but she didn't. She had been beside herself after hearing why JJ had spent his entire sentence in prison. After all, her investment in his future had been wholly consuming. Helping him get a foothold had invigorated her, and, truth be known, the thought that the man might be able to help her escape her own prison had surfaced. She'd built him up to be some poor, long-suffering, misunderstood person. But assaulting a prison guard…that changed everything. He wasn't who he appeared to be. *But Alice says I should...*Quiana shot out a text to JJ, asking him to meet her in the backyard. Securing her armor and satisfied no one was in the main part of the office, the clerk quietly went outside and settled into a lawn chair, facing away from the door.

JJ stood on the steps of the porch. "Why do you want to see me?"

"Alice said I should hear you out about what happened with Royce's cousin."

"I don't know why she would say that. Nobody believes me anyway. I'd just be wasting my time."

"What's with you? You act like you don't care about anything."

"Why should I? I'm about to lose my job. That's all I have. I've already lost my family. All my friends in the world are right here."

"At least you can sit down."

JJ complied. Quiana sat in quiet contemplation, listening to the noise of the neighborhood: dogs barking, car doors slamming, pedestrians laughing, the sounds of living. *I could cut JJ out of my life right now. But do I want to?*

"At least you can tell me what happened. I'll decide if I want to believe you or not."

JJ told the story in a low, monotone voice. "I just lost it. I know I shouldn't have."

"Thanks for telling me."

JJ rose and went back into the office.

Quiana didn't know what to think. Her angst grew. She rose to seek out Dexter. Maybe he could lower her unease.

***

When everyone had left the office, Alice headed to Rebels. *Just one drink.*

Perched on her stool, Alice sighed while sipping the sweet nectar. The fact that Royce hadn't said anything in a week was a concern. What was he up to? Had she pushed too hard? So far, things were quiet between him and JJ. They seemed to be avoiding each other. But how long would that last? *Should I press Royce, or just let sleeping dogs lie?* They couldn't have any real teamwork as long as the two of them were at odds. The chill in the atmosphere was palpable. And then there was Quiana. This whole thing with JJ had upset her terribly. Alice had hardly gotten any "pet" time with Dexter because Quiana had him occupied. Fortunately, Simon was available as a substitute.

And what about Espy? She was frequently gone, and when she was there, she didn't seem engaged. Alice knew a discussion about her performance was long overdue, but the thought of it was just too stressful. Her drink wiped out, Alice chewed her cherry.

She started to wave to Jake to bring another life saver, then hesitated. Her unease erupted into the heebie-jeebies. The therapist at the hospital had told Alice not to imbibe at all because her family history of alcoholism hampered her ability to control her consumption. While she'd been aware of this on some level, Alice had found no other way to handle the immense pressure hanging over her head. Ordering another pick-me-up made her feel guilty, but her cravings for the deep relaxation just one more would bring won out.

A text pinged Alice's phone. Saitou! The auditor, Laura Smith, would be in the office at 8 o'clock tomorrow morning. Alice waved to Jake to bring another lifeline.

***

Alice's head was throbbing from the double dose of drink last night. Now, her nerves were raw, on edge. Would this be the beginning of the end? Alice hadn't doctored the books; everything was right there. Someone would have to be extremely thorough to figure out that expenses were charged for two travelers instead of three, which was a violation.

She heard a knock at the door, which JJ answered.

"What's that awful odor?" Laura said. JJ locked the door behind her.

"Uh, sorry about that. We've done everything we can think of to cut the smell, but it just keeps coming back."

"What is it? It's disgusting."

"Well, bar hoppers have used the entrance to take a leak—uh, excuse me—go to the restroom…Hi, I'm JJ."

"So, where is Ms. Arden?"

"Her office is on the left."

A woman straight off the pages of *Elle* magazine walked into Alice's office. Stunningly gorgeous, blond, tall, and perfect model size. She wore an expensive-looking blue suit with a white oxford, forward point-collared shirt. "Ms. Arden, I presume?"

"Yes. Have a seat, Ms. Smith. Can I get you some coffee?"

"No, thank you." Laura handed her card to Alice.

"I need to get right to work. My boss wants me to complete the audit as quickly as possible. I must say, however, that I find the office in a deplorable neighborhood. And that smell—"

"Ms. Smith, it was not my decision to put the office here. My understanding is that this was the only space available for the budget we have. As for the odor, maintenance has tried everything. He tells me the only way to get rid of the smell would be to replace the wood in the entryway. I don't see that happening. Now, what can I do to help you get started?"

"First off, I will need a private room. I have a list of files I want to examine."

"A room is going to be a problem. You see, I already have investigators sharing offices and one sitting at the conference table."

"No problem. I'll use your office."

Alice was stunned. Gathering all the control she had left, she said, "No problem. Just give me a few minutes, and I will clear my desk. In the meantime, I'll have Mr. Jordon introduce you to the rest of the staff."

After the woman left, Alice looked at her business card. "Office of the Inspector General at the EEOC." *Oh, crap, I'm in trouble now. I thought they were sending one of Saitou's flunkies.* The OIG only got involved when they suspected fraud, waste, abuse, that kind of stuff. *There's a good chance that I'll be sniffed out.*

Alice's head reeled, and the pains bombarding her leg wreaked havoc. Her champion elixir beckoned. But Rebels wasn't even open yet. She sent a quick IM to Gaye, asking for help with the move. As they were finishing, Alice heard the dogs, who had just come in from a bathroom break, growling, and she swiftly maneuvered her scooter into the conference area. Royce struggled to hold Dexter while corralling Simon. *Hmm. They must have gotten bad vibes from the frigid inspector,* Alice thought. *My worst fears are confirmed.*

She's going to do us in.

"What are these dogs doing in the office?" Laura asked.

"Reasonable accommodation animals," Alice said. "Headquarters approved them."

"I don't see why they would approve attack animals. Do they know how these mutts behave?"

"I think you just startled them," Royce said. "We seldom have visitors. I'll just take them outside while you get settled."

"Ms. Smith," Alice said, "Quiana will get you all the documents you need. I think I have everything out of my office, so you're all set."

Laura stared at Alice, long and hard. "Here's the list of what I need."

"Just put it in the inbox for Quiana." Alice pointed to the table outside the Chinese screens.

Laura deposited her paper and went into Alice's office, slamming the door.

Chapter Twenty Two

JJ observed Royce leaving for lunch promptly at 11:30 a.m. *That man s as regular as clockwork,* JJ thought. He'd be headed for the trans-friendly dive ɔar down the street. *I guess it's now or never.* JJ waited for about five minutes ɪnd made his way to the tavern.

Entering, he saw Royce sitting by himself with a glass of iced tea. JJ walked to the table. "Mind if I join you?"

Royce nodded, a look of surprise on his face.

JJ settled in. "I heard the hamburgers here are great."

"Uh, yeah, they are. BBQ isn't bad, either."

JJ placed his order and then turned to Royce. "First off, I want to ɪpologize. I shouldn't have unloaded on you. I have no excuse, really. I've ɔeen doing some reading on the Internet, and know you've had it hard. I ɪhouldn't have said the things I said."

"Actually, I owe you an apology as well. I called Shawn, and he ɔonfirmed he grabbed your privates. I can see why you took a swing at him. He's always been a bully."

"You're kidding? He admitted to it?"

"I couldn't believe it, either."

"Say, Royce, could you tell Quiana that Shawn admitted grabbing me? told her he did, but I'm not sure she believes me. I know that still doesn't make what I did right, but at least she'll know I was pushed into it."

"Well, I—"

"Oh, please. The people in the office mean so much to me, and I feel like I've let them down. They're my only family."

"Sure."

Lunch arrived. As they ate, Royce asked JJ about what it was like coming out of prison. JJ explained his fear and how Quiana had helped him get on his feet.

"But I'm worried. I have a home here, but with the audit, I'm afraid Alice is really going to get in trouble. She's been so good to me; I don't know what will happen if she's no longer my boss."

"You think there are some more problems the audit is going to turn up?"

"I hope not." JJ looked at his watch. "Oh, I gotta run. I have a telephone interview to conduct at one o'clock, and I need to prepare." He stood and reached out his hand to Royce. "Let's call a truce. No more fighting. We're family."

Royce shook his hand. "See you in a bit."

***

Royce watched as JJ left, then he got a refill of his iced tea. *The guy is growing on me,* he thought. Jorge was right. JJ had had his own issues trying to put his past behind him. Royce's mind wandered to Alice. She'd really treated him civilly, despite his threats. Where else was he going to find a group of people who would accept him? Even Jorge was coming around. If they were able to rally around JJ, they could possibly embrace him, too. But only if he let his guard down and quit expecting the worst. But could he do it? Being wounded once more was a terrifying proposition.

His mind drifted to his mother. When he'd tried to talk to her about being uncomfortable as a girl, she'd brushed him off. Then, when Royce persisted, she took him to a deliverance ministry. The outfit attempted to exorcise the trans obsession out of him and turn him into a follower of Christ. Shortly after, he attempted suicide at age twelve. His mother was unmoved, telling him he needed to try harder. God was not wrong, she said. God made you as a woman, and you should live as a woman. At sixteen, Royce left home and lived with the family of one of his high school friends. His mother never tried to contact him. He had not seen or heard from her since. And his father just went along with his mother. *I never want to suffer that kind of pain again.*

When Royce returned, he asked Alice, "Got a minute?"

"Sure," Alice said. She gathered Dexter into her arms and began stroking his coat. "Uh, do you think we could talk in private?"

"Inman is out to lunch. We can use his office."

Royce sat in Inman's chair as Alice parked next to the desk. "JJ and I had a talk. I think we've worked things out, so no need to do anything further. For what it's worth, my cousin admitted to doing what JJ said he did."

"Thanks for letting me know. Now, if you have any further concerns or problems, please tell me. I want us to be like a family. Our work here is too important, and we do our best when we're a team."

"I couldn't agree more." Royce rose. "Thanks." As he left Inman's office, he shot off a text to Quiana, confirming JJ's story.

Chapter Twenty Three

Royce checked his GPS. They still had some miles to go before arriving at the tortilla factory. Going on another onsite had raised some trepidation with him, but surely this one would be more mundane than the last. He yawned and looked over at Gaye, who had her head deep in a textbook.

"Gaye, do you mind if we get some coffee?" Royce pointed to the Starbucks ahead.

"Oh, no, that's fine. Sorry, I don't mean to be unfriendly, I've got a test tomorrow and haven't studied. I thought I'd try to do a quick review before we got there."

"No problem." Royce pulled into the drive-in window and ordered two café Americanos. "Sugar, right?"

"Thanks." Gaye closed her book and stuck it in her bag.

Shortly, Royce eased back onto the freeway. "We should be there in about twenty minutes," he said. "So, tell me, exactly what are we looking for?"

"First," Gaye said, "it appears that we have a number of non-Hispanics who have applied for jobs but didn't get hired. We're going to have to look at all the applications and then do an analysis. There are at least twenty boxes of applications to go through. Also, we need to take a look, as it appears that the job classifications are segregated."

"How?"

"Well, it looks like women aren't allowed to do jobs that involve any lifting because they have a seventy-five-pound weight-lifting requirement. However, when I toured the factory, I didn't see anyone lifting near that much. Anyway, I can't imagine a box of tortillas weighs that much."

"I'm assuming the non-lifting jobs pay less."

"That's something we need to check. Thanks for reminding me."

Royce peered into the rearview mirror and then passed a slow-moving car. "I can't wait. I haven't worked on a good case in a while."

Gaye's phone rang. She grimaced, then answered. "Hi, Mom."

"You what? Really, is that necessary?...But you promised...Look, I'm at work, can we talk about this tonight? ...I promise I'll call as soon as I get off." Gaye gave a big sigh.

"Trouble?" Royce asked.

"It's my mother. She was so upset about me marrying Tommy that he suggested she plan a Hindu wedding for us. She's gone absolutely overboard."

"Yeah? How so?"

"We had a big argument about the ceremony length. I finally got her to cut it to one hour rather than the traditional two to three hours. That's about the only argument I've won. Now she's insisting we have a white horse for Tommy to ride to the venue. It's just ridiculous and a waste of money."

"A horse? You're kidding, aren't you? I didn't know the ceremonies were so elaborate."

"I kid you not. She wants a groom procession where Tommy arrives on a decorated white horse. Then our guests will be expected to dance around him while someone beats an Indian drum. She's even chosen a turban for him."

Royce laughed.

"And that's not all. She's working with a consultant who has lined up a Bollywood dance troupe. Can you believe it?"

Royce hooted. "I never dreamed it would be so tough to get married."

"Me, neither. I guess I'm lucky, though. My mother seems to be coming around. I only hope I can live through all this nonsense."

Royce put on his blinker and turned into the factory. *She's lucky,* he thought. *At least she has a family who loves her.*

After Gaye introduced Royce to Andy Rojas, the duo settled into an empty office. Gaye and Royce sorted through the applications, looking for those with non-Hispanic surnames and setting them aside to copy. They also kept count of the total number of applications.

"There are plenty of non-Hispanics applying," Royce said. He perused an application. "I can't see any difference in this non-Hispanic candidate and the one they hired for the forklift operator."

"Look," Gaye said. She pointed to the notations on the application of a successful candidate, noting the date and time of the interview. "None of the non-Hispanic applications I've seen have any marks. Doesn't look like they bothered to interview them."

"Mine are looking that way, too." Royce stood up and stretched. "I'm going to head to the restroom. Could I get you some coffee or anything?"

"No, I'm fine, thanks."

Royce sauntered into the hall and, seeing no one, made his way to the factory area. A large plate-glass window allowed him to view the operation. As he eyed the process critically, Andy Rojas came around the corner.

"Some operation," Royce said. "You are state of the art."

"Great, isn't it? My dad stayed old school, but mechanization has allowed us to increase sales and keep costs down."

"So, how many tortilla packages go into each box?"

"This line is processing twelve flour tortillas to a package. We put twelve packages into a box to make a case."

"Interesting. Thanks."

"Let me know if I can answer any other questions."

"I will."

After Andy left the area, Royce grabbed his cell phone, surfed the web, and did some calculations. *Hmm*. Each case of tortillas should weigh no more than twenty-five pounds. That's nothing. Women can lift that.

After stopping by the restroom, Royce returned to the office and shared his calculations with Gaye. Around one, they slipped out for lunch.

"So, Royce," Gaye said, "have you settled in?"

"More or less. It's just hard moving somewhere where you don't know anyone in town. I thought a clean break would be good for me, but now I'm not so sure."

"It was the same for me when I moved to Austin. But, between work and school, I've been busy and have managed to make a few friends."

"And get engaged."

Gaye laughed. "Seriously, it's hard making new friends when you're an adult. Have you thought about doing some volunteer work?"

"I don't know. I'll think about it." Royce thought about how people looked at him queerly when they first met; his size and his male dress didn't match up. Right now, he wasn't sure his ego could stand the questioning looks.

Gaye glanced at her watch. "Let's get going. I want to get this wrapped up as soon as possible. I can't wait for us to get this case written up. It's going to be big."

Chapter Twenty Four

Espy boarded the nonstop five o'clock p.m. flight to New York City, settling into an aisle seat. *Can I go through with it?* In her mind, because this was her first trip to New York, spending Hank's money even if the abortion didn't happen was his problem. The bastard. She hadn't yet booked a return flight. *Maybe I'll just stay there and never come home—just disappear into the masses. Then I wouldn't have to answer to anyone but myself.* An appointment with a clinic in lower Manhattan had been set for tomorrow morning.

Hank hadn't objected to her demand that he pay for the hotel and other expenses. That was the least he could do. Not caring about the cost, Espy had booked herself into an upscale hotel near the center of the city.

She waved off the bellhop and headed to her room. Just the thought of having to make polite conversation unnerved her. Besides, her small bag was effortlessly managed. Fumbling with the key card, she finally made her way inside. Her gaze was quickly drawn to the city view out her window. Dropping her carryall, Espy eased onto the bed with its goose down duvet and leather headboard. Deep browns and oranges were accented with a marble-topped nightstand featuring a retro alarm clock. The funky wallpaper appeared to be an attempt at putting clouds into the middle of Manhattan.

Gathering what was left of her energy, Espy drew warm water into the tub and soaked until it chilled. Then, wrapped in a luxurious terry bathrobe, she sat on the bed and perused the room service menu. Nothing appealed to her, but eating was essential. Finally, she chose an omelet.

While waiting, fatigue engulfed her, causing her to doze. Knocking startled her, and she struggled to the door to admit the server. After managing to get down half of her dinner, she snuggled beneath the covers. But sleep wouldn't come. Thoughts of tomorrow assaulted her, pulling her this way and that. No answer came.

Early Saturday morning Espy took the subway to Battery Park and sat on a bench, gazing at the Statue of Liberty. What did it say? Espy quickly googled: "Give me your tired, your poor, your huddled masses yearning to breathe free, the wretched refuse of your teeming shore. Send these, the homeless, tempest-tossed to me, I lift my lamp beside the golden door!"

Ever since she'd found that Hank did not want her to keep the baby, Espy had felt trapped. The inertia was maddening. She just couldn't see her linked to that bastard for the rest of her life. Sure, raising the baby by herself without any financial assistance was a possibility. But sooner or later, the baby would want to know who her father was. Then, what would her response be?

But having an abortion…She was Catholic but didn't practice. During her childhood, the sanctity of human life had been paramount. *I wouldn't wish that decision on my worst enemy.*

Espy lingered, watching the boat traffic and tourists wandering through the park. *Will I ever be free?* Glancing at the time on her phone, she rose and drifted to the subway.

***

Inman was ecstatic and, at the same time, scared. Martha had sent him an e-mail requesting a relationship with him. Her birth mother and the anger she'd harbored for so long were on her mind. While she understood intellectually why Grace made the adoption decision, Martha was still trying to grapple with it emotionally. At this point, Martha was willing to have a telephone conversation with Grace.

Inman was petrified. He must inform Shirley, but how would she take the news? Perhaps telling her in person was the way to go. But he didn't have time to be out of the office—the Bighorn Outfitters case was heating up.

His boss had had a long conversation with Three V yesterday, and they had threatened to expose the entire operation in Austin to Congress.

They'd also hinted that they had some negative information on the staff. Inman shuddered. *Do they know about my illegitimate child?* Then, he dialed Grace.

"I received an e-mail from Martha. She said she understands why you gave her up, but she is still grappling with her anger over it. She is willing to speak with you over the phone."

"Oh. I'm so torn. You don't know the guilt I feel over the whole situation," Grace said.

"She's really a wonderful woman. You should reach out."

"I suppose you're right. If you give me her e-mail address, I'll write to her to set up a phone call. I don't want to catch her off-guard by calling."

Inman provided the information. "Let me know how it goes. I've got my own dilemma. Martha said she wants to be a part of my life, but now I have to tell my wife and children. I don't know how they'll react."

"You better tell them as soon as possible. Their reaction will be worse if they find out you've been holding out on them."

"You're right."

The two then spent some time talking shop. Inman saw a call on his screen and, realizing it was his boss, quickly told Grace goodbye.

"Hi, Stan. What's up?" Inman asked.

"Those sons of bitches. We should have never issued 'cause' on that Bighorn case. Now they've contacted their congressman in Texas complaining about how so-called 'shady' the Austin operation is. And it isn't just any congressman, its Lawson Garrett, the Tea Party darling."

"He's chair of the House Committee on Oversight and Government Reform, isn't he?"

"Yeah, and I've been hearing rumblings that he wants to shut EEOC down. His view is that there's no more discrimination in the workplace. Companies can take care of any possible problem themselves and don't need government oversight.

"Anyway, he's sent me a congressional letter of inquiry, demanding answers. Three V must have sent spies to watch the office. They are accusing us of running an illegal office stuffed with promiscuous drunks, sex offenders, perverts, fornicators, and adulterers, not to mention wasting taxpayer money on frivolous cases."

Inman's heart sank. They knew about him. How did they find out? He'd have to tell Shirley as soon as possible before this became headline news. "Sounds like they're pulling a diversion tactic, personally attacking us to keep anyone from looking at the merits of the case."

"Well, that leaves us in a pickle. At this stage, we can't divulge the facts in Bighorn. We'll have to wind up conciliation fast and file a lawsuit so we can fight back at these SOBs. I wish we had more to go on, though."

I wish we had more evidence, too, Inman thought. "I have a settlement offer out, but I haven't had a response. They have until Tuesday to respond. My assumption is that settlement is a no-go."

"I agree. I want you to have the lawsuit ready to file Wednesday, first thing. Send your draft to Jason and me for a final review before you file it."

"Will do."

"Also, I need you to gather up information so I know how to address this bullshit about the debauched staff. I have no clue who they're talking about. I need to come up with some kind of response to the esteemed congressman."

Inman put his phone on the coffee table and began to pace the apartment. It was all so overwhelming. Where to start? Telling Shirley was his first priority, in case the news leaked when the lawsuit was filed. No telling what slimy Three V would do once that occurred.

Gathering his courage, he dialed his wife. After pleasantries, he began. "Shirley, I know this is going to come as a shock to you, but I recently found out I have a child from a relationship I had way before I met you." Silence ensued.

"Say that again."

"Look, I had a one-night stand when I was in high school. I didn't know anything about the child until recently. But I've actually met her. What a wonderful woman. I want her to be part of our family."

"I'm so confused. Why didn't you tell me about her earlier?"

"I didn't know if she wanted to have a relationship with me, so I didn't say anything about it."

"How did you find out?"

"I, uh." At that point Inman wanted to die. His choices were to make up an elaborate lie about making contact with Grace or come clean. Either way did not bode well. "I ran into the birth mother, and she told me."

"Where? I didn't know you had gone back to Tougaloo? What else have you not been telling me?"

"No, I didn't go there. I ran into her in Austin."

When Shirley did not immediately respond, Inman realized he was doomed.

"So, you wanted to go to Austin so you could take up with the old girlfriend. After all these years…I can't believe it."

"Shirley, it's not like that. Shirley, are you there?"

The phone was dead. Frantically Inman called back, but Shirley wouldn't pick up.

***

A nurse called Espy's name and led her to a consultation room. They began the paperwork. "Do you wish to speak to a counselor about your decision?"

"No."

***

Gaye was weeping when Tommy walked into the living room. "What's wrong?"

"It's Mother, as usual. She just won't listen. This wedding is out of control. I feel like I'm cast as a bit actress in a large Bollywood stage production. And Mom's the director. She's just railroading this. It's all for her friends and family, not our marriage. I wish you'd never agreed to it."

Tommy sat next to Gaye on the couch, taking her in his arms and giving her a long, soft kiss. "So, tell me, if you could wave a magic wand, what would your ideal wedding look like?"

Gaye thought awhile. "I'd go to the Zilker Botanical Garden. It's just beautiful there. So peaceful. Just the two of us. No one else to deal with. That's what I'd do."

"That's a long way from what your mom has cooked up. I'm sorry. I didn't realize how you felt. I apologize. I was out of line offering to let your mother plan the traditional wedding."

"Oh, it's not your fault. It did help soften her up. I don't really blame you."

Gaye heard a ping on her cell and glanced at an incoming text message. "I need to go to the office. Apparently that law firm I was telling you about has sent a congressional to the general counsel. Alice is asking for volunteers' to help prepare a response inquiry and help Inman get the papers ready to file a lawsuit."

"Hmm. Volunteer means unpaid, right?"

"Right. Don't wait for me for lunch. It may be a long day."

***

Gaye entered the office to find everyone except Jorge and Espy at the table.

Quiana said, "Jorge has an afternoon of soccer games, and he's the coach. I haven't heard anything from Espy. Strange. Hope nothing's wrong."

Me, too, thought Gaye. Time was short, and last she'd heard, Espy couldn't make up her mind.

Inman had printed out the inquiry for each of them. He was grimaced, all business. "Go ahead, read it."

Gaye couldn't believe it! Drunks? Sex offenders? Perverts? Adulterers? Fornicators? This Three V was scum, alright.

"General Counsel Weber has asked me to investigate the accusations and give him feedback so he will know how to respond," Inman said.

"I guess I'm the sex offender," JJ said, "unless anyone else wants to claim that role."

"Pervert? Is that what they're calling me?" Royce balled up his fists. "I'm going to sue the bastards."

"We don't have time for that. I'll just tell Weber I have no idea what they mean by perverts."

"Maybe they're talking about me," said Quiana, "and in that case, I want to sue as well."

"My response still stands," Inman said.

Everyone sat silently.

JJ said, "Well, that leaves adulterers, fornicators, and drunks. I guess that could include most of us in the room."

"I have a confession," Alice said. Gaye could see that her hands were shaking. "They are referring to me. I've been under so much stress lately that I've been drinking too much. That's why I was out of the office earlier. I was in rehab."

Gaye was shocked. "But alcoholism is a disease, and you're getting treated for it. How can they hold that against you?"

Alice shrugged.

"I wonder if that blonde we've seen around dug up all this information," Gaye said.

"Oh, I just think they're throwing a bunch of shit against the wall to see if it sticks," said Inman. He rose and leaned on the table. "I'll take responsibility for being the fornicator." Then he told the whole story of finding his daughter.

Gaye squirmed. "I guess I'd be a fornicator, too, Inman," she said. She knew Espy was the target for the adultery accusation, but it wasn't her right to tell everyone. She sent Espy a quick text to call.

Inman then divided the work, assigning Gaye to partner with him and Quiana on the court filings. Alice was responsible for the inquiry, and she gave both JJ and Royce questions to answer. He warned them they needed to finish by Sunday so the auditor wouldn't see what was going on. He and Alice didn't trust her.

By three o'clock, Gaye had not heard from Espy despite a follow-up text. Concern mounted. She then sent an e-mail from her personal account to Espy's, explaining what had occurred. A shudder ran through her. Had Three V tapped their personal phones and e-mails? She quickly processed new passwords.

***

Espy rolled over and looked at her phone. It was after seven. She still felt groggy, but the bleeding had slowed. Her breasts were tender; her nipples damp. Goddamn Hank! Checking her texts and e-mail, she found Gaye's messages. As she quickly perused it, her heart sank. The ordeal wasn't over— it was just beginning. Would the whole world know what had occurred? Quickly, she texted Gaye to let her know that she was OK and would contact her later. Espy made her way to the bathroom and climbed in the shower, huddling on the floor. Could the water wash away her guilt and self-loathing?

***

As Dexter and Simon snuggled around her, Alice stared at the rum and coke sitting on the end table. Her promise of just one had been satisfied, but only because the cocktail was extra strong, with just a splash of coke.

What have I gotten us into? Am I going to ruin everyone's life? Jorge, Espy, and Gaye were the only ones they hadn't found dirt on—yet.

Art wasn't due back until Monday afternoon. She had finished her portion of the work for the general counsel and faced being alone tomorrow. Her nerves were shot, and guilt permeated her wretched body. Especially after Gaye had voiced that Alice had obtained treatment. But the course of therapy was incomplete, though her intentions were honorable.

Idly she thought about returning to the inpatient facility. That was the right thing to do, rather than continuing to depend on Art as a crutch. But that would mean spending time out of the office. Maybe attending some AA meetings would work. *I need to be strong.*

And then, there was no telling what that witch of an auditor was going to come up with. The woman was cool, devoid of humor or smiles. Just sitting in the same office with her gave Alice the willies. Only two more days to go. Thank God an end was in sight.

Maybe she should just resign. That might take the pressure off the office. But she'd made the mess by shoving Bighorn Outfitters through and needed to stay to clean up the pieces.

Suddenly her hands shook, and a fierce pain shot up her leg. Alice grabbed the poison and took a big slug.

Chapter Twenty Five

Inman finished some paperwork and shut down his computer. Attempts to reach Shirley on both the house and cell multiple times had fallen flat. Inman had considered calling his son to intervene, but he'd thought better of it. Providing an explanation to his children seemed unnerving at this point in time. But he didn't feel like being alone tonight. *How can I keep from dwelling on this mess?* His phone rang. Hope soared but crashed when he discovered it was Grace.

"I talked to Martha this afternoon," she said.

"How'd it go?"

"I'm not sure. I don't know what to think. I'd like to talk to you about it if you could meet me for lunch next week."

"Say, I was just about to walk down the street to a bar near my office. Why don't you meet me there?"

"Uh, I guess so. Fine. What's the address?" Inman gave her the office address and told her Rebels was just up the street. "You're going to a bar named 'Rebels'?"

"Yeah, funny, isn't it? It's so close, and some of the people from work have been there. I really don't know anywhere else to go."

Inman arrived and looked around, thankful there was no Confederate paraphernalia adorning the place. The crowd was building, but he spied an empty table in the back and commandeered it.

Watching anxiously for Grace, he ordered a Crown on the rocks from the harried server. Spying Grace just as he finished his drink, he waved her over.

"Have a seat. What can I get you?"

"White wine would be fine."

Inman flagged down the waitress, ordering Grace's drink and another for himself. "So," he said, "How was the conversation with Martha?"

"Rather stilted. I explained to her about how it was back then. How I didn't know what else to do. I think she sort of understood, but she couldn't understand why I hadn't tried to find her later like you did. You know? I just couldn't answer that question."

Inman took a sip, sitting quietly.

"Why didn't I?" Grace asked.

"I'm sure you were afraid of the rejection. After all, I could look for her without guilt because I didn't know she existed. You did. You knew."

"I guess. I don't know. I've been beating myself up ever since I talked to her. I don't have any other close family. I was an only child, and my parents are dead. The older I get, the more family matters."

They both sipped their drinks in silence. Inman waved for another round.

"You're right about family. I may have just lost one part in trying to have the whole enchilada." Then Inman explained his conversation with Shirley.

Tears trickled down his cheek, and Grace leaned over, rubbing his hand. They discussed different things Grace could do if she wanted to bring Martha around.

"Inman, see that lady over there on the barstool—the blonde?"

"Yeah, what about her?"

"I've had the feeling she's been watching us. She just turned around as soon as you looked toward her."

"Who knows? You know what they say? Keep Austin weird. Takes those kinds of people for the city to live up to its reputation."

Grace glanced at her watch. "Inman, I need to go. It's late. Call me when you know something. I hope you can work everything out with Shirley."

As she rose, so did Inman. Grace gave him a hug. He clung to her, feeling she was the only human being who understood him right now.

Inman watched Grace leave, then glanced at his glass. Rather than going home, he lingered. Besides, his current level of inebriation left him sure that driving was dangerous. An infrequent drinker, the Crown had him reeling. Before he could wave the waitress to bring coffee, a woman sauntered to his table.

"May I join you?"

Inman looked at her, the blonde from the bar who had been eyeing him. "Well, I—"

"Thanks." She sat down quickly. The bartender approached the table and put another Crown in front of Inman.

"I'm sorry. I didn't order this."

"No problem. The lady here is taking care of it."

Inman stared at the bartender and shrugged. He then turned to the blonde. "I don't think I know you."

"You do now. My name's Brittany."

"So, what do I owe this pleasure?"

"I could tell you're going through a tough time and thought you might need a little company. I'm a good listener."

Inman took a long sip of his drink. Something didn't feel quite right. Why was this woman so interested in him? He wasn't used to that kind of attention from attractive women—especially white women.

He looked at her questioningly. "So, what brings you to Rebels?"

"I just moved to Austin about three months ago. The bar is listed as one of the best dives in the area. I haven't met many people yet, so I thought I'd come check it out. Better than sitting at home, watching TV. And you? Have you been in Austin long?"

"No. Just about nine months. I transferred here for my work."

"Your job is going well, I hope."

"About as well as could be expected. I really don't feel like discussing it. Nothing you would understand."

"Try me."

Inman drained his glass, only to realize another was waiting for him.

"Please, Brittany, I've had enough to drink tonight and a big day tomorrow. I really need to get some coffee."

"Wow! What could be so important that you have to work on

Sunday? You must have a boss who's a slave driver."

Inman began to unload.

Chapter Twenty Six

Alice woke to whining dogs and a killer headache. Not only her head but her whole body was wracked with pain. Every noise, every movement made her ballistic. She'd put out doggie pee pads, thank goodness, but it was way past the boys' breakfast time. *I can't go on like this. I've turned into my mother. I can't handle it anymore.*

Alice first contacted rehab and arranged to check in later in the afternoon. Then she called Quiana, asking her to retrieve the dogs and keep them until Art returned home Monday evening.

"So, what do you want me to tell Laura, the Aryan goddess?" Quiana asked.

"Aryan goddess?"

"Yeah, she reminds me of an uptight Nazi woman guard in the movies."

Alice sighed. "I really don't care. Tell her I'm sick, which is the truth. I can't deal with it anymore. Leave Jorge in charge."

"Will do."

Alice took some Aleve and was able to get out of bed about thirty minutes later. Feeding the dogs and packing a small bag left her exhausted. Easing onto the couch, she relished the silence. Any noise set her on edge. What about Art? He needed some kind of explanation, but what?

Alice couldn't bear to face the man. Finally, she sent him an e-mail explaining her return to rehab. It wasn't his responsibility to police her drinking—it was hers. She respected—no, loved him too much to put him in the position of a policeman. The note ended, "I love you and hope that our relationship continues for the rest of our lives."

***

Quiana eased into the office before seven o'clock. With Alice absent, chaos would erupt. The Aryan goddess was only supposed to be at the office two more days, but Quiana was already worried. The woman had gone over the travel records and then asked for them again late Friday. That didn't bode well.

So far, she hadn't interviewed anyone. At least Alice had made it perfectly clear they were to answer the auditor's questions truthfully.

Poking around, Quiana noticed piles of trash in the kitchen. Someone, probably Inman, was here Sunday. Quiana quaked. Having the office shut down and being forced to transfer would be a disaster. After all the trouble in the Houston office, she didn't want to go back.

Hearing a rattling at the door, Quiana slipped behind her Oriental screen, a tad surprised someone was here so early.

"Quiana?" asked Gaye.

"Good morning," Quiana said. "I'm glad you're here early. I have an eerie feeling all hell's going to break loose today."

"You and me both. Let me get some coffee, and we can talk." Quiana heard Gaye settle next to the Oriental screen.

"Alice has gone back into rehab," Quiana said. "I probably shouldn't tell you, but you already knew she had been. And with the Aryan goddess still here…I'm not sure what will happen."

"Oh, no! That's so upsetting. I'm really worried about her."

"Me, too, but we've got to hold down the fort."

"Have you heard from Espy?"

"No, why?"

"I tried to get hold of her Saturday and finally got a text that she was OK and would contact me later. But that was Saturday night. I haven't heard from her since."

"Hmm…Anyway, Jorge is in charge."

The two heard a knock, and Gaye opened the door. Laura strode in and stood in front of the Oriental screen.

"I thought I told you to get that foul odor taken care of," Laura said. "Why didn't you?"

"I contacted our maintenance man and he said he'd send someone out, but we're not high on his priority list," Quiana said.

"Where is Ms. Arden? She was supposed to be here this morning so I could conduct an interview with her."

"She's sick today, Ms. Smith."

"Call her and tell her she needs to be here by noon. This interview is extremely important. Tell the others I'm moving their interviews to today."

Quiana paused, thought about objecting, and then changed her mind. "Yes, ma'am."

"I want all the attendance records for the office, including the sick leave slips." Quiana heard the goddess stomp off and slam Alice's door.

"Oh, no," Gaye said. "There's no way Alice can be here."

"I know. I'll see how Inman wants to handle it."

Gaye rose. "Let me know if I can do anything. I need to get to work." Quiana's fingers flew across her phone as she texted the rest of the group:

THE GODDESS IS HERE. Will interview staff today.

She quickly gathered the attendance records and then froze. Alice had been marked as using sick time for the first rehab gig but had never signed a sick leave slip. That document required the approval of Director Saitou. And, of course, Alice probably didn't contact the director about going back into rehab. Quiana started to call the chair's secretary to report Alice was taking sick leave, but she dreaded the grilling about why Alice wasn't calling herself. Everyone knew the score at the office, but Quiana had no idea how much Saitou knew.

She sent JJ a quick text telling him to see her as soon as he arrived so he could deliver the attendance records to the auditor.

***

Espy aimlessly wandered through Central Park. Failing to contact

Gaye bothered her. Also, asking for a few more days off was paramount. She hadn't expected the decision to affect her so much. And, just as the relief of being rid of Hank forever had surfaced, Three V had gotten wind of their affair. No telling how they were going to use it against her. Settling on a park bench away from prying ears, she called Gaye.

"Hold on. Let me go outside. The Aryan goddess is here…Now I can talk. I've been so worried about you. Are you OK?"

"Who's the Aryan goddess?"

"The auditor from the OIG. Quiana thinks she looks like those Nazi females in World War II films. So, how are you?"

"I thought I'd be OK, but I'm not. I went through with it."

"I know it was a difficult decision for you. Just don't be second-guessing yourself. You did what you felt you needed to do."

"Maybe. But I feel lousy about it. Now I'm just plain scared. Sounds like Three V knows about my affair."

"I don't know what to think about them. How could your situation have any bearing on the office performing poorly on a case you didn't even work on?"

"They're such scum. Somehow they'll find a way to use it against us. Can you tell Alice I need a few more days off?"

"Alice isn't here. You missed Saturday. Turns out when Alice was gone earlier, she was in rehab for her drinking. Quiana said she checked herself back in yesterday. Jorge's in charge. I'll tell him."

"Oh, no. I'd noticed Alice hadn't quite been herself lately. How's that going to affect the audit?"

"I'm not sure. The goddess was none too happy this morning when Quiana told her Alice was sick. She's moved up the staff interviews to today. She'll be wanting to interview you, for sure. Quiana said she's gone over the travel records with a fine-tooth comb."

"If I don't show by Wednesday, the goddess is likely to ask for a doctor's note. I simply can't provide one." Tears ran down Espy's cheek. "Tell Jorge I'll be in the office Wednesday morning."

"I will, but Espy, I'm really worried about you. What can I do?"

"Nothing. This is something I have to handle alone."

Espy slowly made her way to the Metro stop at Columbus Circle.

Hesitating before the underground entrance, she googled Catholic church. The church of St. Paul the Apostle was only a block away.

Easing into the back pew, she soaked up the quiet calmness while gazing at the predominately blue stained-glass windows in the front, which seemed to cool her burning soul.

How long since I've been in a church of my own volition? I can't even remember. I only go to make my mother happy, so she won't pester me. Instinctively Espy lowered the prayer bench and got on her knees, but she couldn't pray.

"Excuse me? Could I help you?"

Espy turned toward the voice to find a priest standing in the aisle. "I see that you've been here quite some time."

"You see, I don't quite know how to start."

"Would you like reconciliation?"

"Yes, if it's at all possible."

"Come with me."

The priest led her into a small, comfortable room that was dimly lit. After she was seated, he gave a short blessing.

Espy made the sign of the cross and began, "Bless me, father, for I have sinned."

Chapter Twenty Seven

Inman stirred when he heard his cell phone. He looked around, confused. Bright sunlight radiated into the room. "Quiana?"

"Where are you?" Quiana asked. "The goddess is on a rampage. Alice isn't here, you're not here. I don't know what to do."

"What time is it?"

"Eleven."

"Oh, my God. I'll be there as soon as I can. Just tell her I was working on a brief at home, and the time got away from me."

"I'll try to keep her at bay, but hurry."

Inman rose. Yesterday had been hangover hell. How long since the last binge? Years. Memories about exactly what happened after Grace left and that blonde, Brittany, came to the table were nonexistent. They'd been talking about bad bosses at work. Sunday morning found him in his office, sprawled out on the chair. Thank God he hadn't tried to drive home.

Half of Sunday was spent attempting to recover from his malaise and the other half trying to finish paperwork in the Bighorn case. And still no word from Shirley. Now he had to deal with that goddammed auditor.

Frowning, Inman called Quiana back. "Did you say Alice wasn't there?" Quiana lowered her voice to a whisper. "She's back in rehab."

"Oh, shit. We're doomed. I'll be there as soon as I can."

***

Inman walked in just as JJ was coming out of Alice's office, a deep scowl cemented on his face. Inman motioned him into his office and shut the door. "What happened in there?"

"She's got the whole travel thing figured out. No sense trying to make excuses about it. She pointedly told me it was against GSA regs. Also, she questioned me real hard about why there were two dogs in the office. I told her I didn't really know and that Alice would have to answer that."

"Uh-oh."

"Inman, I feel so bad, I feel like I betrayed Alice. She's the one who's given me a chance, and what do I do? I drop her in the grease."

"We all talked about this. No lying. Lying doesn't do any good, because they'll find out the truth anyway. We'll just have to hope that the good we did outshines the bad for headquarters. Just keep me posted about anything else that happens, OK?"

"Sure." JJ slipped quietly out of the office.

Inman sat down, trying to calm his nerves before the confrontation with the auditor. Was telling the truth the right thing? If he'd fudged a little on the story to Shirley, said Grace lived in Los Angeles and that they'd accidentally met at a seminar, maybe his wife would be speaking to him. But that wasn't what happened. What was it Quiana liked to say, "What's done is done?" Inman left his office to face the music.

"So, Mr. Parker, I see that Ms. Arden authorized three individuals to go to the onsites in the Hyperion investigation when headquarters had only authorized two individuals. Why did she do that?"

"You'll have to ask Ms. Arden. My understanding is that she sensed a reluctance for Mr. Macias to pursue the case. Later, we determined that her concerns were founded, as Mr. Macias has religious objections to and takes a dim view of homosexuality. Ms. Gomez was the real champion of the case."

"What does that have to do with any of this?"

Inman selected his words carefully. "The case involved the owner of the company forcing his employees, who were undocumented, to perform oral sex on him."

"I see. But why send Macias at all?"

"Ms. Gomez doesn't speak Spanish."

"What? A Hispanic who doesn't speak Spanish? That can't be right. You'd better not try to pull anything on me, Mr. Parker."

"You can ask Ms. Gomez herself. The victims spoke little or no English, and a translator was necessary."

"I would, but she doesn't seem to be here."

They both sat in silence as the auditor stared at Inman. He stared defiantly back. "So, Mr. Parker, did you expend any of your personal money to cover per diems for the trip? I'm assuming you must have since it would be hard for three people to travel on the money meant for two. While the per diems are adequate, they are certainly not generous."

Inman wanted so badly to say "no," but he'd given his word to the team that he would tell the truth. "Yes, and it was worth every penny. Ms. Smith, have you read the case? Do you realize what this scumbag was doing to his employees? Forcing them into oral sex and, if they resisted, threatening to call immigration on them? I believe in the 'cause,' and if I have to throw my personal money into righting wrongs, I'll do it every time. What would you do?"

"Mr. Parker, what Ms. Arden did was against GSA regulations, and you went along rather than reporting a violation. That will be duly noted in the report." The woman proceeded to ask Inman a wide range of questions regarding the office and staff. He gave as little information as he could. "One last question, Mr. Parker. Why were two dogs in the office when I arrived? I understand that only one has been authorized by headquarters as an emotional support animal."

"I don't know. You'll have to ask Ms. Arden."

"I would, but she doesn't seem to be here."

Inman left, feeling as if his world were collapsing. Now he'd be in hot water for not reporting Alice. No one cared whether they'd made a difference in anyone's life.

***

Around three, Quiana heard the door to Alice's office open, followed footsteps approaching her screen. She cringed.

"I ordered you to tell Ms. Arden to report to the office. Where is she?" Laura asked.

"I did send her a text, but I haven't heard back," Quiana said.

"I don't trust any of you in this office. You're trying to cover up something here, and I'm going to get to the bottom of it. You'd better not be lying to me."

"I'm not." Quiana grabbed Dexter, who had taken up residence beside her desk, and began to stroke his fur. Her anxiety was higher than it had been in months.

"Where is Ms. Rohatqi? I want to interview her now."

Quiana panicked. She hugged Dexter until he squealed. "She's out of the office."

"But she was here this morning. Where is she?"

"She's at school. She leaves early two days a week to continue her graduate studies."

"Then give me her leave slip."

Quiana felt like a Judas. The final betrayal was about to begin. "She doesn't have one. Alice allows her to leave early, and she makes up the time by staying late when she doesn't have class."

A long silence ensued. Quiana ran her hands rapidly along Dexter's back, praying the torture would soon end.

"I see. I don't see any documentation concerning this type of schedule for Ms. Rohatqi."

"Everything's on the up and up. You will see that she works her eighty hours in the pay period."

"It'd better be."

Quiana breathed a sigh of relief as she heard the goddess retreat into Alice's office and slam the door.

***

Espy sat in her car, sipping a caramel latte and trying to get the courage to enter the office. Her interview with the auditor was scheduled for nine o'clock. Gaye had tipped her off about what to expect and reminded her to tell the truth. While she watched the entrance, an imposing blonde entered. "Must be the Aryan goddess," Espy muttered to herself.

Still, Espy lingered. While dreading her interview, she was absolutely terrified of her coworkers' concern regarding her absences. *What am I going to tell them?* Despite her confession, Espy continued to wallow in self-loathing, still trying to convince herself that her decision was the right one. Getting back to work might help get her mind off the subject. There was no turning back now. Sighing, she took the last swig of her drink and headed into the office.

After what seemed like an eternity, Espy was summoned to the torture chamber. Without any pleasantries, the woman lashed out questions in a rapid-fire manner. While Espy had expected the interview to be contentious, she wasn't prepared for the woman's condescension or her outright hostility. She grilled Espy over the travel expenses, asking why Jorge was sent.

"Alice sent Jorge because I don't speak Spanish," Espy said.

"But you are Hispanic, aren't you?"

"Yes."

"So why don't you speak Spanish?"

"My family is eighth-generation Texan. Why should I be able to speak Spanish? My family assimilated a long time ago. Where's your family from? Sweden, Germany? Do you speak your family's native language?"

The goddess glared until Espy lowered her eyes and began to fidget. "You'd better not be lying to me," Laura said.

"I'm not."

The auditor ended the inquisition by grilling Espy about Alice's whereabouts and Gaye's work hours. Espy made assurances that Gaye put in a full workweek. And Alice? No clue. After all, Espy didn't know the facility's location. After an eternity, she received a curt dismissal.

Espy stopped by Inman's office and filled him in on the interview.

"Damn," he said. "The pressure is on, for sure. I don't think we can hold out much longer on Alice's whereabouts. I don't want to tell them, but maybe it's for the best. Alcoholism is a disability, after all. And she does have a good excuse for not getting her sick leave approved ahead of time."

Espy sighed. "I really don't think the auditor cares whether Alice has a good excuse or not. Look, I need to get to work. Talk to you later."

Espy plopped into her chair and began to stow her belongings. Gaye said, "How was it?"

"Worse than I imagined. I bet she grilled you, too."

"It was absolutely awful. She still doesn't believe that I work my full forty hours a week despite leaving early. Enough about me. Are you OK?"

"Truthfully, I don't know. I feel empty, depleted. Depressed."

"If you want to talk, I'm here. Have you thought about using the employee assistance plan, you know, talking to a counselor? You get some sessions free. The number is on the bulletin board in the kitchen."

"That might be a good idea. Let me see how it goes. How's the tortilla factory case?"

"It's a winner. Royce and I are writing it up as we speak and hope to be able to turn it in by the end of the week."

"And the hip-hop case?"

"I just got notice the company isn't going to settle. I plan to get it to Iman by tomorrow afternoon."

***

Quiana perused the text Espy had sent to her personal number regarding the highlights of her interview with the goddess. She shivered.

Inman's voice boomed across the office. "I finally got approval from headquarters to file the Bighorn case in court. I'll be back after lunch."

"OK," Quiana said.

About fifteen minutes later, Laura came out of Alice's office and announced the investigation was finished for now. Relief surged through Quiana. She couldn't take another day of that obnoxious woman and would be glad to see her gone.

Minutes later, Quiana received a phone call from Jane at headquarters. With trepidation, Quiana answered.

"The chair would like to speak with you," Jane said. "One moment."

Quiana almost heaved and began taking deep breaths to curb her uneasiness. She looked around furtively for Dexter, but he was nowhere to be found.

"Quiana," the chair said. "I demand right now that you tell me everything you know about Alice's whereabouts before I put her on AWOL. If you don't, you will be written up for insubordination."

Tears rolled down Quiana's cheeks. She had no choice but to come clean. "She checked herself into alcohol rehab. She went in Sunday and didn't have the time to contact you ahead of time. She really is ill."

The silence on the other end of the line was deafening.

"This other sick leave that was recorded right before the shooting, but for which I have no leave slip or doctor's excuse—was that also rehab?"

"Yes, ma'am."

"As the recordkeeper, it is your responsibility to assure all documentation is in order. And it obviously isn't. It's bullshit to say that Alice didn't have time to contact me before she checked in over the weekend—or the time before, for that matter. She could have sent an e-mail or text. At any rate, the appropriate paperwork for the time before should have been completed: leave slip and doctor's note."

"But, ma'am, things have been so chaotic with the shooting and all. Anyway, Alice hasn't cheated on her leave. She had been correctly marked with sick leave, and she's got lots of it."

"That's not the point. The paperwork is not in order, and she failed to follow procedures."

"Yes, ma'am."

"If that happens again, I will hold you personally responsible."

"I understand."

Saitou hung up the phone without so much as a goodbye.

Quiana felt as if the world were moving in slow motion. *I've done what I vowed not to do—snitch on Alice.* Shame left her wondering how to face the others in the office.

Lured by soft calls, Dexter eventually came trotting behind the Oriental screen and allowed his friend to pick him up. The ferocious intensity of her grip caused the dog to whimper.

Immediately loosening her hold, Quiana said, "Sorry, Dex." IM'ing Jorge, she feigned illness and headed home.

Chapter Twenty Eight

Gaye rolled over and looked at the clock. Eight-thirty. She must have really been tired. The week had been a nightmare. The way the auditor relentlessly quizzed her about everything from the dogs to travel to the camera trained on the conference table still bothered her. She didn't think the goddess believed her explanation that Quiana could participate in the meetings that way; it was merely another reasonable accommodation. The woman probably thought the camera was set up to spy on her! At least the tortilla factory case was finished and ready to submit Monday.

After a leisurely shower, Gaye went into the living room to see what Tommy was doing. To her surprise, he wasn't there. A note lay on the table: Running errands. About ten minutes later, the door key jingled.

"You sure slept late. That's a first," Tommy said. Then he gave her a long, leisurely kiss.

"What's gotten into you this morning?"

"You just never know." Tommy grinned. "Put on something nice and summery. We're going out."

"But I just ate breakfast."

"We're not going to eat. Hurry, we have to be there by ten, before it gets too hot."

"Where are we going?"

"It's for me to know and you to find out."

Just before ten, Tommy eased in front of the Zilker Botanical Garden. He turned to Gaye and said, "Will you marry me?"

"I already said I would, silly."

"No, I mean right now."

"Now? But the wedding is already planned…"

Tommy put his fingers to Gaye's lips. "I've been thinking about what you said. You are the love of my life, and you are going to have the ceremony you longed for. We'll have the party your mother craves later on. Will you marry me?" Tommy reached behind the seat and produced a beautiful wedding bouquet.

"Now I know why I love you so much! Of course."

"An official is waiting to perform the ceremony anywhere in the garden your heart desires."

"I choose the bridge in the Japanese Garden. That's my favorite place."

"So it shall be."

Tommy took Gaye by the hand, and they made their way into the gardens, joining a slightly built woman in a white robe.

Tommy reached out to shake her hand. "Ursula, this is my bride, Gaye. Gaye, this is Ursula."

The wedding officiant smiled warmly at Gaye and grasped her hand. "You look lovely today. Have you chosen a spot?"

"Yes, the bridge in the Japanese Garden," Gaye said.

"Perfect! It's known as the bridge to walk over the moon. Follow me."

Ursula took the lead as Gaye held tightly to Tommy's hand. Contentment enveloped her; she was going to have the wedding of her dreams. It was comforting to know that Tommy cared that much.

Several people were wandering around the area when they arrived. Ursula leaned over and quietly spoke to them. Smiles broke on their faces, and a man spoke up. "Good luck, we wish you the best." The group then left.

Ursula motioned for Gaye and Tommy to stand at the top of the bridge. Then she began, "Tommy, do you take Gaye as your wife, in friendship and in love, in strength and weakness, to share the good times and misfortune, in achievement and failure?"

"I do."

Tommy, will you cherish and respect Gaye through all the changes in your lives, forever giving thanks that you found each other?"

"I will."

Ursula then turned to Gaye and said, "Gaye, do you take Tommy as your husband, in friendship and in love, in strength and weakness, to share the good times and misfortune, in achievement and failure?"

"I do."

Gaye, will you cherish and respect him through all the changes in your lives, forever giving thanks that you found each other?"

"I will."

Tommy reached into his pocket and brought out both the wedding rings, handing his to Gaye.

"Tommy, as you place the ring on Gaye's finger, please repeat after me: You are the love of my life, and you are my very best friend."

As Tommy repeated the phrases, he gently held Gaye's hand and slid the simple band on her finger. The words they had uttered now came to life as Gaye eyed the golden circle.

Ursula leaned in and gently took the bouquet from Gaye's hand.

"Gaye, as you place the ring on Tommy's finger, please repeat after me: You are the love of my life, and you are my very best friend."

Trembling, Gaye repeated the words, trying to keep from releasing tears of joy. She placed the band on Tommy's finger. Both turned expectantly to Ursula.

"Gaye and Tommy, you have expressed your love to one another through the commitment and promises you have just made. It is with these in mind that I pronounce you husband and wife.

"You have kissed a thousand times, maybe more. But today, the feeling is new. No longer simply partners and best friends, you have become husband and wife and can now seal the agreement with a kiss. Today, your kiss is a promise. You may kiss the bride."

Tommy quickly enveloped Gaye and gave her a long, leisurely kiss. Spine tingling, Gaye reluctantly pulled back.

"Congratulations," Ursula said. "Now, why don't you hand me your phone so I can take some pictures?"

The couple posed as Ursula snapped several shots. Gaye was glad Ursula had suggested the picture taking. The officiant even snagged a passerby to take a picture of the three of them.

With a small wave, Ursula departed.

Tommy led Gaye to a bench, and they both sat, holding hands.

"The ceremony was wonderful," Gaye said. "The vows were perfect."

"I picked them out."

"I can't believe it. Oh, this is so perfect. I never want this day to end."

"Oh, it's not going to end. I have one more surprise in store."

"What?"

"Not going to tell you." Tommy stood. "Come, my lovely bride." He reached out his hand and helped Gaye from the bench.

Chapter Twenty Nine

JJ anxiously looked at his watch, another possession that Quiana had coaxed him into buying. Timepieces weren't necessary in prison, and wearing one felt awkward. While other people used their cell phones, the idea wasn't for him. Besides, he was always forgetting the gadget.

It seemed like forever since he and Quiana had watched the movie together at his apartment. His attempts to arrange another meeting had fallen flat, however, because of his flap with Royce. Although Royce had assured JJ that Quiana was aware of what really happened, she hadn't been as friendly as before.

Now his angel had, at the last minute, asked JJ to meet her in the office on a Saturday afternoon. Not wanting to sound snarky, he hadn't questioned her request. He'd paid optimistic, special attention to a new outfit and meticulous grooming. He'd even arrived at the office early, not wanting to be late. Getting Quiana a small gift had crossed his mind, but that would signal his desire to be more than a friend.

He contemplated the goddess's warnings. She had interviewed Espy first thing Wednesday morning, departing for Washington, DC, later that day. Furious because Inman was not present for her departure, she had called him the next day and blasted him and the office. The auditor informed Inman that the staff had been totally uncooperative and that there were massive irregularities. JJ shivered, memories of the look of total contempt on the woman's face invaded his feelings. A key turning in the lock led him to see Quiana fastening the door behind her.

"Is anyone else here?" Quiana asked.

"Just us. I guess everyone took Inman at his word to stay home this weekend."

Quiana slid behind the screens. JJ could hear her put her purse in a drawer. The ensuing silence unnerved him. Then weeping poured from behind the screen. "Quiana, what's wrong?"

"I'm scared."

JJ had never heard his friend in such a state before. He had no idea what to do. "Quiana, come sit next to me so you can tell me why you are so upset. I won't look at you. Please."

After what seemed forever, Quiana freed herself from the Chinese screen and eased next to JJ, hat hiding her face. Then she burst into long, shrieking sobs.

JJ wanted to grab Quiana and hug her tears away, but he held back. Instead, he moved his hand over and gently took hers. No resistance. Then Quiana threw her other arm around JJ, who drew her into his chest, encircling her with his arms. As her cries turned into sniffles, JJ cradled her softly, not daring to move.

Finally, Quiana said, "I've gotten Alice fired."

JJ rubbed her back. "No, it wasn't just you. It was all of us. We agreed to tell the truth. We had no choice—you said so. I'm just as guilty of saying things that would get Alice in trouble as you are."

Quiana gently disengaged herself and sat back in the chair. "No, you don't understand. Saitou called and forced me into admitting Alice was in rehab."

"Oh, shit. I see what you mean. But, Quiana, it wasn't your fault you told Saitou. You had no choice. They can't fire her for not filling out the paperwork, can they?"

Quiana frowned. "They shouldn't. Hmm. Let me take a look." She rose and went to her desk, gliding behind the screen. Glum, JJ ached for her nearness.

Her nails clicked across the keyboard for a while. Finally, she said, "They can't fire her for taking family medical leave, and, in case of an emergency, she only has to tell them as soon as practicable. Alice is just going to have to let them know it was an emergency and come up with a doctor's excuse. That way, they can't ding her for not reporting in. She checked in on Sunday. That doesn't excuse the paperwork for the first time, though."

"Have you heard from her at all this week?" JJ asked.

"No. I've tried not to bother her. I don't even know if they let her keep her cell phone with her or not."

"What about Art?"

"I didn't know whether Alice told him; he would be so disappointed. I was just afraid to say anything to him Monday when he came to pick up Simon."

"Did going down to one dog satisfy the goddess?"

"I don't think anything satisfied her."

Both sat silently. Finally, JJ spoke. "Look, I don't want to be alone. This craziness has gotten to me. What if we go to the Domain and see a movie? I'd love to go for a walk, but it's just too hot outside. They've got one of those fancy theaters where you can get something to drink and eat while you're watching a movie. I've never done that before, I mean, eating something besides popcorn or hotdogs."

"Sure. Let me get my things."

"And tell your sister I'll drop you off at your apartment."

***

Alice felt chilled in the air conditioning and rolled onto the patio to seek relief. The enclosed area felt stifling, but the heat was welcoming. Their group therapy session today had been brutal, and Alice was totally drained. Eventually, being outside started to feel like being in a sauna. With luck, the accumulated toxins would drain out in her perspiration.

The decent food and lack of booze had definitely put her in a better place. Her physical well-being had been restored. All week she'd been trying to concentrate on conquering her inner demons rather than worrying about the office. Ultimately, a plan was hatched to complete another week of therapy and then take a monthly injection designed to knock out the pleasure of her slings.

In a way, that made Alice sad. Jake's sage advice was a welcome breath of air. These visits with Jake were the pleasurable aspects of drinking.

Unfortunately, besides Art, her only friends were her coworkers and those at the bar. And Art couldn't guard her 100 percent of the time. She'd been working with her counselor to find an AA group to attend after their dog park visits.

What would she say to Art after being discharged? Naturally, he would be disappointed about her inability to stay sober. But hadn't he urged her to check herself back in right after they returned from College Station?

What on earth was going on at the office? Had they survived the audit? Frankly, Alice didn't want to know, the answer would only cause angst, and there was nothing to be done anyway. Not having access to her cell phone had made it much easier to cope.

Realizing that sweat was trickling down her face and back, Alice went inside in search of a towel. Then, a call to Art was in order. She owed him that much.

***

After stopping at the apartment to grab overnight bags, Tommy helped Gaye into the car.

"Where are we going?" Gaye asked.

"It's a surprise. You'll see soon enough."

"Did you tell anyone about the wedding?"

"Not a sole. It's just our secret. Do you want to tell our parents before the extravaganza?"

"Oh, I hadn't thought about it." Gaye grimaced.

"Well, you'll have to decide for yourself, but my advice is that you don't tell them."

"That means we'd have two wedding anniversaries, then."

"That works for me. What could be better than celebrating marrying the love of your life twice a year? I know, we'll just have one celebration each year like a Texas couple and the second like an Indian couple. That should keep our life spicy!"

"I'll just have to talk to the pandit ahead of time. Doing that without having Mom around might be a real trick."

Tommy eased his car in front of the Driskill Hotel and stopped.

"This is where we're staying?" Tommy nodded. "It's much too expensive. You shouldn't have."

"We're here now, so let's just enjoy it. Look, let the bellhop unload the luggage, and I'll be back. I'm going to park in a cheaper lot. That way, we can splurge on dinner."

Gaye laughed as she climbed out, genuinely excited. What a beautiful end to a horrible week. It was love at first sight with the stately hotel. Its grand lobby of marble and stained glass was adorned with white colonnades and accented with potted palms. The cool, serene interior seduced her. Her American honeymoon would indeed be special.

Chapter Thirty

Royce parked near the office and, after looking around, climbed out of his car and leaned against the fender. Bat Hollow, his favorite dive, didn't open for another thirty minutes. He'd gone last Saturday night and actually enjoyed himself for a change.

That evening, while entering the bar, Royce had spied a blond woman helping Inman down the street; the man was obviously trashed. But, when "Brittany" as Inman called her, attempted to enter the office, the attorney had shooed her away, citing the top-secret information inside. Locked out, Brittany had made a call. Later, a white Mercedes had picked her up and sped off.

Royce almost said something about it, but everyone was so stressed; he had kept his mouth shut. *I wonder if that was the same woman Espy and Gaye thought were following them?*

Peering at Rebels, Royce thought he'd walk down and have a drink. He commandeered an empty barstool and ordered a beer. Looking around, he saw Brittany deep in conversation with an older man dressed in what appeared to be an expensive suit. Royce studied the man's features, committing them to memory. She brought a manila envelope out of her oversized bag and slid it across the table. The man opened it and thumbed through what appeared to be pictures. Smiling, he reached into his jacket and extracted a white envelope, handing it to Brittany. She then produced something, perhaps a thumb drive. Royce wasn't sure. The man deposited it in his inside jacket pocket and rose, dropping a few bills on the table. As he was leaving, Brittany waved to the server to bring a glass of white wine.

Turning back to his beer, Royce took a sip. What was going on? Had this woman taken compromising photos of Inman? What about the others? As he thought about it, his indignation rose. *I wonder if she's taken any photos of me?*

Draining the beer, he paid his tab and sauntered over to a table near her in order to get a good shot. Fumbling with his phone, he turned off the flash. No sense in calling attention to himself. When the woman looked down, he hit the screen and heard the whirring noise confirming mission accomplished.

Brittany then glanced at him, and a flash of recognition spread over her face, and, just as quickly, it was gone. Emboldened, Royce walked up and sat down. "Hi, Brittany."

"You've got the wrong person. That's not my name."

"Well, what is it?"

"Uh, Susan."

"Strange, you told Inman your name was Brittany."

"What's it to you? Why do you care?"

"He's my friend, that's why. Someone got you to spy on us, didn't they?" Royce was not about to tell the woman that he didn't care for Inman at all.

"Hey, a job's a job."

Susan started to stand up, but Royce put his hand over hers and said, "sit." She lowered herself into her chair. Without taking his eyes off her, Royce told the waitress who delivered Susan's wine to bring him a Bud Light. When it arrived, he took a long gulp and said, "Start talking."

"There's nothing to tell. Now, if you don't leave me alone, I will yell and tell everyone you're trying to sexually assault me."

"Go ahead. No one will believe you. Look at me... You're taller than I am. Did you know the group you've been spying on are federal investigators?"

Susan blanched. "No."

"I figure spying on federal investigators and trying to force your way into a federal facility might just get you a little jail time."

"I didn't try to force my way into any building."

"Just so happened, I saw you trying to push your way into the office down the street when you were helping Inman. And I bet you had a gun in your purse. You almost got yourself into a situation of armed forced entry. That's a federal office building. You can't carry weapons in there even with a license to carry."

"That stinky place?"

"Yes, ma'am."

Royce was relieved to see that she was becoming a tad nervous. He was not sure whether she could get into any trouble for attempting to go in, but it sounded serious. He reached into his back pocket and jerked out his shield, flipping it in front of her face as he'd seen cops do on TV.

She glanced at the badge and back at Royce. "So, what do you want?"

"I want to know who you really are and who hired you."

Susan sipped her wine. Royce feared there would be no response, and he had only one other trick he could use. He played his ace in the hole. "Three V's your client."

Sighing, she reached into her purse, produced a business card, and handed it to Royce.

Karen Gentry Private Investigator
Houston, Texas

"They had you come all the way from Houston? Why not just hire someone here?"

"I do lots of work for Three V in Houston. I guess they were afraid someone would recognize an Austin PI."

"Wow, they don't spare any expense, do they?"

"No, they don't. They're not very nice people, but they sure pay well."

"So, what do they know about me?"

"Look, they know everything. They have other sources, not just me. They have your medical history, they know who you've dated, and they even know you hang out at Bat Hollow."

"The bastards." Royce was so angry he began to shake and felt an urge to punch his fist through the window next to them. "I'm trying to start fresh. Make friends who see me for who I really am, not who I used to look like."

"Hey, it's nothing against you. I'm lesbian. I get what you've been through. It's just a job." Karen's phone rang. She answered and then said, "I'm on my way." Putting down the phone, she looked back at Royce. "My ride's here. Just take care of yourself." She left a twenty-dollar bill on the table and walked out.

Royce sat as if frozen. A roaring noise crashed through his head. *I'll never escape my past. It will follow me to my grave.*

After settling the tab, he walked back to the office and slithered in, the smell causing his already upset stomach to take its turmoil to another level. Silently feeling his way down the hall, he glided into his desk chair. With his laptop on, he began the search for the man he'd seen at Rebels in earnest. The first stop was the directory of the Austin Three V office.

He was puzzled when no one resembling the stranger surfaced. Then, recalling that Big Horn's main office was in New York, Royce began to peruse the Manhattan staff. Bingo. Johnathan Patton, Partner. They were so screwed. Royce took a screenshot and e-mailed it to his personal address.

How bizarre. Patton had flown all the way to Austin to get the information. But why? Meeting the detective at the scene of the crime seemed draconian. Was he trying to keep the surveillance under wraps? But everyone knew Three V was sleazy and did ugly things. Was it to gloat over his victims? Mark the territory like a dog?

Troubled, Royce sat back. What next? His urge was to fight back, to go after those bastards who were out to ruin his life. But how? He didn't feel comfortable with Inman and was reluctant to tell him. Some part of Royce felt the snob got what he deserved. But they were all under attack.

After some contemplation, Royce decided to try to have some fun tonight and worry about what to do tomorrow.

Chapter Thirty One

The maître d' led Tommy and Gaye to a booth in the back corner, and Tommy quickly ordered two glasses of champagne. As they waited, Gaye took in the decidedly western ambiance, complete with a Longhorn head mounted on the wall. Antlers adorned a modern, metal light fixture that ran the length of the bar. Contemporary two-tiered circular chandeliers with candle-shaped light bulbs hung over the tables of the main dining room.

The server set down the champagne and asked what appetizers they would like.

"We'll start with the fettine trio," Tommy said.

"Very good," the server said. "That's my favorite."

"What is fettine?" Gaye asked.

"The ingredients are pressed together and then thinly sliced."

"Oh, OK. Gaye studied the menu carefully. One had rabbit-rattlesnake sausage, pistachios, and figs. Maybe she could handle the one with the wild boar, lamb, pine nuts, and mozzarella better. What had gotten into Tommy? And the prices…

"We'll need to study the menu more thoroughly and make a decision after the fettine," Tommy said.

"Not a problem," the server said.

When she had departed, Gaye said, "Tommy, this place is so expensive it makes me nervous. And the menu…Why in the world did you choose this place?"

"Interesting, huh? One of the guys in my class has been raving about it. I think his dad has lots of money, and they eat here regularly."

"But it's so expensive."

Tommy looked down for a minute before he spoke. "I know, but today is special. I thought we'd eat some things we've never had before. You know, as a sign of how I hope our life together will be. Getting out of our comfort zones and trying something different. So, we'll try some rabbit and rattlesnake. And besides, I get so tired of hearing that smart ass brag about where he goes to eat, I thought I could shut him up by letting him know I'm well-off enough to go to those places, too."

Gaye reached over and grasped Tommy's hand. "I love you whether we're eating at a hole-in-the-wall or at an upscale venue. One day, between the two of us, I'm sure we'll be able to eat at places like this."

"I know. But let's just have fun tonight. Besides, my grandma Pat gave me some money, so don't worry about picking anything you want on the menu."

"How sweet of her. She's your mother's mother, right? When am I going to get to meet her?"

"She'll be down for the Bollywood extravaganza. Said she wouldn't miss it for the world. She'll be dressed to the hilt in the latest Indian fashion."

Gaye choked on the sip of champagne she was taking. "You're kidding, right?"

"No, and I'm stone-cold sober. I haven't really told you much about her, have I?"

"You haven't. How come?"

At that point, the waitress arrived with the fettine. Gaye tried not to stare as she eyed the beautifully displayed dish, wondering which was the rattlesnake. She started to ask but decided she'd rather taste and not know. Tommy ordered more champagne

She watched as Tommy took a bite. As he chewed, his face lit up. "Oh, my God, this is good." He savored his mouthful and then continued, "Grandma Pat is something else. My grandfather, Roger, was a Baptist minister, and Pat was a long-suffering minister's wife. Downright mousy, according to my uncle. Anyway, my grandfather dropped dead of a heart attack in 1996. About six months later, her friends realized she was profoundly depressed and coaxed her into a trip to Vegas. It was beginner's luck. Within thirty minutes she'd hit the jackpot at a slot machine. Grandma refused to say how much she won, but my uncle swears it was around eleven million dollars."

"Really?" Gaye asked. She was now all ears, intently paying attention to Tommy.

"So, anyway, she took about a million of it and went to a stockbroker who was a church member. He invested it in the IPO for Amazon and bought her a lot of Apple stock, among other things."

"Then she's fabulously wealthy." Gaye sipped her champagne, finishing the last of the fettine. "If the rest of the dinner is as good as this is, I can't wait for the next course."

Tommy sat back and sighed. "Since she got all that money, she's gone wild."

"What do you mean?"

"Well, she has a penthouse on Fifth Avenue in New York and hangs around with a rather eclectic group of people from all walks of life."

"It could be worse." Gaye reached over and patted Tommy's hand. She eyed him critically. "What's bothering you?"

"I just hope she behaves at the wedding, that's all. She insisted on paying for the Friday night festivities, and I have no idea who she's bringing or what she's got planned. My mother and I are spooked."

"Whatever she does, it can't be that bad."

"I hope you're right."

$$***$$

Alice fidgeted, repeatedly checking her watch. A visit from Art was possible as therapy sessions were on a reduced schedule on Sundays. She'd made an extra effort to look attractive, although having no access to makeup had made that next to impossible. *He's seen me at my worst, so it doesn't really matter. He'll just have to accept me as I am.*

Finally, a few minutes after two, Alice was summoned to the meeting room. Art was already seated. When she rolled in, he rose.

"You look good," he said. He returned to his chair.

"Thanks." An uncomfortable silence ensued. Then Alice said, "Art,

I'm so embarrassed. You're so important to me. I'm sorry I disappointed you."

"I'm just glad you got back into treatment. From the looks of you, it's been a good week."

"It has, but the question is, where do I go from here?"

"Like they say, one day at a time."

"You're right, as usual."

"I called Quiana, and she said Dexter was fine, but a little mopey. He must be missing you."

"I miss him a lot, but I also missed you." Alice couldn't believe her boldness. She desperately needed to know how Art felt about her. Earlier her confidence in his love had been high, but now...

Art drew close to Alice's scooter and took her hand. "Alice, you're the best thing that's happened to me in a long time, and I haven't given up on you. But you've got to stay sober. Why don't we take a little mini-vacation in the fall?"

Relief coursed through Alice, expanding into joy. "I'd love that." He leaned in and gave Alice a long, leisurely kiss.

Chapter Thirty Two

Espy reread the latest case she'd been given. A young, white male had filed a sexual harassment complaint against his African American supervisor. According to Hal Strong, CP, his boss continually told sexually oriented jokes and used offensive language. Additionally, the man had taken to calling CP "pinkie." It had caught on, and now everyone on the construction crew was calling him that.

Pinkie. Pinkie? She was unfamiliar with the term. Looking online, Espy found several meanings. European with pink features, white Caucasian, pink and hairless baby rat, or white man's penis.

Suddenly the case became more interesting. She put in a call to CP, but he couldn't talk and said he would call in about ten minutes when his break started. At least maybe this case would help take her mind off her own problems. Besides, they needed more "cause" cases, and this had the makings of a good one.

Work these days was so depressing. The mood in the office was dismal. Alice was still gone, and they'd heard no word about the results of the audit. The consensus was that the team needed to prepare for the worst. If the office closed, where would she go? The last thing Espy wanted was to return to El Paso. Maybe she could get them to move her elsewhere.

While following up on correspondence from a few other cases, her phone rang. CP was on the line. "So, Hal, tell me, how many people are on your crew?"

"There's six of us, including the boss, Sylvester."

"OK, give me their names and races."

Hal explained that he was the only white person on the crew, and the four others were Hispanic. He also said the boss would say things like, "If you don't get moving, I'm going to stick a shovel up your ass."

"Do you think the others will speak up?"

"I really don't know. It doesn't seem to bother them, and I think they're scared for their jobs."

"How's their English?"

"Two of them don't speak much English at all. One of the others is always doing the translating."

"So, what do you think your boss meant by calling you 'pinkie'?"

"I don't really know, but he laughs when he says it, so it can't be good. It just bothers me."

Espy hung up the phone and leaned back. If you don't know what something means, how can you find it offensive? On the other hand, if he's saying "pinkie" and just means white man, it could still be considered derogatory. *I need to amend the charge to include race.*

While planning the interview questions, she heard the door open and the whir of Alice's scooter. Dexter was yelping what could only be cries of joy. Closing the case, she hurried out to the conference room. The staff had gathered as Alice, armed with *marranitos*, called a meeting. Espy's mouth watered. The pig-shaped Mexican gingerbread cookies were simply to die for.

Gaye hustled into the kitchen to make fresh coffee, and Alice told everyone to have a seat. As Espy looked around, she realized that the crew wore a grim look.

"I apologize," Alice said. "I have let each of you down. It's my fault Three V is on our backs and that Saitou sent the auditor down. I just hope you can forgive me."

Quiana said, "I'm the one who needs forgiveness. I spilled the beans and told Saitou you were in rehab. I didn't want to, but she scared the bejesus out of me."

"Quiana," Alice said, "I'm the one who failed to fill out the sick leave paperwork properly. You did what you had to do. Have we heard any results from the audit?"

"I've been asking around," Quiana said, "but HQ is really tight-lipped. That can't be good."

"I'm sure we're in deep trouble," Inman said. "The witch auditor was simply horrid. I felt she'd already made her decision before she heard any of the circumstances surrounding the travel issues."

"And where are we with Three V?" Alice asked.

"I filed the lawsuit, but HQ is handling the case; I think Three V has them by the throat."

Espy watched Alice closely. Her boss appeared lost, a look of desperation crossing her face. Was she holding herself responsible for all that had happened?

"Alice," Espy said, "you're not responsible for all of this. If I spoke Spanish, three of us would not have gone. You're not the only one Three V is using to smear the office's reputation."

All at once, a chorus of voices began to confess their wrongdoings.

"Stop!" JJ said. "What's done is done. We can't take it back, so there's no use beating ourselves over the head about it. I, of all of you, should know. The question is, where do we go from here?"

"You're right, JJ," Alice said. "Inman, where should we go from here?"

"At least we all told the truth, so things won't get any worse. I say we produce more 'cause' cases and let the bastards know we're the best office in the country. How can they disband us when we do such good work?"

Alice sighed. "I agree. Let's see what we can get on the books. Espy, where are we with the hip-hop case?"

"The settlement offer is out," Espy said, "but I haven't had a chance to follow up yet. I'll do that today. Fortunately, it doesn't seem as if they are too interested in settling."

"The tortilla case?" Alice asked.

"On your desk," Gaye said.

"Any others?" Alice asked. When no one responded, she said, "Let's get to work."

Espy returned to her office and immediately put in a call regarding the settlement. Then she put all her effort into "pinkie."

***

Alice rolled into her office and stowed her belongings. She grabbed Dexter and nuzzled him.

"Dex, look at this pile of work. What am I going to do? Even thinking about Three V leaves me nauseous. I so want a sling, but I know I can't. It would ruin everything." At least they had the wedding to look forward to. Everyone needed a diversion.

Reluctantly, she eased her canine companion onto his bed and turned to the task at hand. Reviewing the tortilla case was her first priority. Fabulous. Royce and Gaye hit a home run. A congratulatory IM went out to the investigators, and the investigation was promptly turned over to Inman.

Before completing the second stack of work, the phone rang. Jane. Alice shivered. It couldn't be good news. Alice reluctantly answered and, after hearing what Jane had to say, laid her head on the desk, sobbing. A straightjacket of anxiety crushed the air out of her lungs. Gasping for breath, she leaned back in her chair and tried to calm herself. Her body screamed for a sling to rid her of her torment. Grasping the armrests of her scooter, she began the desperate fight against the urge to flee to the safety of Rebels.

Alice was being called to testify before Congress. *Can I handle the pressure? I should just quit.* Then she thought about her staff and Ms. Lipscomb. Minutes passed. Wrestling with her demons, Alice managed to crank her edginess down a notch, enough to think rationally.

On September 15 at ten o'clock in the morning, she was to report to committee room 2154 in the House of Representatives to testify before the government operations subcommittee of the House Committee on Oversight and Reform. Steadying her hands, Alice googled the panel to discover that Lawson Garrett was the chairman, while his Tea Party protégée, Sylvia Swanson, was chair of the Government Operations subcommittee.

Reading about Swanson drove Alice's desperation to a fever pitch. The woman was anti-government, anti-gay, and anti-anything Alice believed in. Sweat prickled on Alice's body despite the brisk air-conditioning. *We are so screwed. I know Three V put Garrett up to this.*

When Alice had mastered her shaking hands, she asked Inman to come to the office. Upon arrival, he plopped down in the chair before her desk and said, "And to what do I owe this invite, A Plus?"

"This is not the time for that. We're in real trouble now."

"I don't see how we could be in much more trouble."

"Yeah? Well, I've got to testify before Congress next month for a subcommittee run by Swanson. The chair of the committee is Garrett."

A look of sheer terror crossed Inman's face. "And Garrett has the power to order Swanson's committee to investigate us. What's the topic?"

"Government waste, fraud, and abuse of power."

Abruptly, he rose and rushed out. "I've got to call headquarters."

***

Jorge studied his notes before placing a call to the owner of Ike's Burgers. The small chain operated in the Beaumont, Texas, area and had four locations. The CP, Ellen McCarty, had said that she was hired as a cashier at the Nederland store. When she appeared on the first day wearing a skirt, her manager told her pants were mandatory. Her explanation that as a Seventh Day Adventist, her religious beliefs required her to wear a skirt fell flat. When CP wouldn't budge, the boss sent her home. Later he called and terminated her.

He dialed Ike Wilke's number promptly at eleven o'clock.

"Mr. Wilke, thanks for speaking with me this morning. Please understand that I am a neutral third party, and my job is to determine what happened. I am going to write what you say on an affidavit and have you read it over, make any additions or corrections, and return it to me. I'll put the password 'hotdog' on it so no one else can open it."

"Young man, that's not necessary. I'm the only one who has access to my e-mail account."

Jorge grimaced at being called a "young man." Was Mr. Wilke trying to put him down, indicating Jorge should not be taken seriously?

"As you wish. Mr. Wilke, please explain to me the reason your manager, Jeff Riley, terminated Ms. McCarty."

"Jeff called me and told me that the little lady refused to wear pants. Something about her religion, which I consider total nonsense. What kind of church would tell women they can't wear pants? Sounds un-American to me.

Anyway, From what Jeff said, she had a long skirt that reached to the floor, so I told him to cut her loose, as it's too dangerous in the kitchen with a skirt on."

"So, exactly what danger did it pose?"

"You know, there's the grill with grease, and it's crowded back there. Someone might step on her skirt and trip her up. She might fall and put her hand on the grill, something like that. Anyway, I require all my cooks and cashiers to wear pants. I have the right to have a dress code."

"Did you actually see her skirt?"

"No, I just went by what Jeff said. Like I say, as a business owner, I can tell my employees what they can and cannot wear."

Jorge decided to keep his mouth shut and not get into an argument with Mr. Wilke at this point. After the interview, he finished the affidavit and e-mailed it.

Then Jorge went to the EEOC website and reread the religious accommodation information:

Religious Accommodation/Dress & Grooming Policies

Unless it would be an undue hardship on the employer's operation of its business, an employer must reasonably accommodate an employee's religious beliefs or practices. This applies not only to schedule changes or leave for religious observances, but also to such things as dress or grooming practices that an employee has for religious reasons.

These might include, for example, wearing particular head coverings or other religious dress (such as a Jewish yarmulke or a Muslim headscarf), or wearing certain hairstyles or facial hair (such as Rastafarian dreadlocks or Sikh uncut hair and beard). It also includes an employee's observance of a religious prohibition against wearing certain garments (such as pants or miniskirts).

When an employee or applicant needs a dress or grooming accommodation for religious reasons, he should notify the employer that he needs such an accommodation for religious reasons. If the employer reasonably needs more information, the employer and the employee should engage in an interactive process to discuss the request. If it would not pose an undue hardship, the employer must grant the accommodation.

Grasping the phone, Jorge called CP. She swore that her skirt didn't drag the floor and was above her ankles. Nothing, she proclaimed, was dangerous about it. When pressed, she gave Jorge the name and phone number of the crew lead, Keyshia Samson, who was present at the time. CP was to have reported to her for daily assignments.

Jorge then called Keyshia to uncover her version of events. CP's story checked out, and Keyshia couldn't think of any kitchen danger the CP's attire would cause. The team lead had been a bit hesitant to speak with him. Still, he reminded her that she was protected by the retaliation laws and that, if something happened to her because of her testimony, she should call him.

Excitedly, Jorge turned to JJ. "Finally, I've got a 'cause' case. Failure to accommodate because of religion." He explained the matter to JJ.

"But doesn't the owner have the right to a dress code?" JJ asked.

"Yes, except in the case of religion. They must make a reasonable accommodation."

"So, what would be an unreasonable accommodation?"

"One that poses an undue hardship. Let's say you work in a shoe store, and their dress policy says you must be clean-shaven, but your religion requires you to wear a beard. There's nothing they can say about the beard because there is no undue hardship about it. However, if you work in a refinery or other area where you are required to wear a respirator, that would be an undue hardship."

"Huh?"

"The respirator doesn't get a tight seal with a beard, and you have to be cleanly shaven to get that seal."

"Wow. So, there's nothing in the restaurant that would be hazardous to CP in her skirt?"

"JJ, just think about it. Women have been cooking in skirts for hundreds of years."

"You got that right. This is good. At least we'll have another 'cause' case to get out this week."

"I'm going to let Alice know. She deserves some good news today."

Jorge entered the main area where Quiana and Espy were in deep conversation. "What's going on?" Jorge asked. He gestured to Alice's door, which was shut.

"I don't know," Espy said. "Alice called Inman into her office, then he left hurriedly. Now he's back in there."

"I was going to tell her I got a great 'cause' case. I think I can finish it by the end of the week, provided everyone gets their statements to me in the next day or two."

"Thank goodness," Quiana said. "Good news is so scarce these days."

"I got another one that looks good, too. Unfortunately, the employees don't speak English," Espy said.

Jorge rolled his eyes. "Let me guess. They speak Chinese."

Espy huffed. "Look, this doesn't involve too much, just a couple of interviews. Besides, if we can find discrimination, we'll have three cases for the month; my hip-hop isn't going to settle, so it can be litigated. That will really help." She began to explain the new complaint to the others.

"Pinkie?" Jorge said. "What does that mean?"

"It can mean a white person or," Quiana said, "a white man's penis."

"How'd you know that?" Jorge asked.

"I looked it up on the Internet," Quiana said.

"And I thought I'd heard every word in the book," Jorge said. Inman softly closed Alice's door and tiptoed to the conference table. In a hushed voice, he said, "Gather everyone, and let's meet outside."

"Why are we meeting out there?" Royce asked. "It's roasting."

"We need to talk privately," Inman said.

***

Inman gazed at the faces gathered around him. Feeling sucker-punched left him unsure of how to proceed. Quiana was off to the side, only her hat visible, revealing more of her than Inman had seen in ages.

"Everyone, shit's hit the fan. Alice has been called to testify in front of a congressional subcommittee, and the chair and general counsel are furious. The take on it from the general counsel is that it's because of the Bighorn case. Alice has been accused of harassing a small business and running a rogue operation."

"Crap!" JJ said. "This is ridiculous. Why can't they just leave us alone? If only the lion could have testified, he'd have told us the truth, and we wouldn't be in this mess."

"What do you think will happen?" Jorge asked.

"I don't know, Inman said. I'm actually worried about Alice," Quiana said. "Just being out of rehab and having this disaster dumped on her... Anything can happen."

"What can we do?" Gaye asked.

"Not much," Inman said. "Just try to keep Alice company, and don't let her go Rebels. I'm sure the Three V spies are all over the place. The general counsel will be preparing possible questions, and Alice and I will be busy trying to come up with answers and practicing them." Inman wiped the sweat off his brow with his shirt sleeve. "It's gross out here. Let's get back inside."

***

Royce went to his computer and roamed the Internet, looking for further information about Three V slime ball Johnathon Patton. Family man...three kids...wife who looks like a model...charitable foundation dedicated to spaying and neutering animals...Nothing.

Thoughts of going to Inman with what he'd learned materialized, but how would that help? Keeping their guard up was crucial, because the sleaze might have dispatched another spy to replace the compromised one.

Funny how his state of mind had changed over the last few weeks. His armor was melting because of his decision to start caring about others. It felt good. For too long, he'd shut down human connections for fear of being wounded.

Looking at the time, Royce realized it was almost noon. He went to Alice's office, and she bade him enter.

"Alice, is there anything I can do? Can I get you lunch?" She gazed out the window without responding. "Look, I can't even imagine how difficult this is for you. Let me help you, be your bodyguard. I'll hang around in the evenings and entertain you, keep you away from Rebels. Anything you need, just ask, and I'll be there in a heartbeat."

Alice looked up with a sad expression. "That's so sweet of you. And yes, if you could bring me some lunch, I'd appreciate it. Now, there is one thing you could do for me. Next Thursday will be Gaye's last day in the office. I'd like to have some sort of get-together. I know we'll all see her at the wedding, but I think we need a going away party for her. Could you get it organized?"

"Not a problem."

Chapter Thirty Three

Espy drew up to Royce's apartment and announced her arrival. Secretly she was glad he had taken her up on her offer to drive him to Gaye's wedding in Dallas. She'd been dreading the extravaganza, as they were a gruesome reminder of her failed attempt at living happily ever after. But not attending would have hurt Gaye's feelings. Besides, the distraction was welcome.

As Royce appeared, Espy popped the trunk open, and Royce put in his bags. As he slid into the front seat, Espy said, "That was a great party you threw for Gaye yesterday. The food was scrumptious. Where did you get it?"

"Thanks. I've made friends with the cook at Bat Hollow. He does some catering on the side. I'll let him know you approved."

"Did he do the cake, too?"

"No, I went to a bakery on 12th Street. They talked me into the lavender icing; I would never have thought of that myself."

"Hopefully, we'll have something good to celebrate in the office again soon so we can order another."

Turning her full attention to the task at hand, Espy dove into the traffic. As they were clearing the city, Espy asked, "Are you excited about the wedding?"

"I guess. Whenever I go somewhere new, people stare at me and it makes me feel uncomfortable. I've never been able to get used to the sensation."

Espy glanced at Royce. She totally understood why he got withering looks; his body did not match his masculine appearance. "I totally understand. Hopefully, everyone will be too busy partying to notice us."

"At least the weather is much cooler. Gaye had been anxious that Tommy would get overheated with the horse stuff."

"Can you believe that? I just can't picture Tommy all dressed up and on a horse. I hope I don't start laughing. Apparently, he's only been on a horse one other time in his life.

"Gaye said she will be so glad to get this over with, it isn't even funny," Royce said.

"I don't blame her. She said she needs time to concentrate on her classes, and this has been one big distraction after another."

"That's not the half of it. Apparently Tommy's grandmother, Pat, has been sparing no expense for the sangeet for Friday night. Gaye's mother, Nila, is feeling a bit jealous."

"Oh, that doesn't sound good."

"Gaye says the bash Pat insisted on throwing is going to be extremely lavish. Pat wouldn't tell Tommy all the plans, and he's worried she'll upstage Nila's after-ceremony spectacular. Poor Gaye. She didn't want this big wedding anyway, and I hope it isn't going to be a disaster."

The conversation soon slowed, and Espy was left with her thoughts. This was her first outing in public since her abortion. Mainly, she'd been staying to herself, wallowing in self-loathing and pity. Gaye had urged her to go to counseling, but Espy had been reluctant. Was it because seeking treatment would be admitting weakness and an inability to handle things herself? The weekend would be challenging. Part of her said she should let her hair down and have fun, while the other part said she did not deserve to enjoy herself.

***

Royce gazed out the window at the horrific traffic on I-35. Would they ever finish the construction? Fortunately, Espy was driving. His recent malaise had been wearing him down. Others would think he was of unsound mind for not looking forward to a weekend full of free food and booze. And, amazingly, with people who actually accepted him. He hadn't been able to say that for a long time. *Why am I not more grateful?* And now, just as things were looking up for him, the office was in jeopardy. If the office closed, what would happen to him? Back to California? Houston was a possibility, but Quiana had related unsettling things about the director there. *I need to do something, but what?*

***

Inman turned into the Marriott's valet parking and sighed. He's been apprehensive about the festivities. His first instinct had been to say no, but the team would never have spoken to him again. Truth be told, the wedding was the only bit of bright news in a summer full of lows.

Inman had tried to talk Shirley into coming so they could start to heal their rift, but she'd declined. The idea of watching the happy couple when his own marriage was in shambles depressed him. He'd just plan to slip out early tonight and leave the youngsters to their party.

After checking into the room, Inman lay on the bed and began mental calculations. These rooms alone cost Tommy's grandmother a fortune. What would it would be like to have that much money? He'd quit his job, of course. But then what? His quest for answers to the sensation that something was missing in his life had led him from one disaster to another. The only bright spot had been finding his daughter, but it had estranged him from Shirley. And now, Bighorn. Three V was stalling, using every trick in the book. At this rate, the case would never see the light of day.

And the congressional hearing? Agitation had engulfed him after he'd been told to attend. That would probably end his career. And then what? Restless, Inman rose and decided to take a shower.

***

Alice gazed out the office window, watching as a couple climbed out of a taxi, no doubt hoping for a good seat during the upcoming happy hour. Alice envisioned enjoying a sling and a conversation with Jake at Rebels. She did miss him.

Deciding to keep the office open Friday in case the chair called, Alice had promised to arrive in time for the Saturday festivities. She was in enough trouble without being forced to explain closing the office on a workday. She and Art would drive to Dallas this evening but not attend the sangeet. Apparently, the event would be full of alcohol, and it would be her first real test of being around drinkers and not imbibing. She'd just postpone that tribulation a day. Thank goodness Art would be there to distract her.

She turned her attention to the computer and continued reading about congressional hearings, even watching a few on YouTube. A glance at her watch signaled quitting time. Good. Her packing wasn't complete. Her thoughts turned to her new dress. Would Art be impressed?

***

Royce slid into his sport coat. He'd thought about a tie, but Gaye had assured him it was not necessary. To her, being comfortable and having a good time was important. He lingered outside the hotel, smoking. The cool breeze from Wednesday's cold front lifted his spirits. The summer had been one of the hottest on record and had fried him physically and emotionally. The large number of couples and families streaming into the hotel, many wearing traditional Indian dress, surprised him. He hadn't taken Gaye for a person who would want a massive crowd at her wedding.

Finally, he stubbed out his smoke and headed inside. As an attendant opened the door for him, Royce gawked. The space was bathed in purple disco light. Above the dance floor, a huge disco ball shimmered, sending fragments of light to all corners of the room. Tables alternating with white and blue tablecloths held snowy flower arrangements. Waiters dressed in white tunics with Nehru collars plied the guests with champagne and hors d 'oeuvres. Open bars were tucked into two corners of the ballroom. A soloist playing the sitar entertained the guests.

Looking around, Royce spotted Espy deep in conversation with Gaye and Tommy. Gaye sported a floor-length, cream-colored silk dress with a wide hem. An overlay embroidered with green leaves covered the bodice. It swooped down asymmetrically to cover approximately one-fourth of the gown. The shoulders and arms were encased in a sheer fabric with embroidering. Tommy wore a similar royal blue tunic that hung to his knees.

The poor man was wearing pants that looked like tights and leather sandals. Royce stifled a giggle. Did Tommy feel like a "Ken" doll that his in-laws were dressing? He hurried over to the couple, giving Gaye a big hug and shaking Tommy's hand.

"Where's this grandmother of yours, Tommy?" Royce asked.

"She'll be down in a bit. She likes to make big entrances." He sighed.

The waiter appeared, and both Espy and Royce took champagne. Gaye, as well as Tommy, declined.

"No champagne?" Espy asked. "I thought you liked it."

"I do, it's just that Grandma Pat has organized a fabulous party, and we need to pace ourselves. We're having a sit-down filet mignon dinner before the dancing. I guess she wanted to blend the sangeet and a traditional American rehearsal dinner. I'm a bit worried about how my mother is going to take it."

"Don't worry, she'll be fine. I'm sure of it." Espy patted Gaye on the arm. "How was the rehearsal, by the way?"

"It's been a long day. We had the pre-wedding religious ceremonies this morning and then the rehearsal after lunch. Mom was so annoying, directing us all if we stepped out of line."

"You're being kind," Tommy said. "Frankly, it was a nightmare."

"Tommy, you're surely exaggerating," Espy said.

"Unfortunately, not," said Gaye. If it hadn't been for the pandit calming her down and pacifying her, I don't know what I'd have done." Looking up, Gaye saw her family enter the room. She grasped Tommy's arm. "Let's go say hello."

"I wish I'd grabbed some of that champagne," Tommy said as he escorted Gaye to mingle with the in-laws.

Royce shook his head. There were some good things about being single, and not having in-laws was one of them.

Inman ambled up, drink in hand. "Have a good trip coming up?" he said.

"The traffic was horrid," Espy said.

As they were making small talk, the music stopped, and a man in a red-sequined tuxedo jacket walked onstage.

"Ladies and gentlemen," he said, "welcome to the sangeet for Gaye

Rohatqi and Tommy Dwyer. I'll be your host this evening. Pat Gentry, grandmother of the groom, welcomes you.

At that point, a spotlight went to the back of the ballroom where Grandma Pat appeared, wearing a stunning purple sari highlighted with gold thread. Around her neck was the most beautiful pearl necklace Royce had ever laid eyes on. Pat waved and made her way to the dance floor next to the stage.

"Please, Tommy and Gaye, come forward," the announcer said. He scrambled off the stage and took the mic to Pat. A waiter appeared with three champagne glasses.

"Everyone, please grab a glass of bubbly. I'd like to make a toast," Pat said. The guests waited expectantly as the waiters hustled to ensure all had a glass. "I'd like to share an old Irish toast so dear to my heart."

"May the road rise up to meet you,
May the wind be always at your back,
The sun shine warm upon your face,
The rain fall soft upon your fields,
And until we meet again
May God hold you in the hollow of His hand."

She then lifted her flute and shouted, "mazel tov!"

The announcer took back the mic and directed everyone to be seated, indicating that dinner would be served shortly.

Royce observed Gaye's mom, realizing that Nila was scowling. Espy had apparently noticed as well, because she began to move toward the unhappy woman. Then he spotted Quiana and JJ, who had secured seats at a table in the back of the room. Quiana had an enormous hat and a veil so dark that Royce couldn't see her face. He hurried to join them, not wishing to sit among strangers. Royce at once felt sorry for Quiana. *It must be a real ordeal for her. I bet people are staring at her as much as they are at me. Are the two of us destined to be the object of scorn for the rest of our lives?* At least she understood his angst.

Eventually, Espy left Nila's side and joined Royce at the chair he had reserved for her. Royce leaned in to Espy. "What happened?"

"This night is quickly turning into a disaster." Royce gave Espy a quizzical look. "First off, while Indians eat beef, lots of them are vegetarian, and Grandma Pat only had a chicken substitute ordered. Fortunately, the wedding planner got wind of the faux pas yesterday and hustled up an acceptable vegetarian menu. But Nila found out and was steamed. Then, the Jewish and Irish blessings? I don't think Tommy has any Jewish in him, but I may be wrong.

"Anyway, I cajoled Nila by telling her it was so 'American' to have a blended wedding celebration like this and what a superb hostess she was."

Royce laughed. "So, you laid it on thick."

"I truly want Gaye and Tommy to enjoy their big day, so I'll do anything I can to avert disaster. Keep an eye out, and if you see Nila looking out of sorts, let me know."

***

After the meal, Royce leaned with his back against the bar, sipping Glenlivet. He watched idly as the Rohatqis and their guests danced to the Bollywood music. Some of the women had removed their shoes as they twirled and gyrated in what appeared to Royce to be choreographed dances. Gaye had tried to entice him onto the dance floor, but he'd declined.

Eventually, the red-jacketed host appeared and quietened the audience. A special treat for the honored couple, he proclaimed. Then he called Tommy and Gaye to the dance floor and told the audience, "The first dance is for the bride and groom."

The curtain opened, revealing a small band. Then Royce gulped as Mary J. Blige stepped out.

"Ladies and gentlemen, Mary J. Blige," the announcer said. A gasp rose from the crowd, and then the soulful words "At last, my love has come along…" enveloped Royce. He watched Tommy gently take Gaye into his arms and maneuver her skillfully over the dance floor. Blige's masterful rendition of the song brought tears to his eyes.

At that moment he glanced down and realized that Grandma Pat and her purple sari were next to him.

"They're a gorgeous couple, aren't they?" she said.

Royce nodded, afraid his voice would crack. He only wished he could find such happiness. Pat motioned to the waiter to bring her a Buffalo Trace on the rocks, and shortly she held the drink in her hand.

"I'm Pat, by the way. I know you are Royce. Gaye has told me all about you."

"Nice to meet you."

"A toast to the happy couple." Pat steered her glass toward Royce and tipped it slightly.

He lightly touched her glass with his.

"How in the world did you ever get Mary J. Blige to perform?" Royce asked.

"Oh, I've known her for quite some time. We met at one of Diddy's white parties. We really hit it off, and we dine together occasionally when she's in town."

"You mean Sean Combs? P. Diddy?"

"Yes, he's my next-door neighbor in the Hamptons."

Stunned, Royce didn't know what to say.

"So, my question to you," Pat said, "is why the sad face? You look like your best friend just died."

"It's a long story."

"I'm listening."

After a bit of hemming and hawing, Royce poured out his heart to Pat, telling her how he hadn't given his coworkers time to prove that they accepted him and how badly he had treated them. Then he laid out the whole Bighorn case and Three V.

"Bighorn? That's owned by that prick, Jack Stewart, isn't it? And his son; he's so pompous, he walks around like he's got something stuck up his ass."

Stunned at Pat's language, Royce stifled a giggle.

"Hmm. And Three V. Who are you dealing with there?"

"The guy I saw in Austin is Johnathon Patton."

"Patton?" Pat broke into a big grin. "Listen, Royce, I've got to attend to some hostess duties, but plan on flying to New York Sunday at my expense.. I'll have my secretary contact you. I just might have a way to get that asshole off your back."

With that, Pat put down her empty drink glass and glided out onto the dance floor to party with Gaye's father.

Chapter Thirty Four

Inman awoke early and headed down to the restaurant for a bite of breakfast. While he sipped his coffee, last night's extravaganza replayed in his head. He felt sorry for Gaye's parents because they couldn't top Grandma's night. It must be frustrating when you are solid upper-middle-class and can't compete with the new in-laws.

He hadn't known who Blige was until he'd texted his son. The response was full of OMGs and exclamation points, telling Inman how lucky he was and to record some of her music. *I must be getting old if I don't know who's who in music,* he thought.

After his plate arrived, Inman greedily dug into his eggs, wishing for one of Shirley's biscuits to go along with it. Would he ever taste one again? With a few hours to kill before Tommy's equestrian show, Inman decided on a stroll through White Rock Park, anything to take his mind off Shirley.

While waiting for the check, he thought about what excuse he could use to retire early from the evening's festivities. Quiana had told him that a professional group of Bollywood dancers would be performing. Try as he might, Inman couldn't get used to the Indian/hip-hop/rap/whatever-it-was sound. Feigning a headache might be a good idea. That always worked for Shirley. Inman contemplated calling his wife, but he changed his mind. There had to be some other way to repair the mess.

***

Alice stretched luxuriously and snuggled deeper into the covers. Art was standing by the window in his hotel bathrobe, looking at the Dallas skyline. She loved watching him and treasured the fact that he was sharing these precious moments with her. Last night had allowed her to forget the sword of Damocles hanging over her head. Giving herself permission not to think of the hearing for the rest of the weekend cheered her.

Art looked over. "Want some coffee?"

Alice shifted her pillows and, sitting up, leaned against the headboard. "Sure." Art then began to operate the in-room machine.

"OK, tell me exactly what's happening at one."

"It's called the Baraat. That's when the groom and his family arrive, and it's traditionally done on a white horse."

"A horse? You're joking, aren't you? A real horse?"

"Yes. Gaye's mother insisted that Tommy ride in on the horse. Gaye lost that round."

"Tommy had no say in all of this?"

"Apparently not." Alice laughed. "At least Gaye got her mother to agree that Gaye would only get henna on the back of her hands and the top of her feet. Usually it also goes up and down the bride's arms and legs."

"That's all that fancy dark artwork, isn't it?"

"Yep."

Art handed Alice coffee and then returned to a seat on the couch. Alice took a sip and, summoning her courage, said, "Art, you haven't spoken much about your past. I know you have no children, but were you ever married?"

He stared at the floor. Alice suddenly felt she'd made a mistake.

After an endless silence, Art said, "Yes. When I was eighteen, I married my childhood sweetheart. After a year, I found out she was cheating on me. We divorced. I was crushed. It was the high school football star. They're still married and have grandchildren." He sighed.

"I'm sorry. It was none of my business. I don't know why I asked."

"No, it's OK. It was a long time ago. I've always wondered what I did wrong, if I could have somehow made it turn out differently. You never married, right? I'd wished I'd never been. It hurt so much."

Alice shook her head and sat quietly, contemplating what Art had said. The beige tones in the room drew her in, giving her a feeling of calm. Marriage had been her goal, but the timing was never right. Now, the idea of matrimony didn't interest her. A piece of paper was not necessary to make her whole. She finished her coffee and put it on the bed stand.

Art rose and approached her, stretching out his hand. "Come, my love. I need someone to scrub my back in the shower."

Alice giggled like a schoolgirl and greedily reached out to the love of her life.

***

Gaye stood in front of the mirror with Nila, gazing at herself. The vibrant red lehenga and sheer-at-the-waist crop top were adorned with ornate silver embroidery. Tommy had settled on it and, she had to admit, he had exquisite taste. Her mother then added an elaborate jeweled headpiece that started from the edge of Gaye's bun and spread to a teardrop pattern surrounding a large red stone on her forehead. The design was repeated in the subsantial earrings and necklace, an heirloom of Nila's family.

"You are so beautiful, Gaye," said Sanit. He put his arm around Nila. "She's a beautiful bride."

Gaye caught a glimpse of a frown on her mother's face. "Mother, what's wrong?" Gaye was alarmed. Nila had been so upset over the ostentatious sangeet that Gaye had feared she'd storm out of the room. Thankfully Espy had spent considerable time calming Nila so Gaye could enjoy herself. Tommy had seen the reaction as well and promised he'd speak to Pat to be sure there were no other surprises.

"It's that Pat woman."

"Nila, that's silly," Sanjit said. "You ought to be thankful for her. She put on a sangeet no one will ever forget. A rock and roll star, can you imagine? It will be the talk of Dallas for weeks, that's for sure."

Gaye reached for Nila's hand. "Mother, Pat was just trying to send Tommy off in the best way she knew. I don't expect you to compete with that kind of money. That's not the point. What's an over-the-top wedding if you're not surrounded by a loving family? Besides, in America, the night of the rehearsal is supposed to be the night the groom's family entertains. I prefer today just as you've planned it." She leaned down and gave Nila a kiss on the cheek. "I love you."

"I'm sorry, Gaye. It's just been so stressful."

"Well, you need to let your hair down tonight and have a good time," Sanjit said.

They were interrupted by laughter and snickering by the window. Gaye turned. "What's going on?"

"It's Tommy on the white horse," her cousin said. "He looks none too confident."

Gaye wedged her way to the window and then broke out laughing. Tommy almost looked distinguished in his ivory-colored *sherwani* with crimson trim and his crimson pants. Funky-looking slippers with pointed, blunt toes and a rather sizeable matching turban swallowed his head. But his grimace told Gaye everything she needed to know. He gripped the pommel tightly with one hand and tentatively waved to the crowd with the other. An attendant led the horse, bedecked in a dazzling red and gold blanket with matching harness and breast collar, through the hotel parking lot and grounds. Sweat was breaking out on Tommy's face despite the cool day.

There'd been some argument about who was to carry the umbrella, as Tommy's male friends wanted to dance while the horse made its way to the festivities. JJ had been elected and was standing as far away from the horse's rear as possible, still keeping the umbrella near Tommy's head. The others jived to hip-hop blasting through a groom's cell phone.

"Take plenty of pictures," she said to her cousin. Gaye giggled. "Mom, I can't believe you made him wear those shoes. They look goofy."

"*Juti* are so traditional and romantic," Nila said. "Isn't he handsome?"

"Yes, he is." Gaye reached over and squeezed her mother's hand. "Thanks for everything."

***

Inman stood to the back of the crowd watching the spectacle. Amused, and then thankful he hadn't had to do anything so foolish on his wedding day. And JJ—how in the world did they talk him into carrying the umbrella?

His thoughts turned to Shirley. How he missed her. The wedding would be much more fun in her company. The Shirley Iman knew would have read up on Indian weddings and been explaining the intricacies of the ceremony.

Glancing down the sidewalk, Inman was taken aback. Had he conjured up the love of his life? No, there she was, strolling slowly toward the dancing crowd. Inman wove his way through the boogying throng and rapidly walked toward her. Her progress halted when they locked eyes. Inman rushed forward despite her troubled expression. Suddenly they were face to face.

"Shirley, what a wonderful surprise. How—"
Shirley put her hand up to silence him. "I had a long talk with Grace Wednesday. She said that you asked her to call me. She told me about the whole situation. We do have lots of things to work out. Frankly, my trust in you has been badly shaken."

Inman hung his head, unsure how he would ever be able to restore Shirley's confidence in him. Then, he looked deeply into her eyes. "We can just take it one day at a time. I'll do anything I can to make it up to you."

"That's a start," she said.

"Do you have bags?" Inman asked.

"I've already checked into a hotel down the street. This one was booked."

"You'll join me for the celebration, I hope."

"I will. I think it's high time I met your coworkers."

Inman looked about, noticing that Tommy had dismounted. The crowd was making its way inside. "This has been a ceremony for the record books, so far." Inman stood to the side and gestured for Shirley to walk with him.

***

Alice looked for a place to park her scooter in the packed ballroom. Art tapped her on the shoulder and motioned to the side of the room where

JJ was waving. They soon joined her coworkers. Sadness enveloped Alice as she spied Quiana in what could only be called a burka-like covering. Alice could see none of Quiana's face, and she couldn't fathom how the woman could even see out of the contraption.

After she'd parked, Art assisted her to a chair next to Royce. She leaned over and made small talk with him. When everyone was settled, the ceremony commenced.

The stage was set with two large chairs accompanied by small sitting areas on either side. Tommy stood ramrod straight on the dais. Prayers were offered, and then Gaye was ushered in.

Alice gasped. She leaned over to Art, putting her hand on his knee. "She's beautiful."

"That she is." Art took Alice's hand in his.

The couple exchanged garlands, and the ritual began in earnest.

Alice noticed the door on the far side of the ballroom open. Inman and a woman eased in and sat against the wall. Watching them intently, Alice realized it was Shirley. She hadn't seen the woman in years. Hopefully, they would work things out. As much as Alice disliked Inman, she didn't wish him an unhappy personal life. In fact, if they patched things up, maybe he would pay more attention to the Bighorn case.

***

JJ looked over at Quiana, wishing he could see her expression. What was she thinking or feeling? They'd gotten plenty of stares last night, but in the end, JJ didn't mind. They'd slow-danced to one of his favorite Blige songs, "We Got Hood Love." Just to be able to hold her as they swayed on the dance floor electrified him.

He looked down at her lap, hoping to grab her hand and hold it, but Quiana was tightly gripping her purse with both fists as if she were afraid it would be ripped away by a mugger.

JJ heaved a sigh and looked around. To him, the ceremony was longer than an African American funeral—way too long. And to think that it would have been longer if Gaye hadn't put her foot down. He noticed Alice and Art were holding hands. That pained him.

***

Gaye simply went through the steps of the ceremony, hardly paying attention as the pandit droned on. She kept her mind focused on her one and only wedding ceremony. Just her and Tommy.

Finally, the pandit said, "May your lives be intertwined with a strong fabric of love, harmony, and peace! May you fully support each other in your life's journey! Go, and lead a joyful life with family, friends, and children! May God bless you!"

Relief coursed through Gaye's body. At last, it was done. One more party tonight, the parting breakfast tomorrow, and then she and Tommy could return to a normal life.

Flower petals landed lightly on Gaye, and Tommy turned to her, brushing them off. In defiance of traditional wedding protocol, he ripped his turban off and swept Gaye into a long, no-holds-barred kiss. The audience erupted with applause and shouts.

When Gaye was back on her feet, she stifled an embarrassed grin. Thankfully Tommy's family had willingly agreed to dispense with the new bride welcome, freeing her to disappear into the crowd.

Sanjit took the microphone. "Honored guests. Thanks for sharing in the marriage of our eldest daughter, and please welcome my new son-in-law into the family." After the applause died, he said, "Please enjoy a drink and appetizers. The buffet will open shortly. We also have a fabulous show arranged in honor of the bride and groom."

Sanjit approached the couple and reached out his hand to Tommy. As they were shaking hands, Sanjit pulled Tommy closer and hugged him with the other arm. "Thanks for suggesting the traditional wedding. Nila is so happy."

Gaye glanced into the audience and realized that Grandma Pat, clad in an eye-popping teal green silk sari enhanced with silver thread and stonework, was heading toward them. Hers was the same color as Nila's sari and, of course, much more ornate. Gaye's heart sank. How to head this disaster off? Alarmed, she looked around for her mother. Fortunately, Mom's back was turned, and she was socializing with one of her best friends.

Pat sashayed to the couple and gave them both hugs. "You are so beautiful, Gaye," Pat said. "Tommy is a lucky man. And Tommy, take good care of her, or you'll be on my shit list."

"Not to worry," Tommy said. "Grandma Pat, thanks for being here and treating us to a fun night last night. We're so honored that you provided rooms for the out-of-towners."

"You're welcome." Pat grabbed his hand and squeezed it.

Gaye looked back at her mother, relieved that she had not yet turned around.

Royce appeared at Gaye's side, looking dashing in a gold tunic. He leaned over and whispered to Gaye, "What's wrong?"

"Grandma Pat has on the same color dress as my mother, but much more elaborate."

Royce nodded and then walked to Pat, keeping between her and Nila's line of sight.

"Pat," he said as he grabbed her elbow. "We have lots to talk about. Mind if I steal your grandma, Tommy?"

"Tommy chuckled. "Be my guest."

***

As Royce was escorting Pat to the far side of the room, he leaned over and said, "Mind if we go to the bar for a bit? It's so noisy in here. I can't hear myself think." Without waiting for an answer, they left the ballroom and found a quiet corner table. Royce waved over the server, ordering drinks.

"So, just what do you have in mind for me to do in New York?" Royce asked.

"Here's what I suggest." Then Pat laid out her plan.

Stunned, Royce sat back. But would it work?

***

Flushed with wine and excited over the Bollywood production, JJ walked Quiana to her room. He'd never been to a live dance show, and it had thrilled him. "Weren't those desserts good?" he said. "I wish I knew what they were. I'll have to ask Gaye. I'd like to get some more of them."

195

"You may not want to know what's in them," Quiana said. "Best to keep it a secret." Quiana opened her door and hesitated. "Want to come in? It's been such a fun evening; I don't want it to end."

"Me neither." JJ followed her and locked the door behind them. He undid his tie and took off his jacket. Looking around, he sat on the couch. Quiana turned her back and removed the heavy veil, trading it for her usual hat disguise. Then, she propped herself on the bed close to JJ.

The idle chatter continued until Quiana looked at her watch. "Oh, it's one. I really need to get to bed. We've got a long drive back tomorrow."

Reluctantly JJ rose. Wistfully, he thought about Alice and Art. Maybe one day. Quiana walked JJ to the door. JJ unlatched it but, before exiting, he turned and faced her. On an impulse, he reached beneath the headgear to touch her cheek.

"Quiana, I had such a wonderful time. Having you next to me was what made the night." She started to interrupt, but his finger on her lips quieted her. "I know you don't date coworkers. We're just friends, remember." Then he tilted back her hat. Quiana looked down but didn't pull away. "I'll close my eyes." JJ leaned down, taking her face in both hands, and gave Quiana a long, lingering kiss on the lips. Then, returning the brim to hide her face, he slipped out the door.

Chapter Thirty Five

While shaving, Inman thought about last night. Shirley had gotten along well with the team, even taking a special interest in Quiana. The evening seemed to put her more at ease. Although she had heard tales about his coworkers, meeting them made it clear there was nothing to hide. Still, they hadn't had a good talk, but his wife had invited him to breakfast, and with any luck, they could smooth out their differences. He was anxious to learn precisely what Grace had said to Shirley, though he dreaded the discussion of her feelings in the matter.

As Inman dressed, he considered buying flowers but thought better of it, instead opting to arrange for his mother-in-law's caregiver to extend her stay. Perhaps Shirley would accompany him to Austin if she knew her mother was in good hands.

Shirley took Inman's breath away when he met her at the hotel restaurant. She was as gorgeous as ever. He enveloped her, and a slow, leisurely kiss ensued. She responded in kind. As they were being escorted to their table, a text came in. Inman read it and sighed with relief.

Once they were seated, she said, "I've given this lots of thought. I realize you didn't know about the baby; there's no way you could have known. I guess I realize that you have taken ownership and are doing the right thing. I'll try to live with it, but it'll take some time. My perception of family has been tossed on its head."

"You don't know what it means to me. I never meant to hurt you. I didn't know what else to do. I guess I handled it badly. Look, why don't you come to Austin with me for a few days so you can see where I live and what's going on. I hope you will feel more comfortable with me being in Texas. Right now, I can't transfer back. There's too much at stake."

"But mother—"

"I've taken care of that. I've arranged for the caretaker to stay a few more days. She'll be fine. Our time is too precious to waste."

***

Royce heard a knock on his door and, looking out the peephole, saw a bellman. Upon opening the door, the man said, "Pat Gentry asked that I give you this." Royce said thanks, closed the door, and sat at the desk where he opened the envelope.

Inside was a first-class plane ticket to New York, leaving at one o'clock that afternoon, along with hotel reservations. Pat indicated she would make contact with him this evening. Royce sighed. His clothes were dirty. He really couldn't afford to be buying any more outfits, but he saw no other way out of the situation.

He finished packing and headed to the wedding party breakfast. All his coworkers were at a table except for Inman. Royce occupied the empty chair near Alice. After the server had poured his coffee, he leaned over to Alice and said, "I've got to take a few days off—not sure how long. I'll let you know as soon as I can."

"Not a problem. Is anything wrong?"

"No, it's just personal business. If you need anything, call Espy. She'll be there to support you."

"Thanks. You've been so helpful. I couldn't have done everything without you. Keep me posted."

Royce looked over at JJ, who was positively beaming. *What in the world happened last night?* Royce thought. Must have been good.

When breakfast arrived, he ate hurriedly and pressed Espy to get on the road.

They said their goodbyes to Gaye and Tommy. *I'll really miss Gaye,* Royce thought. *She, of all of them, accepted me immediately without reservations.*

When they were en route, Royce explained the detour.

"Whatever for? Where are you going?"

"Look, Espy, I'm headed to New York, but I can't tell you why. It might be important to the office, I don't know. Thing is, if something goes wrong, the less you know, the better it will be for you and everyone else in the office."

"Isn't that a bit draconian?"

"Not really. I'll give you a call when I'm ready to leave New York. I'll be flying back into Austin. And please, could you hang around Alice more? I don't want her backsliding."

"Me neither."

***

Quiana looked out the window as they passed from the suburbs into the countryside, heading south. She'd avoided JJ at breakfast and hadn't said two words since they left the hotel, despite his attempts at conversation. Her confusion was boundless. Letting him kiss her had been a bad idea. They were no longer friends. But what were they? Truthfully, the kiss was divine, awakening something in her that had been suppressed for years. And now that the genie was out of the lamp…How was she going to handle it?

Quiana swiftly glanced at him, then steered her eyes downward. Suddenly remorse enveloped her. Why punish JJ for something they both desired? If she really wanted a relationship but continued to rebuff him, he would undoubtedly retreat into his shell. And what if the office were closed? *Then, I'd never see him again. Is that what I want?*

"JJ, I'm sorry. I really enjoyed your company last night. It's that…I don't know…I'm scared, scared of moving forward and scared not to. I'm sorry. I guess I'm just no good at saying how I feel."

JJ continued to watch the traffic, saying nothing. Quiana became uncomfortable. Not knowing what to say, she turned to stare out the window to her right.

Finally, he said, "Quiana, I had fun last night, too. I like you very much. No, that's not right. I'm in love with you, and I want more time with you than I've been getting. I'm putting myself on the line saying this. I've been so terrified that you'd reject me that I've kept quiet. You know, we've both been locked up in our own hell, but that's no reason we can't find some peace.

"Just think about it. Think about where you want to go and whether you want me with you. I know you can beat the sociophobia, and I can help you get there. You've helped me stop thinking I was a worthless ex-con; now let me help you."

Overwhelmed, Quiana closed her eyes as visions of what could be jumbled through her brain. "JJ, give me some time. I need to think."

***

Alice glanced at the text she'd just received. Inman was going to take a few days off. Her first impulse was to text back, saying they were too busy. But he and Shirley appeared to be patching things up. Let him do what he needed to do; the office mess wasn't his fault. She sent an "OK."

"How much further?" Alice asked.

"We'll be home in about an hour. I thought we'd get the dogs sprung out of jail and then go out for an early dinner. Will that work for you?"

"I really don't feel much like going out, thanks. I'll just hang around home. You're welcome to join me."

"You're worried about testifying, aren't you?"

Alice sighed. "I'm so haunted I even dreamt about it last night. I have this fear that something dreadful is going to happen."

"I'm sure everything will be fine. I don't see how anything could happen."

"You never know."

***

Espy exited the interstate and went through the Starbucks drive-thru. While sipping coffee, she replayed the bizarre weekend. The wedding was as over-the-top as Tommy's Grandma Pat. Idly, Espy wondered how her own life would change with that much money. Would endless travel satisfy her? Where would she live? A large mansion on Lake Travis with an infinity pool was a must. An apartment in Paris?

But what was the use of all the riches in the world without anyone to enjoy it with? Seeing everyone paired up had left her depressed. At least hanging with Royce had eased her angst. But he'd been reserved. And this New York jaunt? What in the hell was going on anyway?

She'd had a couple of dances with one of Tommy's friends, Mason, who'd asked if he could call her. Saying no had been her first instinct, but she'd acquiesced. He was just probably saying that in the heat of the moment, and Espy would never hear from him. While she wasn't bowled over by the man, he was decent. It was time to end the pity party and restart her social life.

Chapter Thirty Six

The taxi rolled up to a four-star boutique hotel on the Upper West Side and deposited Royce. Panting, he lugged his bag into the lobby only to see Oriental rugs, plush leather couches, and candles giving the interior an inviting look.

The clerk handed Royce an envelope and package at check-in. When in the room, he tore open the packet and found a terse, printed command. Bar at seven-thirty. A prepaid Visa card was also included. The bundle contained underwear, socks, three shirts, and jeans—his exact size. *Who in the hell is this Grandma Pat?*

He was drained from his flight, but a shower revived him somewhat. And, amazingly, Pat's outfit complimented his complexion. Settling at the bar, Royce ordered two Buffalo Traces on the rocks. A few minutes later, a plainly dressed woman approached and slid into the chair opposite him. He did a doubletake. Grandma Pat had on no makeup, no jewelry, and mousy gray hair.

"Did I startle you? This is what I look like without my paraphernalia. It makes the perfect disguise," Pat said.

"You think someone is watching us?"

Pat frowned. "Never can be too sure." She took a long draw from her bourbon. "Johnathon lives about two blocks from the hotel." She offered a piece of paper. "My sources say he goes out on Monday evenings by himself, but they couldn't tell me where. He apparently has several hangouts." Pat also passed along another paper with the names of several bars. "Be sure you throw these away when you're finished. I can't be caught helping you. It would be bad for my reputation."

"Any idea what he looks like as a woman? Hair color? Anything?"

"I have no earthly idea. Apparently, he leaves the house, stops at an apartment he rents, and then changes. Your best bet, though, is to get a good full face and pictures of him with his alternative friends. His proclivities are carefully guarded. I don't even think his wife knows."

"How do you want me to get in touch with you?"

"Don't. Your bill is being paid with a special account. Just charge everything to the room. Stay as long as you want, and don't worry about the cost. Just take him down. I've hated that bastard for a long time."

"Why?"

"Best you not know." Grandma Pat rose and disappeared as quickly as she had appeared.

Royce swirled his drink, finished it, and ordered another. He felt conflicted. Exposing the great Mr. Johnathon Patton, Esquire, as a cross-dresser would inevitably end his marriage and possibly his career. And Royce hated ruining a man for pursuing a lifestyle that felt comfortable. On the other hand, the bastard had judged everyone in his office and implied they were subhuman. *What had he called us?* The words were seared in Royce's mind: promiscuous drunks, sex offenders, perverts, fornicators, and adulterers. And for that, the man had it coming.

Royce considered ordering food, but backed off, preferring the buzz. Suddenly it struck him: Patton knew what he looked like from the surveillance photos. Fretting, Royce realized he had precious few hours to come up with a way to get pictures without being recognized.

***

Exhausted from a lack of sleep, Alice forced herself to work Monday. Thoughts of being grilled by Sylvia Swanson had left her with a sense of foreboding. She hated calling other women "bitches." However, the term perfectly described that sanctimonious heifer with the trademark June Cleaver pearls and scrupulously coiffed hair. Despite her petite size, the woman had a sharp tongue that had been trained to tear witnesses apart in a court of law.

When she entered the office, it was eerily quiet. Quiana was not behind the screen, and Inman and Royce were gone. Where were the others?

"Hello! Anybody here?"

Espy came into the open area. "Good morning. Looks like we're the only ones here. Jorge stepped out to pick up some breakfast tacos. You want me to call him and tell him to get you one?"

"No, I haven't had much of an appetite lately. What about JJ and Quiana? Where are they?"

"Quiana called saying she was sick, and JJ said he would be in after lunch. I'm really not sure what is going on."

"So, how's the 'pinkie' case going?"

"Actually, Jorge and I are leaving as soon as he gets back. The case is in Temple, which is about an hour's drive. I wanted it on the fast track. We're splitting up the interviewing, so we should be finished this evening. There's not much documentation, and they've agreed to give it to me when I'm onsite."

"That's fabulous." Alice's spirits lifted a bit. "That case, if it pans out, and Ike's Burgers, if it can be completed quickly, would make three cases for September. "OK, sounds good. I'll be in my office."

Alice retreated into her sanctum and noted Dexter's sullen look. "Missing Quiana?" She embraced him, rubbing his silky coat. Contentedly, he cuddled in her lap. "Sorry, Dex, got to get working on the hearing." Avoiding those eyes begging for attention, she set him on the ground. Finally, he wandered off in search of an eager hand.

About thirty minutes later, Jorge stuck his head in to tell her they were leaving. "You'll be OK?"

Alice smiled. "I'll be better if you can bring back another 'cause' case. Be safe."

Jorge waved, and Alice heard the door shut and lock. Dexter then slunk in and settled in his bed, ignoring her. *No doubt he's still mad about being left at the luxury kennel over the weekend,* she thought. Alice then heard the office phone ring, but thought nothing of it. She'd check the voicemail later.

Alice then noticed a new e-mail from Saitou. The hair on her neck stood on end. With dread, she read:

Hearing moved up one week. You are to be in DC on Friday to go over the materials Weber has obtained from the OIG so he can prepare you for questioning. He is not happy.

Alice began to quiver. The bosses now had everything the Aryan goddess found. *I am screwed.* The quiver turned into outright shudders. Alice desperately tried to grab Dexter but couldn't manage to control her spasms. The angry bonds of anxiety lashed at her chest until she thought about screaming. She closed her eyes. A sling beckoned her.

"Dex…forgive me" Alice grabbed her purse and fled the office.

***

Royce finished breakfast and, lingering over cappuccino, made a list of supplies and surfed the Internet for a secondhand shop. Next, a trial run past Patton's apartment to look for places to loiter discreetly was in order.

After a brisk walk, he arrived at a tannish building replete with gabled roofs, windows, turrets, and arches. A castle amid skyscrapers. The doorman wore a navy-blue double-breasted suit with eight brass buttons, a white dress shirt, and bowtie. The outfit included a billed blue cap with gold braid. The bouncer lurked near a sign that read, "Authorized Persons Only Beyond This Point."

Looking around for a vantage point across the street, Royce realized that a HOHO bus was disgorging passengers with cameras in hand, making a beeline for the building. Chuckling, he fondly remembered his friend, Felix, who loved to call the Hop-On Hop-Off tourist busses "HOHOs."

Between the tourists and other street traffic, Royce calmed. Remaining invisible would be easy. He sauntered over to a woman who had just departed the HOHO.

"What's the big deal with the building?" he asked.

The incredulous look on her face made him want to hide under the bus. "This is the Dakota, the most iconic residence in New York. John Lennon was killed here. You have to be approved by the board to live here. Says in this brochure that Antonio Banderas, Alex Rodriguez, Billy Joel, and Madonna were rejected. Can you believe that?"

The woman appeared eager to engage in further conversation, so he started to ease away. "Thanks. I didn't know all that." Royce hurried to Central Park and found a bench.

Checking his phone, he confirmed what the woman had said. Patton was a big fish, all right, and Royce didn't know if he dared to take him down. Wearily, he made his way to the closest subway station and, after many agonizing minutes, decided what line would take him to the secondhand shop.

***

Alice drove her scooter into Rebels, parked in the corner, and, with Jake's help, made her way to her favorite stool.

"Alice, how are you?" Jake said. "I've missed you. Have you been OK?"

"I'll be better with a drink," she said.

"The usual, I assume."

Guiltily, Alice nodded. While Jake fixed the luscious elixir, Alice tried to calm her jittery nerves. Heart pounding, she willed herself to think about something else. Still, visions of the House members grilling her, interrupting her, and humiliating her kept up a running commentary.

Jake set the drink in front of her and headed to tend to a new customer. Grabbing the glass, Alice took a healthy pull from the straw and then sat back, waiting for relief to wash over her....Nothing happened. She downed the drink.... No euphoria.

Alice was now genuinely panicked. For most of her life, alcohol had eased her incertitude. And now, with that damn injection, nothing happened. The desire to release a primaeval howl and run down the street gripped her.

***

JJ entered the office and, finding it a tomb, quickly checked to see if anyone was there. As he peeked into Alice's office, a barking Dexter bounded from his bed, nosing JJ. Scooping up the dog, he asked, "Dex, where's Alice?"

Dexter began to lick his face, and JJ pushed his muzzle away. Then he carried the spoiled pooch to the backyard to do his business. While waiting, JJ plopped into a lawn chair and started to dial Quiana but thought better of it. Instead, he called Jorge to see what was going on.

"Hi, JJ. Look, I can't talk now. We're in the company's parking lot, and we need to get set up for the interviews."

"I won't keep you. I'm at the office, and no one else is here."

"Just a minute…Espy said that Quiana called in sick and that Alice was there."

"She's not here now, only Dexter."

"Here, Espy wants to talk to you."

"JJ, see if you can find out where she's gone. She really looked stressed this morning. I hope she's not at Rebels."

"Me, too. I'll let you know what I find out."

JJ shooed Dexter inside and headed to Alice's favorite watering hole.

Slowly opening the door, JJ peered in. Spying Alice, he cringed, fighting back the tears. She was sitting over an empty glass, not moving. JJ occupied the stool next to her.

"Alice, is everything OK?"

"No, nothing is right. I feel like I'm going to shatter into a million pieces."

"Let's get you out of here." JJ threw a twenty on the bar and, grabbing Alice's arm, helped her to the scooter. On the walk back to the office, he wondered how to handle this broken woman.

When the door opened, Dexter let out a wail, jumping and barking. JJ lifted him and directed Alice to the conference table. Then he dropped Alice's best friend into her lap. She absentmindedly ran her hands along his silky fur.

"Anyone you want me to call?"

Alice said nothing. Freaked out, he stepped into his office and called Quiana. "Alice is in trouble," he said. Then he explained what had happened.

"I'll be there as soon as I can. You said she had a drink?"

"Yes."

Put on some coffee. Put in an order at the Subway down the street, and I'll pick it up on my way in."

JJ returned to the conference room and watched helplessly as Alice stared at the table. Then, remembering Quiana's missive, he brewed coffee. The cup sat, untouched. Eventually, Alice took a sip of the beverage.

Relief flooded JJ as he heard the door open and saw Quiana bustle in, face hidden. She spread lunch for the three of them on the conference table, all the time making small talk.

"Eat," Quiana commanded. JJ jumped and grabbed his sandwich.

"I'm not hungry," Alice said.

"I get it, but at least take a few bites. It will absorb the alcohol you drank."

"It didn't do anything," Alice said.

"What do you mean?" Quiana said.

"I'm taking a monthly shot to stop the alcohol cravings. Nothing happened when I took a drink."

JJ was confused. "That's good news, isn't it?" JJ asked.

"Yes and no. Yes because I didn't have another drink but no because I am so stressed and strung out with torment that I feel paralyzed. Now I don't know how to get rid of it."

Both JJ and Quiana sat in silence. Then Quiana said, "I know those feelings. I get so stressed out when someone is looking at me, I go into complete panic mode. The only way it stops is if no one is looking at me."

JJ said, "It sounds like both of you need to figure out how to get rid of your stress in other ways. Drinking and hiding don't work that well." He dared not look at Quiana, who he suspected was giving him the evil eye.

Alice toyed with her sandwich and then took a nibble. They finished their lunch in silence.

"Alice," Quiana said, "What triggered your attack?"

"The hearing has been moved up a week. I report to headquarters Friday. Worst of it is, the general counsel has all of the OIG's audit."

"Oh, shit," Quiana said.

***

Quiana crept into Inman's offices and made some phone calls. Unfortunately, no one could tell her what headquarters was going to do with the audit information. A call to Inman confirmed he was aware of the schedule change. However, she stayed mum about Alice's liquor run. Inman promised to be at the office tomorrow to help Alice prepare even though headquarters had insisted they do the prep work. Then she slid next to Alice. "Are you feeling any better?"

"I guess. I just don't know whether I can go through with the hearing."

Chapter Thirty Seven

Assuring himself that no staff was in the lobby, Royce grabbed his shopping bag and made a beeline to his room. Would his gamble pay off? After showering, his painful transition back to Royce Ann began.

An hour later, he stared at himself in the mirror. The auburn wig was perfect; a blond one would have attracted too much attention. Casual jeans and a silk tie neck, long-sleeve blouse in cool turquoise rounded out his ensemble. Royce didn't overdo the makeup, fearful of standing out in the crowd. Satisfied, he removed the cosmetics.

Off came the wig, and he stuffed it into a large purse along with thong sandals and the makeup. Throwing on a light, oversized jacket, he slipped into tennis shoes and jammed a baseball cap low upon his head. *It's showtime.*

Royce set up shop at the corner bus stop across from the Dakota entrance, playing with his cell phone. Use of the its zoom feature afforded him a good look at the faces of the doormen. Continuing his charade, he occasionally glanced up, on alert for the asshole.

His patience paid off. Around six-thirty, Patton exited the Dakota, looked both ways, and headed to the corner. Patton passed within feet of him, forcing Royce to duck his head and concentrate on his phone. When the danger had passed, pursuit of the bastard began in earnest.

Soon Patton entered a nondescript brownstone. Royce took note of the fact that the top of the man's head was level with decorative bric-a-brac on the doorframe. Even after removing his cap, Royce feared the sparse cover would not conceal him. Moving a far distance away was his only prudent option. *Will I be able to recognize Patton in drag?* While waiting, he googled trans bars.

Minutes passed, and several people exited the building. Finally, a striking blonde emerged wearing a flattering green dress. She was the same height as Patton. Heaving a sigh of relief, Royce watched as Patton turned away from him and sauntered down the street. *Funny,* Royce thought, *the bastard appears to be headed to the bar I would have chosen.* Royce tailed lengths behind until he confirmed Patton's destination.

Royce desperately searched for a restroom where the transformation into Royce Ann could occur. Finally, he scurried back to Central Park and, satisfied his transition was complete, made his way into the bar.

Royce Ann blinked, taking a minute to get used to the darkened atmosphere. The brick walls were covered with modern art for sale, and a DJ was spinning the latest dance music. The slightly curved bar was well stocked with her favorites. After selecting a bar stool, she started to order her usual but decided against it. Patton probably knew more about her and her habits than she did. Instead, she chose a pre-Royce standby: a margarita.

Drink in hand, Royce Ann took a sip and then relaxed, casually looking around. The bar was filling up fast, and most of the tables were taken. Gay couples mingled with trans couples.

Eventually, she spotted Patton at a table in the back of the lounge, deep in conversation with a dark, heavyset man wearing a dress shirt with no tie and a sport coat. While talking, Patton repeatedly touched the man, who laughed at what he was saying. *Wonder if he knows she's a cross-dresser?* Royce Ann thought.

Convinced that the couple was unaware of their surroundings, Royce Ann pulled out her phone and took a selfie, careful to get the couple in the background.

Unfortunately, the picture was of poor quality. *Now what? How can I get closer without being obvious?*

A trio of men entered and took a seat at the table next to Patton. After they were served, Royce Ann grabbed her drink and walked over to them. The only chair left put her with her back to Patton and company.

"Mind if I join you?" Royce Ann said.

"Uh, sure," the short man said.

Introducing herself, she told them she was visiting New York for the first time and was lonely. Asking them questions allowed her to engage them in conversation. After she paid for a round of drinks, they were bosom buddies.

Royce Ann wasn't able to hear any of the conversation behind her. Fear that the couple would leave without her getting clear and convincing evidence stirred her anxiety level.

Rising, she said, "Guys, thanks for a wonderful chat. I need to get going. I have an early business meeting tomorrow. Mind if I take your picture?"

"Sure," the short man said.

Royce Ann snapped a picture of the trio and then suggested a picture of the four of them together. Mustering all her courage, she turned to Patton and said, "Would you take a picture of us?"

A look of annoyance crossed his face, but he complied. Holding Royce Ann's phone, Patton snapped several pictures.

"Oh, thank you," Royce Ann said. "Could I get a selfie of us?" A look of pure evil emanated from Patton.

"Oh, please, you're so gorgeous—and I just love that dress. This is my first trip to the Big Apple."

"Oh, go ahead, Patton," his companion said. "Make the little lady happy."

Royce Ann quickly snapped two selfies and thanked Patton profusely. Then she said her goodbyes and made her way to the ladies' room. Satisfied the images were clear, she immediately e-mailed them to Espy's personal e-mail address along with a warning not to ask any questions.

Washing up, Royce Ann wondered about the other man. He had called Patton by his name. Why didn't Patton have an alter ego? Just in case, she decided to get a good photo of Patton's companion.

As Royce Ann emerged from the restroom, she saw a thin man approaching Patton's table. The companion rose and gave the newcomer a kiss. Obviously a romantic interest, as the swarthy man held the newcomer's hand.

Going for broke, Royce Ann approached Patton's table, snapped a picture, and ran for her life. Angry shouts followed her out the door. With footsteps gaining ground, she made a beeline for a nearby bar and ducked in. In the bathroom, the transformation occurred.

Royce stuffed his purse into the trash can and exited the facilities. Moving to the bar, he ordered a Buffalo Trace and watched as the thin man scoured the bar looking for Royce Ann. As the bartender was serving Royce, the pursuer approached and asked the bartender about a short woman with auburn hair and a turquoise blouse. The bartender answered no. Then the skinny man turned to Royce. "You seen anyone by that description?"

Unnerved Royce said, "no," and hurriedly took a sip of his drink. He praised God for the foresight to have been a brunette instead of a blond who would have attracted more attention.

"I know I saw her come in here," the thin man said. "She has to be here somewhere." Then he wandered off for another tour of the lounge.

By the time Royce had finished his drink, the follower had vanished. Relieved, he ordered another beverage and checked the last photo on his phone. It was a beaut! The three faces were crystal clear; the thin man was snuggled with Patton's companion. Then he e-mailed it to Espy along with his plans to return tomorrow, arrival time unknown.

After paying his tab, Royce found a drugstore, where he purchased some plastic bags and a disposable phone. He dropped his personal cell into the plastic bag and made his way to the hotel.

A bite to eat and another drink helped steady him. After purchasing his airline ticket online, he perused Amazon and, satisfied with his find, completed his purchase. Grandma Pat received a "mission accomplished" text. With luck, Royce Ann was out of his life forever.

Chapter Thirty Eight

Alice sipped coffee and tried to concentrate on the latest spate of e-mails. Avoiding Art by declining a visit to the dog park would allow an opportunity to process the loss of her long-cherished elixir. The injection had done its job; the trick was to have enough strength to continue the shots. Figuring out how to lower her edginess without alcohol was paramount. While the cravings were gone, the panic remained. Maybe gym visits, working the upper half of her body, would reduce her stress level.

Espy poked her head into the office. "Alice, Jorge and I would like to chat with you about the 'pinkie' case. Do you mind coming into the conference room?"

Glad for a distraction, Alice assented and steered toward the table. When settled, she asked, "So how'd it go?"

"The supervisor said he did call CP 'pinkie,' but he was just funning, and it didn't mean anything. When I asked him where he got the idea for the nickname, the supervisor said he couldn't remember. He said he told jokes just like everyone on the crew and denied they were sexually oriented."

"What else would you expect?" Alice asked.

"Oh, this is good. He denied saying that if people didn't work faster, he would shove a shovel up their ass or whack their peckers with it."

"Ouch. Did anyone else verify this?" Alice asked.

Jorge said, "Only two of the Hispanics would back up CP on the shovel business. The other two said the boss was just joking around and wasn't offensive."

"What did they say about 'pinkie'?" Alice asked.

"That it was a nickname. One of the other guys said the boss called him 'taco' but that he just blew it off."

"Did they think pinkie was offensive?" Alice asked.

"They didn't, but they said that CP really got angry when anyone called him that. He asked them to stop, but the boss just laughed and kept on doing it," Jorge said.

"My question," Espy said, "is whether, if CP didn't really know what was meant by 'pinkie,' we consider it to be harassment based on sex or race rather than just mere teasing? I know if someone tells jokes about Texas Aggie football players until an Aggie fan is sick and tired of it, it's not covered because it has nothing to do with a protected status."

"Hmm. I think in this case, since he was the only white person, it could be inferred that the term was used because he was Caucasian. Also, he called someone else 'taco,' so obviously the supervisor did take race and national origin into account when assigning nicknames. Go ahead and get it written up. The sooner, the better."

Alice headed to her office and realized that, for a few minutes, she had forgotten all about her distress.

***

Inman tried to squelch his sense of a tragedy in the making. He'd been on the phone with headquarters all morning and found that somehow the preliminary results of the audit had been leaked to Garrett's office. The congressman was on a scorch and burn mission and would be joining the hearing, as was his prerogative.

Headquarters had provided an outline for the statements he and Alice were to submit to the committee beforehand. The way Weber had explained it was that, because Alice and Inman were equals in the office and the highest-ranking employees, Garrett wanted both to testify.

Their best draft was due by noon on Thursday, and headquarters would review it with them Friday. The hearing would start at ten o'clock Monday morning.

Disturbed, Inman switched his thoughts to Shirley. They'd had a divine time last Monday evening. After an exquisite dinner, she had shared his bed. With great reluctance, he had dropped her at the airport this morning, the hearing needing all his attention. Shirley promised to think about how to break the news of a half-sister to their children.

While Inman didn't want to see the office go under and Alice penalized, his primary goal was now to return home. His malaise had disappeared, and he no longer felt something in his life was missing. The sheer drama was wearing him out.

Dutifully Inman trudged to Alice's office and took a seat, saying nothing.

"It's bad, isn't it?"

"Worse than you know."

***

While in the airport's cell phone lot, Espy rechecked the status of Royce's flight. Still on time. She perused the pictures he had sent once more but hadn't a clue why Royce had taken them. Upon receiving Royce's call, she pulled into the pickup area. Shortly, Royce hopped in.

"What the hell's going on?" Espy asked.

"The blonde in the picture is none other than Johnathon Patton, managing partner of Three V," Royce said.

"You've got to be kidding. How did you find out?"

Royce then related the story, blow by blow, about his escapade the night before.

"But how did you find out about Patton being a cross-dresser in the first place?"

"I think it's best I don't tell you. I don't want to compromise my source."

The urge to protest welled within her because he had dragged her into this mess. Instead, she asked, "Have you told anyone else yet?"

"No. Frankly, I'm not sure how I'm going to handle the information. I thought maybe you could help me think this through. Tell you what. I have a package that is supposed to arrive tomorrow, so why don't you come to my place after work."

"Package?"

"Yep. I ordered a fingerprint kit. Patton held my cell phone, and I want to get his prints off of it in case he denies he's the woman in the picture. Extra insurance."

"Wow, I'm impressed. We've got other troubles. Alice's testimony before Congress has been moved up, and she's paralyzed with fear."

"Will this nightmare ever end?"

***

As Espy knocked on Royce's door, the feeling of being a character in some clandestine spy movie overran her. The situation was unreal. She didn't know what to make of it.

Royce let her in, and Espy was taken aback by his apartment. The tastefully done décor had a decidedly masculine feel. A light-gray couch accented in brush nickel furniture nails commanded her attention. The throw pillows accented the burnt orange colors of the mosaic wood chest that served as a coffee table. A matching chair sat to the side.

"Come in," Royce said. "I've just been unpacking the fingerprint kit and reading the instructions."

"So, how are you going to be able to match Patton's prints on your phone to a set taken when he wasn't in drag?" Espy asked.

"Good question. I don't know. At least we have them in case we need them. I think you should film me taking the fingerprints off the phone. That way we'll have a record of what we did."

"Great idea."

Espy began filming with her cell phone as Royce made a speech about obtaining the fingerprints. The first step was to dust the phone gently, covering as much of the surface as possible. Next the lifting tape was applied. Upon its removal, he transferred the adhesive to the fingerprint backing cards. Espy immediately sent a copy to Royce.

"OK, so what are we going to do with all of this?" Espy asked.

"I'm torn. I want to tell Alice but, from what you said, she's a basket case."

"I agree. What about Inman?"

"I don't trust him."

"He's a bit pompous, but he believes in the 'cause.' Besides, he's the only other person who has the power to do anything with the information."

"I guess you're right."

"Look, why don't you put all this on a thumb drive and give it to Inman first thing in the morning so he'll have it before leaves for Washington?"

"That's a plan."

"Don't forget to include information about where the pictures were taken. That's a really important piece of the puzzle."

"Will do."

Espy took her leave, driving aimlessly. Not wanting to go home, she decided to stop at a wine bar. It was still a bit warm and muggy, the last cold front a distant memory. Nonetheless, Espy opted for the patio, tired of the canned air. The sauvignon blanc flight led her to opt for a glass of Pascal Jolivet to go with her capellini and shrimp.

While sipping her wine, she let her eyes drift over the patio crowd. One group of women were in a lively discussion, laughing. Numerous couples were dining, and several were riveted to their mobiles.

Espy sighed. *Will I be alone forever?* Perhaps that was God's way of punishing her. Suddenly, a text appeared from Mason, the wedding guy, asking her for a date Saturday. Feeling undeserving of joy, she started to decline, but then she remembered what JJ had said. "What's done is done." While he didn't excite her like Hank or her ex, Enrique, he was a nice man. What was it that drew her to attractive, emotionally distant men? Maybe she did need therapy after all.

Espy texted, "Yes."

Chapter Thirty Nine

Royce stood behind Espy as she knocked at Inman's door. An irritated voice emanated from the office.

"We have something important to speak with you about before you leave," Espy said. "Can we come in?"

"Can't we talk in the conference room? This office is so tiny," Inman said.

"I don't want anyone else to hear what I've got to tell you," Royce said.

"OK, but make it quick."

Espy urged Inman to hand her his mouse and insert the thumb drive into his computer as Royce told his story.

"See, Inman. Royce has put Patton's photo as a cross-dresser next to his photo from the firm. Check the nose, the shape of the mouth," Espy said.

"Oh, my God. It appears identical. And the woman who bought me the drinks was a spy for them? Why didn't you tell me sooner?"

"Sorry, I just wasn't sure where this was all going," Royce said. He had no intention of telling Inman the truth. "So, any idea what we should do with the information?"

"I don't know. I'm so angry at how Three V used us. They got all that information out of me by getting me drunk. Frankly, I'm stunned."

"Inman," Espy said, "don't blame yourself. They got stuff from all of us. You didn't know about Alice's drinking. They got all that from somewhere else."

"If I can ruin the bastard, I will," Inman said. He took the thumb drive out of his computer and stowed it in his briefcase.

At that moment, Quiana called from the conference room that the food had arrived. Relieved to have unburdened himself, Royce joined the others around the table.

JJ stood as the group gathered. Looking at Inman and Alice, he said, "Quiana and I wanted to share a 'last lunch' with you both and wish you well. I know this has been a tough week for all of us. We know, Alice, you've done your best, and whatever happens, happens. We're behind you one hundred percent, and we'll be rooting for you. We wish we could be with you in person, but since we can't, we'll be watching from here."

"Gaye sent a good luck e-mail," Quiana said, "and wanted you and Inman to know she was thinking about you."

"Any idea when you'll be back?" Jorge asked.

Alice shook her head. "I want you all to know I appreciate your support, but if things go as bad as I think they will, take care of yourselves. I'd rather not bring the rest of you down with me."

Royce started to say something to Alice to ease her torment, but he couldn't think of a thing. Realistically it would be the end of the office as they knew it. The audit and all the surrounding publicity would be too much. A sense of desperation was in the air. Everyone picked at their food, keeping conversation to a minimum.

Jorge said, "Feels too much like the last supper to me. I'm going to my desk so I can finish writing up Ike's. Inman, if it's OK, I'll do the predetermination interview tomorrow."

"I'm fine with it," Inman said.

Royce watched as Jorge gathered his plate and made his way to the back. It was funny—despite everything that had happened, Royce was beginning to like the guy.

***

After the remainder of lunch had been disposed of and the others had left the conference room, Quiana donned her hat and tiptoed to Alice's office. In another twenty minutes, JJ would be driving the duo to the airport.

The door was closed, and when Alice didn't respond to Quiana's soft rap, Quiana pushed the door open a crack. Alice, sitting in her chair with eyes closed, looked up.

"Quiana, come in. My therapist suggested I try deep breathing and meditation for my anxiety. Also, lavender aromatherapy. Want to try some?" Alice edged a bottle of lavender oil and a cotton ball toward Quiana. "Just put some on the cotton ball and breathe it in."

Quiana did as Alice suggested, not expecting much to happen.

"You sure you don't mind keeping Dexter?" Alice asked. "If it's a bother, I can ask Art."

"No, no, it's fine. That way I can bring him to work. He's my lavender." Quiana emitted a nervous laugh. "So, anyway, I thought long and hard about what JJ said about us learning to handle our distress in other ways. I'm going to read up on meditation and deep breathing and talk to my therapist to see what she says. Anyway, it's a start. I was hoping that when you get back, maybe you and I could get together during lunch or something and talk about our progress. I've realized there are things in life I want to do that I can't do until I conquer my sociophobia."

"I'd love nothing better."

"Alice, don't let those people get you down. They're just political hacks, doing what they think will rile their base and not what they think is the right thing to do." Quiana turned to leave and, as she was stepping out, said, "No matter what happens, I will always believe in you. You've been wonderful to me."

***

Jorge settled at his desk and realized the place was disconcertingly quiet. He had an uneasy feeling about Monday's hearing and was glad the Ike case would keep him busy. If the hearing went badly, they'd probably close the office. Being shipped back to San Antonio did not appeal to him. The challenge here had rekindled his passion for "the cause." Besides, his coworkers were great, and Alice was the best supervisor he ever had.

Sighing, he called Ike Wilke about the results of the investigation.

After the pleasantries were over, Jorge said, "Mr. Wilke, we were unable to identify any hazards caused by Ms. McCarty wearing a skirt to work. By law, religious views must be accommodated unless they cause an undue hardship. We were unable to find any hardship that her skirt would cause."

"What do you mean? I have the right to expect her to wear pants. It's in my written dress code."

"Mr. Wilke, you are allowed to have a dress code, but you must make a reasonable accommodation for religious beliefs."

"Skirts are too dangerous. She could have tripped or gotten her dress caught on something."

"Sir, I spoke with the lead at the store. She told me that Ms. McCarty's skirt was above her ankles and that she was unaware of any danger issues involved in working in the grill area."

"That's absolutely not right. So, what are you trying to tell me?"

Jorge winced, as Mr. Wilke's voice had become defensive and shrill. "We will be issuing a finding that your company is in violation. We'll be contacting you later to see how we can settle the matter."

"This is preposterous." Wilke abruptly cut off the phone call.

Taking a deep breath, Jorge walked into the common area and grabbed a Coke out of the fridge. Then he wandered over to Quiana's fortress.

"Tough interview?" Quiana asked.

"Yeah, but now I can get the letter of determination out. I really don't think he's going to settle."

"Well, that's good. Then we'll have another case to take to court."

"That should please Inman."

Jorge finished his drink and returned to his desk. He wrote the letter of determination and signed it on behalf of Alice. As he was about to mail the letter, his phone rang. It was the lead, Keyshia Cummings, at Ike's.

Through sobs, she told him that Jeff, her manager, had fired her. He'd said that her work performance was poor and they no longer needed her. Jorge's body prickled.

"Had he said anything about your performance before?"

"No, actually, I just got promoted to team lead in April because he and Ike were so happy with my work. They hadn't said I was having any problems."

"OK, we're going to need to take a complaint from you. I can get it written up, but I'll need you to sign it. Do you have an e-mail address I can send it to?"

"I do, but I don't own a computer. All I have is my phone."

"Let's do this. I'll just come Monday to take your statement and get your complaint filed."

"Please. I've been living paycheck to paycheck as it is, and now, without a job, I don't know what I'll do."

Jorge anguished over the termination. *It's my fault. I told Ike about what Keyshia said.* He vowed to do everything in his power to make it right.

Reluctantly, he called Mr. Wilke about his visit to Nederland and his desire to speak with both Mr. Wilke and the manager about the termination. A belligerent Ike informed Jorge that he was not welcome on the property and not to call again.

Jorge wished he could ask Alice's advice, but dared not call her. Making his way into Royce and Espy's office, he explained the problem.

"Geeze, that's a hard one," Espy said. "If he isn't going to cooperate, you're going to have to subpoena all the documents and the testimony."

"And Saitou will hit the roof about the testimony being subpoenaed," Royce said.

"The timing's so immediate—couldn't you just write it up?" Espy asked.

"I'm not sure that would fly. I could see if Keyshia had another coworker who could vouch for her performance, but then I'd be afraid that person would be fired, too. I can't risk it. I'm going to make a run to Nederland Monday to get the charge and her testimony. I'll have the document subpoena written up by the time Alice and Inman get back. Maybe it will fly if we just have the documentation and not the testimony."

"That's what I'd do," Royce said, "but I understand we're out of travel money. If you want to get reimbursed, you better run it through Quiana first."

"I don't care. I'll pay for it out of my pocket if I have to."

"Inman will be happy. We needed some more litigation just to show we aren't screwups," Espy said.

Chapter Forty

Alice took a seat at the elongated witness table next to Saitou, noting that its elliptical ends were chopped off. *Just like my head will be in a few minutes.* Several bottles of water sat next to her elevated nametag, with "Ms. Arden" in large black capitalized letters on a white background. The mic on a flexible arm intimidated her. She shoved it away from her face.

She gazed at the two rows of high-backed chairs rising before her and curving around the witness table. Shortly, members of Congress would be sitting behind the solid wood railings and peering down at the witnesses. A quiver flooded her. Chairwoman Swanson would be enthroned in the position of honor, the seal of the United States marking her spot. Two American flags stood on either side. She glanced past Saitou, who had said nothing to her since her arrival in DC. Inman, who was sitting on the other side of Saitou with General Counsel Weber, studied his notes.

Alice didn't even bother; it was going to be a disaster. Swanson entered the room, causing pain to attack her battered leg. Breathing deeply with eyes closed, she dug out a handkerchief from a plastic bag in her purse and wiped her face, inhaling lavender. Only then was she prepared to face Swanson. The woman was wearing blue, the color of trust. *Go figure.* And those pearls.

Garrett was one of the last to enter, and he took his seat next to Swanson, shoving her a stack of papers. The meeting was called to order, and Alice was sworn in.

"Do you solemnly swear or affirm that the testimony that you are about to give is the truth, the whole truth, and nothing but the truth, so help you, God?"

"I do." Alice said.

The chairwoman then ceded the questioning period for the Republicans to her staff member. He directed all his inquiries at Alice, ignoring the other witnesses at the table.

***

Inman listened to Alice being peppered with yes-or-no questions without a chance to explain. The man must be a trained lawyer, he thought.

With a sneering voice, the man launched into the final assault. "You opened an office in Austin, which was not a designated EEO location, didn't you?

"You sent three people and only paid the employees travel money for two, shorting the employees their rightful travel expenses, didn't you?

"You took leave without signing out for it or informing your supervisor, didn't you?"

Inman's anger increased to the point that he had to fight an urge to stand up and scream at them. They didn't care; they just wanted to humiliate Alice and the EEOC. At least she seemed to be holding up better than expected.

As the bashing continued, Inman tried to shut it out, afraid of losing his temper and embarrassing them all. He glanced at Alice and, in the corner of his eye, caught sight of a dark, heavyset man sitting at the far end of the first row behind Alice. A smirk on his face indicated he was enjoying Alice's torture immensely. Something was familiar about him…but what? Then, Inman clicked. He was the man in the picture with Patton. Inman had to find out who he was. But how?

At last, a break was called before the Democrats could begin their questioning. Inman hoped they would lob softballs, but the charges of misappropriating money and the secret nature of the office were probably troubling to the Democrats as well.

He rose and walked over to Alice, who was wiping her face with a handkerchief. "You OK?"

"I don't know. I expected questions, but I'm a bit stunned at the man's ferocity. He didn't give me a chance to explain. Well, hopefully that will come with the next round of questioning." Inman looked over to see that the smirker was still there, talking on his cell phone. *It's now or never.*

Bounding over to the man, Inman reached out his hand. "Johnny, I'm so glad to see you. It's been a long time." Inman tried to be as excited and cheerful as possible.

The man looked at Inman, a puzzled look on his face. "You must have me mistaken for someone else."

"You sure?" Inman asked. "I could have sworn you were Johnny Hightower."

"No, I'm not."

Afraid of not getting what he needed, he said, "Sorry. My name is Inman Parker. And yours is?" Again, he stuck out his hand.

"I'm Miles Vinson," the man said. "Excuse me, but I need to finish this call before the break is over." He ignored Inman's outstretched hand.

Inman waved and retreated. Miles Vinson…Miles Vinson…Could he be some relation to the Vinsons in Three V?

Inman returned to his seat and sent Royce a text to find out about a Miles Vinson, recommending he check the Three V website first.

***

Quiana stuffed her tears as she watched Alice being butchered. For once, she was thankful to be behind the screen and not at the witness table. Then, the reality of what was occurring hit her. Closing the office was a real possibility. Where would that leave her and JJ? The experience in Houston had been a nightmare, and returning didn't appeal to her. And JJ? He was still in his probationary period. Would they keep him on?

Finally, the hearing stopped for a break. Quiana looked at her camera on the conference table and saw Royce respond to a ding on his phone.

Royce looked up. "That was Inman. He told me that he thinks he saw the heavyset man who was at the table with Patton. He told me to research the name, Miles Vinson."

"What are you talking about?" JJ asked, and Royce explained about the picture.

"I'm so confused," JJ said. "How in the world did you get all this?"

"It's a long story. I'll explain everything later."

As Quiana listened, her fingers flew across the keyboard. No Miles Vinson on the Three V website. She then turned to LinkedIn. Bingo.

"I found him," Quiana said. "He works for Three V as their Chief Financial Officer. He's been there for years. I bet he's somehow related to the partners."

"Nice work, Quiana," Espy said. "But what are we going to do with all this information?"

"It won't help the hearing, that's for sure," Royce said. "It's been a disaster. I'll let Inman know what you found."

Quiana took screenshots of the information on Miles and forwarded it to Royce and Inman. Then she reached for Dexter, who was sitting next to her. Concentrating on stroking his sleek fur allowed her to chill out. *What's done is done. I've never felt so alone.* Being able to sit next to her coworkers at a time like this would bring her comfort. She vowed to do everything in her power to break out of her cage.

***

The hearing break over, Alice had a bit more time to answer questions from the Democrats. The members had decided to ask their own, and she was able to explain a bit about why three investigators were sent instead of two. Still, they didn't seem to understand, or care, for that matter. At least Saitou was forced to answer the questions about why the office had been established and whose idea it had been. But Alice was afraid the first round of questioning would be all the public heard. While watching the facial expressions of her questioners, she realized they didn't want anything to do with this issue. It would make them look bad to throw their support to an agency that skirted the OPM regulations.

Hours later, the hearing adjourned. Alice sat, numb, unable to process everything that had happened. Then it struck her. This hearing wasn't about her. Her wrongdoings were small potatoes. She was simply a pawn in the red and blue wars. Neither side cared about what was right or about the victims of discrimination. They just wanted to win. And she would be a casualty. *If I'm going down, I'm going with my head held high. I've given my life to "the cause," and I'm proud of it.*

Saitou leaned over and said, "You'll be hearing from me about how the agency will handle your transgressions." Then she left, her staff trailing behind her.

Dazed, Alice remained in her seat, her mind blank. Then she felt a tap on her shoulder. "Are you OK?" Inman asked.

"I don't know. This was worse than I imagined."

"Let's get out of here. Weber said we should return to Austin and not even bother to go to headquarters." He gently took Alice by the elbow and helped her to her scooter.

Chapter Forty One

Exhausted, Alice slept in the next morning. The dread of facing her colleagues caused her to linger in bed. Cutting corners had torpedoed their venture. Fretting, she wondered what would happen to them all. One bright spot was that Art had insisted they meet for lunch. They'd settled on the Mexican restaurant near the office.

Immediately after arriving at work, Alice slipped out a bit early to the eatery. Settling in, she munched on chips. Funnily, a margarita didn't even interest her. Art arrived with a small bouquet of flowers.

"For you." Art leaned down and kissed Alice before he sat.

"What's the occasion?"

"I watched the hearings. They gave you quite a beating. It really made me mad. They didn't care about all the fantastic work your group was doing. I know you must be devastated."

Alice sighed. "At least I survived. I don't know what's going to happen to the office, though."

They spent the rest of the meal making small talk and catching up on what had happened since the last time they saw each other. After the table was cleared, Art reached for Alice's hand and said, "Alice, let's move in together. You don't have to give me an answer now, but I've been thinking about it hard and long. You've put a spark back in my life, and I'd like to move our relationship to the next level."

***

Alice called a meeting upon her return. The group was glum, and Alice wasn't quite sure what to say to them. To her relief, Inman took over.

Inman asked Royce to tell everyone the story about his New York visit from the beginning. Royce divulged everything except Grandma Pat's involvement.

Stunned, Alice said, "I cannot believe that scum Three V would stoop so low; what hypocrites. All the time, they're bashing us for our personal lives when they are 'perverts' as well. Now what?"

"I don't know. I'm not sure I want to tell headquarters about any of this," Inman said. "They'd probably read us the riot act about spying on opposing counsel. And everything with Three V is going through headquarters. I can't even speak to them."

"If we do anything with it," JJ said, "it will look like blackmail. Then we'd really be in trouble."

"You're right, Alice said. "So, where are we with all the other cases?"

"We had a blowup at Ike's," Jorge said.

"What happened?" Alice asked.

"After I did the predetermination interview, the owner fired one of the witnesses. He is now refusing to cooperate. I've taken a retaliation complaint from the new CP, and I got a subpoena signed by the San Antonio district director. I'm ready to issue it if you are OK with it."

Inman reached for the subpoena and briefly perused it. "Nice job. Glad you made the turnaround time for the documents short. Go ahead and send it. Hell, overnight it. What he did was disgusting."

"Are you sure about that?" Quiana asked.

"I'm sick and tired of penny-pinching. A woman got fired because she cooperated, and I want to go after the bastard."

"What about witnesses?" Jorge asked. "Ike has told us we are not to come on the property. And, according to the CP, everyone is afraid to talk to me for fear of being fired."

"I'm not even going to go there," Alice said. "Let's just see if we can find 'cause' on the documentation. I know Saitou will not let us subpoena witnesses."

"You got that right," Inman said.

"Royce, what's going on with the tortilla factory?" Alice asked.

"I thought they were all hot to settle, then they hired an attorney who put the kibosh on it. We can file suit. I'll bring it over to you in a few."

"I think it's going to be a great case. At least I'll have that and hip-hop to work on," Inman said.

"Anything else?" Alice asked.

"Just got off the phone on the 'pinkie' case," Espy said. "They're anxious to settle. I'll get the agreement written up and over to them later this afternoon."

"Fabulous! Great work, gang. Inman, anything on Bighorn?"

"Apparently Three V filed a motion to dismiss, and the judge is still reviewing it. I haven't heard anything else."

Alice looked around the table and steeled herself. "About the hearing…"

"Look," Espy said, "you don't need to say anything. We'll just have to wait and see. Anyway, I'm tired of talking about it. What about the rest of you?"

A chorus of assents rose, and Quiana's camera rotated up and down. Relieved, Alice said, "Let's get back to work."

Chapter Forty Two

JJ parked his car in front of Quiana's apartment. Things had been a bit tense between them after the fabulous wedding weekend. But her dinner invitation had sent him into a frenzy. Her apology for the spur-of-the-moment offer had been unnecessary.

Quiana answered the door in her floppy hat and motioned him in. JJ took in the ambiance and the pleasing aromas emanating from the kitchen.

"Where's Chivann?" JJ asked.

"Oh, she's on an all-night study bender at the library. She's got some big exams tomorrow."

JJ was thrilled. "So, what's for dinner? It smells great!"

"I thought we'd go New Orleans tonight. Red beans and rice. It's a recipe my grandma always fixed. Would you like a glass of wine?"

"Yes, please." JJ sat on the couch, surveying the room. It was sparsely furnished with what appeared to be Ikea furniture, which made sense. Chivann probably needed to save all she could to put herself through law school. Then, JJ became anxious, unsure what to say or do.

Quiana handed JJ a glass and joined him. "Have you been thinking about what you're going to do if the office closes?"

He took a leisurely sip. "This is good. I've tried to put it out of my mind. There's not much I can do but see where the cards fall."

"You know you're on probation, right?"

"I hadn't thought about that. Do you think they would just terminate me?"

"I wouldn't think so, but then, the way headquarters has been acting, I truly have no idea what they'll do."

JJ closed his eyes and tried to hold back tears that were threatening to flow. "I've worked so hard, tried to fit in...I don't know where I would go or what I would do if I didn't have this job."

Quiana reached over and took his hand in hers. They sat silently. Eventually, JJ said, "Enough of this. We can't control it, so we'll just have to wait to see what happens. Let's eat. I'm hungry."

The two talked and laughed as they devoured the meal. Quiana explained that her grandma always said that Monday was wash day and red beans and rice day because you could put the beans on to cook while you handled the laundry.

JJ cleared the table while Quiana worked on the dishes. Then he crept behind her, encircling her, pulling her close. "Quiana, let's be a couple." He then gently removed her hat and laid it on the counter. Quiana didn't stop him. Nibbling her ears, he felt her ease into him.

Quiana then loosed his grip and slowly turned to face him. For the first time, JJ looked into the eyes of the love of his life.

***

Alice hurried to the dog park after her AA meeting. As she sat on their favorite bench, the muggy warmth irritated her. Would the Indian summer ever end? Contemplating Art's proposal, she wondered whether their relationship would eventually cool as the weather inevitably would. Committing to someone after all these years unnerved her. What if he'd made the offer simply because she might lose her job?

Recalling her stress level, she marveled at her ability to handle it without drinking. Tomorrow was injection day. Being deprived of the relief alcohol delivered was like losing an old friend, but sometimes you needed to move on. Not wanting to disappoint Art, she planned to go through with it. Perhaps it would even be possible to hang out at Rebels with a nonalcoholic drink. Her visits with Jake and her ability to bounce things off him had brought a bit of sunshine to some otherwise dreary days.

Art and Simon approached. Art leaned to unleash his friend, who bounded toward Dexter. The two yelped and circled each other, heading out to sniff the bushes. It had been a while since the two had seen each other. *They need a companion just like I do,* she thought.

After a bit of small talk, Alice said, "Art, I'm both excited and scared about your proposal. You are also the best thing that has happened to me in a long time, but I'm afraid you're just doing this out of pity for me, knowing I might soon be unemployed."

Art took her hand. "Alice, I don't pity you at all. Yes, you've been through a rough patch, but I have the feeling you're the kind of person who can bounce back from anything thrown at you."

"Thanks for the support. The answer is yes."

***

When Inman got off the phone, his excitement was palpable. He ordered all to the conference table.

"What in the world is going on?" Alice asked.

"I'll tell you when everyone is here." He waited impatiently, yelling at JJ to hurry up. When all were seated, he began. "I just got a call from headquarters saying that the judge in Bighorn has ordered the case to mediation."

"What does that mean?" JJ asked.

"That means that he wants us to try to settle the case," Inman said.

"But I thought they had no intention of settling," Jorge said.

"This is big," Inman said. "Don't you see? The judge read the motion to dismiss, and he could have done that, but he didn't. He's forcing them to mediate instead. They don't have to settle, but in my way of thinking, if the judge didn't feel there was merit in our case, he would have granted the motion to dismiss. That should send a big message to Three V."

"So, when's this happening?" Alice asked.

"It's been scheduled for the end of the week."

"Are you going?" Royce asked.

Inman frowned. "Weber did not say he expected me to attend. I need to call and see if I can go."

"Keep us posted," Alice said.

Inman returned to his office and called Weber. "Sir," he said, "I'd like permission to attend the mediation."

"Inman, you and the office are on the shit list up here. I don't want you anywhere near it."

"But that's not fair. I know this case backward and forward. I know I'll be able to contribute to the settlement. Besides, I volunteered for this assignment when no moving expenses were paid. You owe it to me."

"Let me think about it."

Chapter Forty Three

Inman arrived at the mediation early to scope out the surroundings. Three rooms had been reserved; one held a long conference table, and the others were to be used as breakout rooms where participants could caucus. Each was accessed from a lounge area with a sofa, chairs, restrooms, and a coffee bar. All areas were painted in a soothing green with artwork on the wall.

Inman helped himself to coffee and settled into one of the chairs, enabling him to see who entered. As he was just about finished with his first cup, Weber and his entourage arrived. Inman stood and greeted them, extending his hand.

"Look, Inman," Weber said. "It was against my better judgment to let you come. I want to set the ground rules. You aren't to speak up, and if you have something to say, you let me know first what your thoughts are. I'll decide whether I want you to proceed."

Inman stuffed his anger. "I understand, sir. I'm just thankful you've allowed me to attend."

After getting a refill, Inman sat, nervously fingering the thumb drive in his jacket pocket. The mediator arrived and pointed out the area where the EEOC could set up shop. Inman dropped his briefcase on the table but scurried back to the lounge area just as Lipscomb and her attorney, Jack Caulfield, arrived. After escorting them to the EEOC area, the duo accepted his offer of coffee. He worked as slowly as possible, afraid of missing his only chance to save the case.

It was almost nine when Patton and a host of Three V attorneys swept in with their client, Davis Cummings. *What a pompous ass,* Inman thought, as he watched the sneering Cummings adjust his shirt cuffs so that his aquamarine cufflinks could sparkle in the soft lighting of the room.

Abandoning the coffee, Inman reached into his pocket and palmed the thumb drive in his left hand, making a beeline to Patton. "I'm Inman Parker." Inman reached out with his right. Patton gave him a cold stare and returned the offered handshake.

Inman swiveled his hand so that Patton's palm was up, and then, as he let go, slid the drive into Patton's hand. "A little something for you," Inman whispered as he turned back to the bar, grabbed the cups, and hustled to the safety of the EEOC's refuge.

A few moments later, the mediator stuck her head in. "All, there'll be a short delay before we begin the general session. I'll let you know when the other party is ready to begin."

Inman heaved a sigh of relief. Maybe Patton was looking at the drive. As the minutes ticked by, restlessness overtook him. A trip to the toilet allowed him to enter the lounge. The area was deserted, but tense voices emanated from Three V's breakout room. The fear of being caught stopped him from moving closer to the door in an effort to eavesdrop. Hurriedly he made way to the restroom and darted back to the safety of the EEOC's sanctum.

After what seemed an eternity, the mediator entered the room. "All," she said, "the other party has agreed to the original proposed settlement. We're working on the paperwork at this moment."

The others looked at each other in disbelief. Weber said, "Excuse me?"

The mediator smiled. "The case is settled. I'll be back in just a bit to obtain signatures." She then left the retreat.

"I don't understand," Lipscomb said.

"We settled the case," Caulfield said. "We're getting everything we asked for."

Lipscomb began to sob uncontrollably. "I didn't think anyone would ever believe me. I can't believe it's finally over, and I can get back to my life."

Caulfield patted her hand and offered a tissue. "We had a strong case, and justice prevailed."

A grinning Inman lowered his head, not daring to look up. He was having a hard time keeping his mouth shut about the sudden change of heart. Then he sent a text to Alice.

***

Alice was perusing her e-mail when Inman's text arrived. Stunned, she savored the victory. Her intuition had paid off, and Ms. Lipscomb was vindicated. After such a stunning victory, there was no way they could close the office. Defeating Three V was definitely a feather in the EEOC's cap. She started to call the team together and tell them but decided to wait. Let Inman do that; for once, he deserved the spotlight.

***

Espy stopped at the receptionist's desk and made an appointment for next week. The therapist had given her ample food for thought. After several dates with Mason, she had begun to wonder what was wrong with her. He was attractive in his own way, interested in politics, funny, caring, and had a good-paying job. While she enjoyed their outings, there was just no magnetism between them.

Not wanting the return to work, she drove to Mozart's on Lake Austin and bought coffee and a fruit tart. A place on the patio overlooking the water allowed her to be alone with her thoughts. At least the terrible heat of the summer was behind them, and the cool of autumn was bringing much-needed relief.

As the therapist had explained it, a man like Hank is attractive because he appears desirable and in control while not being fully present. This trait leaves a woman feeling she has discovered someone special, pushing her to seek a deeper relationship. These men are not always remote, however. At times they are charming, sweeping the woman off her feet, leaving her wanting more.

Thinking about Hank, Espy could see the pattern. About the time Espy became fed up with his lack of availability, Hank would surprise her with an overnight getaway or shower her with attention by buying her an expensive piece of jewelry.

And the bit about how they play into women's fantasies of the perfect life: a physically desirable and in-control man who can take care of the woman, allowing her to live happily ever after. Espy could see all this, but what the therapist suggested next troubled her.

Did Espy have a lack of self-esteem on some level? *Am I afraid I can't be happy without an alpha male? Do my insecurities push me toward that type of man?* She'd always thought of herself as a capable, take-charge woman.

Espy recalled the pressure her mother put on her to marry up. Was her mother's underlying message that Espy couldn't take care of herself and needed a strong man to protect her? Had this subliminal message defined Espy and given her self-doubt in her relationships? Had she chosen to read romance novels to reinforce this belief?

The breeze rose, bringing a ripple along the lake. A feeling gurgled within her. *I'm actually taking care of myself just fine.* A dominant man wasn't necessary to secure her place in the world. It was time to decide what she really wanted from a relationship. After all, a partnership should simply add extra joy to her already rich life, just like the dessert sitting in front of her.

***

Later that afternoon, the fax machine rumbled, spewing out documents. Surprised, Quiana rolled her chair over to the printer/copier/fax machine. So few people faxed these days. She read the papers with interest.

"Jorge, come here," she said. "It's your evidence in the hamburger joint from hell case." Quiana stuck the papers in her outbox, wishing she felt secure enough to sit at the table with him as he reviewed the documents.

Royce and JJ followed closely behind Jorge and gathered at the conference table, waiting impatiently for the verdict.

"I think we've got that bastard," Jorge said. He looked up. "She got a promotion and a raise, and there is no documentation in her file that shows any poor performance whatsoever. The others they've fired for poor performance have writeups in their files."

"The timing was too close to make it a coincidence," Royce said.

"*Yahoo!*" JJ yelped, bringing Alice out of her office.

"What in the world is going on?" Alice asked.

"Hamburger Ike is dead meat," Quiana said.

Jorge gave Alice an overview of the evidence.

"That's fine. We won't even bother with testimony," Alice said. "Quiana, could you help Jorge with file preparation? I'd like to be ready to present Inman with the conciliation agreements when he gets back in tomorrow."

"Sure, no problem," Quiana said. "Have you heard from Inman yet? The mediation has been going on an awful long time."

"I have," Alice said. "Inman will be back tomorrow morning, and I'll let him tell you all about it."

Quiana peered into her camera and detected a slight smile on Alice's face. They settled it, didn't they?" Alice hesitated. "I know they did. You just gotta tell us."

"Yes, but I want Inman to be the one to give us the blow-by-blow tomorrow. Quiana, plan us a breakfast fit for champions. Everyone be here by nine."

Quiana released a huge sigh of relief as she listened to the excited chatter on the other side of the screen. How could they possibly close the office now? They'd knocked Goliath to his knees and would soon have the hamburger, hip-hop, and tortilla cases ready to go to court. Maybe there was hope for her and JJ after all.

***

Back at her desk, Alice called Royce into her office. "Great job on the Bighorn case," she said.

"Thanks."

"I must tell you how grateful I am for your help."

"I must tell you, Alice, that I still feel a bit ashamed. I'm not proud of the blackmail."

Alice sighed. "Funny, isn't it. Three V had no problem using our personal weaknesses against us even when they bore their own. In some ways, it's fitting. What goes around comes around."

"I hope I never have to do it again."

"It's amazing, isn't it, what we'll do for 'the cause'?"

Alice's phone began to ring. She looked down and, not recognizing the number, frowned. Probably some telemarketer. "Let me get this."

Alice answered the phone as Royce closed the office door behind him.

"Ms. Arden?"

"Yes."

"This is Janine Lipscomb. Do you remember me from the Bighorn Outfitters case?"

"Indeed, I do, Ms. Lipscomb. Congratulations on the settlement."

"My attorney said it was OK to call."

"Sure."

"I just can't tell you how much it meant to me that you believed in me and kept on fighting for me. I finally feel I can get on with my life."

"You're welcome. That's my job."

The two chatted a bit more before concluding the conversation. Finding justice was what Alice lived for, and she'd do it all again.

Perhaps this big victory would give them a reprieve and slow down talk of shutting the office. They'd have a new president next year and perhaps a new chair. She wondered if Hillary and Saitou had any ties? Hopefully not. Maybe a new boss would give her a fighting chance. But still, Alice knew she wasn't out of the woods yet, and that the odds of surviving the audit unscathed were slim.

If you enjoyed this book, please leave a review at your favorite book review website. Even if it is just a sentence or two, it makes all the difference.

Follow Marie and her stories about life at:

Newsletter Signup: https://mailchi.mp/8eec9d6c8b15/newsletter

Website: https://www.mariewatts.com

Bookbub: https://www.bookbub.com/profile/marie-w-watts

Facebook: https://www.facebook.com/mariewattsbooks/

Instagram: https://www.instagram.com/mariewattswriter/

Twitter: https://twitter.com/MarieWattsBooks

ALSO BY MARIE W. WATTS

An American Salad

The Cause Lives: Warriors for Equal Rights

La Grange (Images of America: Texas)

The Story Ends In:

RAPTURE BY REVENGE: WARRIORS FOR EQUAL RIGHTS

Alice's cell rang. Saitou! Panicked, she motioned for everyone to be quiet. "Chair Saitou, how are you today?" Alice fought the urge to vomit.

"Ms. Arden," the chair said, "you're obviously aware that you have been accused of gross abuse of power and mismanagement of the office. After serious discussion, a determination was made that you are being placed on an indefinite suspension pending the outcome of the OIG report and the house committee report. Pack your belongings and exit the office. Inman is to be in charge until further notice."

Click.

Just like that, Saitou was gone. Tears began to stream down Alice's face.

"What's wrong?" Espy asked.

Alice could barely breathe; the bands tightening in her chest hadn't been this strong in weeks. "I've been suspended indefinitely."

"Oh, no," Espy said.

"That can't be right. You didn't do that much wrong," Inman said. "I'm going to call General Counsel Weber and get to the bottom of this." He reached for his cell phone and began walking to his office.

"I wouldn't do that if I were you," JJ said. "You need to let those fools in Washington calm down a bit. You think she's gotten pushback from Three V's buds on Capitol Hill?"

"Damn, I hadn't thought of that," Inman said. He returned and sat with the stunned crew. Alice felt their eyes on her as she summoned the courage to speak. "I need to leave now, but I want you to carry on."

Follow my progress at http://www.mariewatts.com

DISCUSSION QUESTIONS

1. Alice cut corners by sending three investigators on money allotted for two and failing to properly report sick leave. Have you ever cut corners? What was the outcome? Does the end ever justify the means?

2. Royce protected himself from being hurt by staying on the offensive and keeping others at arm's length. How effective was it? Have you, or someone you know, ever used this defense mechanism? What was the outcome?

3. Throughout the book, the characters reveal their own biases and prejudices. What are Alice's biases? Inman's? Jorge's? Royce's? JJ's? Why do you think their biases evolved?

4. Gaye chose not to tell Espy what she should do. When a friend is faced with a life-changing decision, what should our role be? Should we give advice? If so, when? If our friend ignores our advice, how should we handle it?

5. Alice continually failed to reveal her true feelings to Art because she feared rejection. Have you ever been in a situation where you have not spoken for similar reasons? What were the consequences? If you were rejected, how did you handle it?

6. JJ stopped trying to succeed in his job because he thought no one would believe his side of the story. Why do you think he caved in so quickly? Is our tendency to judge a person by his/her past useful or fair? If not, what can we do to ensure this does not happen?

7. If someone like Royce joined your church, social club, or workgroup, how would you react?

8. Inman openly accepted his daughter. However, not everyone reacts in the same way. What would you do if you suddenly found you had a sibling or relative you were unaware of?

9. Have you ever been pressured by a boss to do something you thought was not the right thing to do? If so, how did you handle it?

10. Were you aware of the EEOC before reading this book? If so, how did you learn about its existence? Does the federal government have an obligation to actively promote the use of agencies that protect employees from discrimination, workplace accidents, or not being paid appropriately for work performed? Are you aware of the Occupational Health and Safety Administration and the Department of Labor?

I am available to speak with book clubs. Please contact me through my website: http://www.mariewatts.com

ABOUT THE AUTHOR

Marie W. Watts is a former employment discrimination investigator and human resource consultant with over twenty-five years of experience. She has trained thousands of employees to recognize one's own biases and prejudices and avoid discriminating against others in the workplace, and she has coauthored a textbook about it: *Human Relations*, 4th ed. Additionally, her work has been published in the *Texas Bar Journal* and the *Houston Business Journal*, as well as featured on *Issues Today*, syndicated to 119 radio stations, NBC San Antonio, Texas, and TAMU-TV in College Station, Texas.

In pursuit of justice in the workplace, Marie has been from jails to corporate boardrooms seeing the good, the bad, and the ugly of humans at work. She now brings her experiences to life in her works of fiction.

She and her husband live on a ranch in central Texas. In her spare time, she is a volunteer first responder, supports a historic house, and hangs out with her grandsons.

Follow Marie and her stories about life at www.mariewatts.com.

Made in the USA
Coppell, TX
02 September 2020